ALL THAT REMAINS

What Reviewers Say About Sheri Lewis Wohl's Work

Drawing Down the Mist

"Vampires loving humans. Vampires hating vampires. Vampires killing humans. Vampires killing vampires. Good vampires. Evil vampires. Internet-savvy vampires. Lovers turning enemies. Nurturing revenge for a century. Kindness. Cruelty. Love. Action. Fights. Insta-love. This one has everything for a true drama."—*reviewer@large*

Cause of Death

"I really liked these characters, all of them, and wouldn't say no to a sequel, or more."—*Jude in the Stars*

"*CSI* meets *Ghost Whisperer*. ...The pace was brilliantly done, the suspense was just enough, and I'm not ashamed to admit that I had no idea who the serial killer was until almost the end."—*Words and Worlds*

"*Cause of Death* by Sheri Lewis Wohl is one creepy and well-written murder mystery. It is one of the best psychological thrillers I've read in a while."—*Rainbow Reflections*

"[A] light paranormal romance with a psycho-killer and some great dogs."—*C-Spot Reviews*

"There's a ton of stuff in here that I enjoy very much, such as the light paranormal aspect of the book, and the relationship between our two leads is very nice if a bit of a slow burn. The case was engaging enough that I didn't really set this title down once I started it."—Colleen Corgel, Librarian, Queens Public Library

"Totally disturbing, and very, very awesome. ...The characters were amazing. The supernatural tint was never overdone, and even the stuff from the killer's point of view, while disturbing, was awesomely done as well. It was a great book and a fun (and intense) read."—Danielle Kimerer, Librarian (Nevins Memorial Library, Massachusetts)

"This thriller has spooky undertones that make it an intense page turner. You won't be able to put this book down."—*Istoria Lit*

The Talebearer

"As a crime story, it is a good read that had me turning pages quickly. ...The book is well written and the characters are well-developed."
—*Reviews by Amos Lassen*

She Wolf

"I really enjoyed this book—I couldn't put it down once I started it. The author's style of writing was very good and engaging. All characters, including the supporting characters, were multi-layered and interesting."—Melina Bickard, Librarian, Waterloo Library (UK)

Twisted Screams

"[A] cast of well developed characters leads you through a maze of complex emotions."—*Lunar Rainbow Reviewz*

Twisted Echoes

"A very unusual blend of lesbian romance and horror. …[W]oven throughout this modern romance is a neatly plotted horror story from the past, which bleeds ever increasingly into the present of the two main characters. Lorna and Renee are well matched, and face ever-increasing danger from spirits from the past. An unusual story that gets tenser and more interesting as it progresses."—Pippa Wischer, Manager at Berkelouw Books, Armadale

Vermilion Justice

"[T]he characters are so dynamic and well-written that this becomes more than just another vampire story. It's probably impossible to read this book and not come across a character who reminds you of someone you actually know. Wohl takes something as fictional as vampires and makes them feel real. Highly recommended."—*GLBT Reviews: The ALA's GLBT Round Table*

Visit us at www.boldstrokesbooks.com

By the Author

Crimson Vengeance

Burgundy Betrayal

Scarlet Revenge

Vermilion Justice

Twisted Echoes

Twisted Whispers

Twisted Screams

Necromantia

She Wolf

Walking Through Shadows

Drawing Down the Mist

The Talebearer

Cause of Death

Avenging Avery

All That Remains

ALL THAT REMAINS

by

Sheri Lewis Wohl

2021

Credits
Editor: Shelley Thrasher
Production Design: Susan Ramundo
Cover Design By Jeanine Henning

It is joy to the just
to do judgment;
but destruction shall be
to the workers of iniquity

—Proverbs 21:15
The Holy Bible
King James Version

CHAPTER ONE

Johnnie Lancaster stared down and thought, "Damn, this is fucked up." At least the thought stayed in her head and didn't come rolling out of her mouth. No need to prove to everyone what a potty mouth she possessed. She and her partner, human-remains-detection K9, Cougar, were professionals after all. Professionals didn't utter words like *fuck* at what turned out to be a crime scene. No, they did not, and her mouth stayed shut.

Bless his heart, Cougar had done his job like a true champion, and for that fact alone she should be grateful. In all the ways that mattered, she was. It was more that no one expected this. It wasn't the first time they'd worked with law enforcement on an active criminal investigation. It was the first time she'd seen anything like this.

"Houston, we have a problem." Deputy Sheriff Rick Tellarude stood with his hands in his pockets, his expression grim.

"No, duh." See, she could keep it clean.

Rick blew out a long breath. "Can you say serial killer?"

"No. Not here and not again." Not another damn serial killer. Johnnie didn't intend to let the words cross her lips, yet they came out anyway, colored with the dismay that filled her. It had happened too many times in this area of Eastern Washington State, where agriculture and mountains co-existed in stunning harmony. Despite the natural beauty that surrounded those who lived here, there had to be something in the water. No other explanation for the killers that decided to make this place their home and their killing grounds—for the wheatfields stained by blood and the wilderness violated by graves.

Rick looked at her and raised an eyebrow. His expression seemed to question her ability to comprehend the obvious. "Who else but a serial killer would bury bodies like this?"

Regardless of how she might wish things to be different, the proof rested in the reality of Cougar's discovery. At their feet, what the forensic-unit folks carefully excavated silently testified to the truth of Rick's words. Cougar had pointed them to the location of human remains in the past. Nothing new in that. The three-and-a-half-year-old was an exceptionally talented HRD dog. However, he'd never pointed them to multiple sets in the same day, and not just buried bodies either. These were disarticulated and piled together like creepy hidden treasures someone went to great trouble to keep hidden. The ME would need to spend some serious time putting the bodies back into place so perhaps their identities could be ascertained. Sooner, rather than later, she hoped.

"When I got into the HRD business, nobody told me about anything like this. I thought we'd just find people and bring them home." She spoke out loud, even though she knew, as did all the handlers she worked with, that the reality of their work never played out that simple.

"Sister, nobody told any of us about shit like this before we signed up. Welcome to my world."

Johnnie agreed. She'd become involved with search and recovery when an elderly neighbor with manifesting dementia walked away and lost his life in the bargain. It took two weeks before a recovery team found him. While he'd been missing, she couldn't think about anything except that he was out there cold and alone, his chances of survival in freezing weather diminishing every passing hour. Her heart had hurt, and she'd vowed then to do whatever she could to bring the lost home. Training with a local team began the day after his body was recovered, and she got her first dog a year later.

"I'm heading out," she said as she tapped Rick's arm. The day had already been long, and the team excavating the remains had work to complete that didn't require her presence. Her part in this matter concluded when she handed over the coordinates to Rick. Despite the clean, fresh air that washed over her, she wanted to put distance between her and what the team was in the process of uncovering.

"Sign out, and if you would, send me your field report by tonight." He squeezed her arm lightly, and she appreciated the gesture.

"You got it." She headed back to her truck, where Cougar waited, the window down partway, his seatbelt hooked into his harness. He knew the drill and never fussed once back in the truck after a mission. Besides, after a long and emotional day, he could rest easy in the quiet the truck afforded him. Dogs internalized the stress of a search as much as the humans did, maybe even more. He needed, and deserved, the downtime.

Johnnie reached in and rubbed the top of the big head of her partner, a stunning bi-color German shepherd. She'd fallen in love with him at first sight. His all-black head and body, along with his tan feet, made him unique and gorgeous, though picking out a search dog based on appearance—a definite no-no. Such dogs needed drive and persistence and, of course, an excellent nose. Fortunately for her, he came with it all.

"All right, buddy. Let's go home." With Cougar in the backseat of the truck, she could talk to him, and thus he rode in a harness and seatbelt versus a crate. The highly rated harness set-up kept him safe.

She negotiated her way through and around the myriad law-enforcement vehicles that crowded the area around the parking lot. A popular location, the trailhead wasn't designed for the number of cars, trucks, and vans there now. When she'd gotten here early in the morning, parking had been a breeze, given the search party consisted of her, her navigator Stan Silver, and Rick. After the first positive from Cougar, they'd called in the forensic unit and, by the time it arrived, had identified a second location. The unit would be working out here for hours.

The drive home turned out to be the easy part of the day. Often, they were called out to remote locations far away from where she lived. Her poor truck registered over a hundred thousand miles, the vast majority logged from training and missions. Once she pulled onto the Pullman Highway, as the locals liked to call it, she made it to the Hatch Road turnoff within a few minutes. Traffic got a little heavy at 57th because of rush hour. Still, it didn't take long to make it to the Palouse Highway and, from there, a straight shot to the farm.

As she turned onto Stoughton, she hit the remote for the driveway gate. When her father built the place some forty-odd years ago, he'd never envisioned the technology she now employed. No need for the security of a gate then. Everyone knew everyone and looked out for each other, even though acres of land separated their houses. Things had changed since those early years when nothing but bare fields dotted by stands of pine trees surrounded the place.

From the outside, the house and outbuildings appeared much as they had when she moved in after her father passed away. Her mother decided to relocate to Arizona shortly after losing Dad, and her brother, living in Seattle for years, never considered a return to Eastern Washington. It all came down to her. She could either take it over or sell it, and since the latter didn't set well with her, she opted for the former. She didn't need this much house or acreage. Thankfully her neighbors leased and tended most of the land. The farm became her refuge and remained as beautiful and well-tended as her father intended without becoming an overwhelming burden. Dad would be very pleased.

In the backseat, Cougar started to whine, and she smiled. He could be sound asleep, which he usually was after a full day of searching, but the minute she turned onto their road, his head popped up. He did love his farm.

As she drove up the driveway, the gate automatically began to close—another nifty piece of technology that made her life easier and safer. She pulled into the garage, put the car in park, and swung her legs out. Her cell phone rang before she could even stand up.

"NO!" Dr. Shantel Kind didn't mean to yell, and she did anyway. How many times did she have to tell Daniel the same thing before it penetrated his thick skull? She would have thought the divorce papers made her decision crystal clear. They were done. Period. End of story. Any reasonable person would have gotten the message.

Not Daniel. Tenacity was his middle name. Yes. He had encouraged her to apply to the anthropology department here at Eastern Washington University. Yes. It had been a good idea. The job granted her the treasured tenure that fulfilled her long-time dream, and after living here for a few years, she could find no fault with his hometown. Spokane was beautiful, and the small town of Cheney, just a few miles west of Spokane and the home of the university, equally as lovely. Did it save their marriage? Not even close. In fact, the move made it easier for her to finally break away from a relationship that had her gasping for breath.

To get through to him, she'd been brutally honest, even as hurtful as she knew it would be. Nobody wanted to hear that their spouse of almost ten years wasn't attracted to them. She'd tried. God knows she'd tried to be what everyone expected of her—a good daughter, a good wife, a good straight woman. She'd only truly succeeded at being a damn good forensic anthropologist. Her students loved her, and local law enforcement began calling on her about five minutes after she arrived. As for the rest, she wouldn't exactly equate it with success.

Coming out had been easier than she envisioned, despite the vocal disappointment of her family and the outright denial that Daniel still clung to. She'd thought it would be hard to at last declare what she'd known in her heart for a long time. Enormous relief came when she put voice to those four words: "I am a lesbian."

Daniel, incredibly handsome, tall, and with a body made for the movies, never understood. For most women, he would be the guy to die for. Unfortunately, she wasn't most women, and she really did hate that she'd hurt him. He'd treated her well in all their years together, despite his controlling tendencies that made him perhaps a little clingy. A lot clingy, in fact, but it beat indifference.

In her defense of all the years of pretending, she always wanted to fit in with her family and friends. She'd made herself believe that her attraction to other women would pass if she ignored it. That all women had those secret moments of desire and longing. For a really smart woman, sometimes she could be clueless.

Not anymore. She stood tall and owned it all without even a glimmer of guilt or shame. No more living her life for others, not in that way, at least. The time had arrived to become the person she needed to be in order to make it through this life. Now if she could just get her ex-husband to move on, her world would be pretty good. So many women out there would love to have his attention, and she tried time and again to channel his energy toward them. The flowers and card she found on her desk when she came back to her office after class told her he wasn't even close to moving on. If she'd been here when they arrived, she'd have made the delivery person take them back. Erin, her graduate assistant, had accepted the flowers and put them on her desk. She probably thought them from an innocent admirer rather than a stalker-like ex-husband.

"Dr. Kind?" In her doorway, Erin, her student assistant, stood holding a slip of paper as if summoned by Shantel's mere thought of her.

She pushed aside her irritation with Daniel and concentrated on Erin. "What's up?"

"Deputy Rick has been trying to get in touch with you. I told him I'd track you down."

Shantel smiled and took the slip of paper that Erin handed her. Rick's office and cell numbers were printed in tidy, legible black ink. Her more-than-able assistant's efficiency came in very handy for the profession she was currently training for. "Thanks. I'll give him a call."

"Does he have another case for you?" Excitement radiated in Erin's voice. Occasionally, she needed assistance and would take along a student, several times in Erin's case, and with her keen eye, she would soon be a most excellent forensic anthropologist.

"It's possible."

"I'm available." Hope bloomed on her face.

"Good to know. I'll keep you posted." No promises, as she didn't have the details yet on what Rick needed from her.

Erin left Shantel's office, pulling the door closed. She didn't call the sheriff's department with her office door open, an invitation to any student who wanted to stop by. Her students were aware that her posted office hours included drop-in meetings when her schedule allowed. The enthusiasm of many of them invigorated her and thus her open-door policy. Not right now, however. This conversation required privacy.

"What's up?" she asked when Rick answered. She'd called his cell because, in her experience, chances he'd be in his office were slim.

"Bodies." Not wrong about him being out in the field.

"Bodies?"

"Yep. Four at the moment."

"What's Dr. Skelton say?"

"He's working on them as we speak and asked me to bring you in."

"Why?"

"It would be better for you to just come take a look."

All thoughts of Daniel and his unwanted delivery vanished. "A hint? You have me mighty curious now."

"Nope. You're not getting a thing out of me at this point. I'm interested in a cold read."

Her curiosity skyrocketed, and she reached for her bag. "On my way."

All the signs were there for a perfect day. Whenever he had a chance to mess with Shantel's head, Daniel considered it a win. She thought he didn't want to move on, and her belief held a grain of truth. Except that rationale simplified it by quite a lot. He didn't refuse to move on. He couldn't, for a very good reason. But he'd never shared that particular detail with her.

The whole commitment thing, the for-better-or-worse part, seemed to have slipped out of her grasp. When they'd married, he'd been one-hundred-percent serious about his vows. Until-death-do-them-part wasn't an empty pledge for him. In his family of choice, death represented the only way out. He could kill her. Then, the move-on piece would no longer be a problem. He wouldn't exercise that option now or ever. She'd been, and still remained, a perfect match for him, and together, their progeny would draw out the best in both of them.

Granted, she possessed one flaw his family found unpalatable. He'd assured his mentor, during numerous trips to see him, that before any children were conceived, he would remove that flaw from the mix. Easy enough to do, and he'd been waiting for the right time. Honestly, she should have caught on by now about what made him far better than any man she'd ever met. That she didn't made him even more determined to put everything right.

His office, in the converted Browne's Addition mansion, was large and boasted a massive view of Coeur d'Alene Park. Most days he enjoyed standing with a cup of coffee and staring out those windows at the park, despite the rising number of the homeless there. Some would call it uncomfortable. He liked to think of it as encouraging. Those were the nameless, faceless people that most in the community turned away from when they passed them on the street. Few took the time to see them as the people they were, and for him, that fact became important. No one would miss them if they disappeared. And they did. On a regular basis.

Like the park he watched now, the city had changed in the years he'd been away. His family still called the massive house and grounds on Rockwood Boulevard home. They'd lived there for generations, and everyone in the city knew their name. Buildings and parks were named after his forefathers. His public face presented an upstanding man of wealth and accomplishment. No one knew his secrets, and his family of birth didn't care to delve into his private activities. Unless, of course, he did something to tarnish their golden name.

He could have returned to the family home and lived in his own wing, just as other dutiful sons before him. Not his style. He required freedom from the prying eyes of his mother and father. He loved the city and the thrill of the hunt on urban streets. He loved being a lawyer and the excitement of defense work. His instincts were spot-on, and he hadn't lost a case since he passed the bar, one of the reasons his father had pushed him to return to the family business. Everyone knew that what Senior wanted, Senior got, and thus, home he'd come.

He turned away from the windows, holding a glass of scotch. Coffee didn't cut it for him. Besides, it wasn't the time of day for coffee, and while drinking alcohol in the office might be frowned on these days, no one dared question the golden boy. Local news on the flat-screen mounted on the west wall of his office provided an easy way to keep an eye out for potential clients. It wasn't quite ambulance chasing, given the clients who came to him needed to meet a certain level of liquidity. Nonetheless, for every twenty-five criminal events reported upon, perhaps one would rise to his level of representation. Today it wasn't the prospect of a client that made him lean in and turn up the volume.

"No, no, no." He slammed the glass down on the top of his desk, and golden liquid splashed onto the spotless surface. This shouldn't be possible. He'd been very careful, both as a young man who'd returned home from exploring the world and as a maturing man excelling in law school. Since the move back, he'd been equally careful. The hunt was too important to not execute things to perfection.

He stood in front of the screen, watching as the news crew filmed from a distance. The familiar yellow tape strung between trees, lots of police vehicles with flashing lights, uniformed and plains-clothes cops standing around, and in the background, a large white canopy erected over a piece of ground he knew intimately.

His jaw ached as he ground his teeth. Any lingering thoughts about Shantel or the flowers he'd sent her disappeared.

CHAPTER TWO

Johnnie groaned at the name displayed on her phone. She'd met Kay in the third grade at Orchard Center Elementary, and their friendship had endured the decades since, at least for the most part. When Kay became a reporter at the top local news channel, it regularly tested their bond. No doubt she'd glimpsed Johnnie at the scene and figured she could get the inside scoop. It happened every time she discovered Johnnie's involvement with a newsworthy case. Every. Single. Time. She did not pick up. Instead, she hit the ignore button and slipped the phone into her pocket. She reached around and opened the door to let Cougar jump out. She'd deal with Kay's drama later, and it would come. Kay never freaking gave up.

Anyone who watched Cougar run the acres of green fields dotted with apple trees and a seasonal stream on the east border would never guess how many hours he'd spent searching. Johnnie sent up a silent thanks. Cougar had been a true blessing.

The moment his paws touched the ground, he ran and jumped, his obsession with birds obviously making him believe he could leap high enough to catch them. Fortunately for the birds, he couldn't. She left him to his game and went inside.

Since Falco crossed the Rainbow Bridge almost a year ago, the silence hit her hard every time she walked through the door. Like Cougar, he'd been a great search dog and an exceptional companion. Cancer took him right before he would have turned ten and only six months after he'd retired from the field. He should have had more time.

She ignored the green plaid bed with the flannel top she'd been unable to take out of the corner of the kitchen. Instead, she stopped at the sink and stared out the window. For at least a week, Cougar had laid next to that bed—never on it—waiting. Someday she'd be able to pick it up and put it away. Today wasn't that day. She wiped away the tear sliding down her cheek.

Espresso, that's what she needed. Good coffee fixed everything.

Half an hour later, she still wasn't able to relax. Today's finds went beyond anything she'd come across to date, and she'd been doing this for a long time. After enough cases it wasn't hard to get jaded. Or so she'd thought. Jaded didn't hit the mark right now. Nope, more like immensely sad.

Emotions tended to overwhelm after the fact. When she and her first dog found a man's body, instinct and training kicked in and left no room for anything else. Only after she left the scene and disconnected did her reactions roll in. The first time the tears came, she'd been driving along a scenic stretch of the Spokane River. Forced to stop by blurring vision, she'd sat there in the small gravel pull-out for a good fifteen minutes, her shoulders shaking. Thankfully, the other handlers and the sheriff's department were a great support network, a resource she'd tapped more than once.

The multiple remains today shook her with the same force. No amount of training could prepare any handler for such a sight. More than the visual proof of unnatural death, something felt off, and she couldn't quite figure out what. Maybe her over-active imagination and the shock of discovering a burial ground versus a single recovery had her mind whirling. Or, maybe not.

The soothing effects of the shower she banked on didn't last much longer than the time it took to dry off. While she might be a lot cleaner and smell a lot better, that was about it. Even her expensive lavender soap failed in its touted calming properties. She'd be having a little heart-to-heart with her essential-oils buddy who swore lavender could work magic.

If warm water, lavender, and a rich, dark roast bombed, one other potential existed. She walked to the kitchen and opened the pantry door. "Hello, my pretties."

Johnnie studied the wine rack, deciding what lovely red would fill the relaxation bill for the evening. More than one way to coax relaxation into existence. Whoever said alcohol was a lazy way to handle stress never imbibed anything in her collection. A California deep-red blend won, and she pulled the bottle from the rack.

By the time she uncorked the bottle, Cougar scratched at the back door, and she let him in and smiled. Dinner time. Pretty sure he wore a watch under all that fur. She might want to relax with her glass of wine. He had his own priorities, and number one on the list was what she referred to as doggy meatloaf. Once a week, she prepared a big batch of ground meat, vegetables, and blueberries. Try to give him regular dog food, and she'd receive a withering look before he put his nose in the air and walked away. Her dogs were not spoiled at all. Considering their work, they deserved only the best.

Dinner dished up and delivered in his sparkling clean stainless-steel dish, she stood with her glass and watched him devour his sustenance. How could he eat so fast and not get sick? Tonight, she wouldn't tell him to slow down. In fact, after he finished, she opened the refrigerator and pulled out a bone. If any night called for something special, this was the one. She handed it to him, and as he opened his mouth to take it, she froze. "Oh, shit."

Shantel put her hands on her hips and shook her head. "This is pretty strange." She stared down at the first set of remains, then walked to the second, the third, and the fourth. She studied them as well as the graves the bones remained in for the moment, her mind whirling.

"You want to explain?"

Dr. Skelton stood back watching her, his hands behind his back. "Do I need to?"

"No."

He raised his eyebrows. "Good. Now humor me and explain the 'strange.'"

Shantel cocked her head and studied the doctor. He was an interesting man who often made her feel like she was back in school. She also couldn't argue that the guy was good and wanted to hear her thoughts. "Okay, Fred. Here's what I've got. Four separate victims."

Fred nodded. "So far. So good."

"Are you grading me?"

He smiled. "Why do you ask? You need the continuing-ed credits?"

"Funny guy."

"I try. Continue." He waved a hand toward the remains.

"Four victims buried at different times."

He nodded. "Agreed."

"Teeth marks on all the long bones."

"Definitely teeth marks."

"What's your initial thought, Fred?" She hesitated before she tossed out the question on her mind. "Cannibalism?"

"I don't know, at this point, and am not inclined to speculate. It'll get dark soon, so let's get these folks out of the ground and back to the lab. Then we'll figure out what's going on and if we have a Dahmer on our hands."

"God, I hope not."

"That makes two of us."

She stepped back and put her hands in her pockets. The techs were doing an excellent job in their excavation. The grid lines were set, and they were slowly and systematically uncovering the remains. The forensic team had exposed the bodies carefully while maintaining the integrity of the crime scene. A crew set up lights, anticipating sunset and the continuing work.

At least now she understood why Fred asked her to come. If she'd been first on scene, she'd also have wanted a second opinion. Even in the face of the many buried bodies she'd seen in the past, the site was unique. A little thrill tickled all the way to the tips of her fingers, followed by the heaviness of guilt.

Four people had died, and her firm religious upbringing told her that being excited wasn't an appropriate response. However, the scientist in her couldn't help it, upbringing be damned. Besides, she'd left that all behind. The moment she'd told her parents why she filed for divorce, the bridge home went up in mile-high flames.

The move here put a thousand miles of distance between her and the family that wanted nothing more to do with her. Even her twin sister turned away, which hurt the most. Not the time. She returned her attention to Fred and far less emotional ground, murders aside.

"Call me?"

Fred patted her shoulder and gave her a nod. "Of course."

❖

Daniel's practice had never been better. His family's name carried a great deal of weight in this part of Washington state, and to his own credit, he was an excellent attorney. Of course, he doubled down on the family skills after his backpacking trip between college and law school. Born with high intelligence, he came home from that trip with all his natural abilities amplified.

His last client, the son of one of the city's richest families who got his dick in a ringer after a tryst with an underage girl, just left. The case didn't require a whole lot of thought. The family possessed enough money to pay for the kind of defense only he could provide. The charges would be dropped within a month.

Daniel paced his quiet office, then turned the television back on so he could watch as the five o'clock news began. The lead story remained the discovery of multiple bodies in the Cheney area. Every channel he clicked to ran the same thing.

He'd always been very careful. How had they discovered his personal burial grounds? Surely, they'd stop with the bodies they'd found and call it a day. If they continued to search? He wouldn't go there. Not right. His secret.

The more he thought about it, the angrier he grew. It was all her fault. Everything had been fine until she decided to change sides and dump him. Nothing about that worked for him, and now this?

In all the years since that fateful trip, no one caught a clue as to his true nature. Not even his pretty wife who didn't lack for brains. She'd had some questions, and he'd had an explanation she bought every single time. No one knew and never would. He was simply that good.

For years, he'd been able to indulge in his favorite game without a problem. Wild game might be fine for most like him. Someone as powerful and alpha as he'd turned out to be required more. Nothing rivaled hunting humans, especially the thrill of the hunt and the taste of the flesh in his teeth. His bloodlust satisfied, he'd covered his deeds right from the start in order to remain under the radar of law enforcement.

And not just law enforcement. Some people took it upon themselves to hunt the preternatural, though most of society wrote them off as crackpots. That perception of the masses worked to his advantage, and he joined in the chorus to discredit them. Few grasped that those folks weren't wrong. Preternatural creatures existed and had for centuries. They lived in the shadows, where their secrets remained safe. They avoided the hunters or, if possible, took them out themselves. One less hunter, one less threat. Another game he enjoyed.

A couple of those annoying hunters rested six feet under near Fish Lake, and that's where they would stay. Those particular hunts turned out to be both enjoyable and utilitarian. Now to figure out how to throw off Shantel and her cronies. When he did that, no more of his prizes would be revealed.

After they finished covering the Cheney discovery and his beloved walked out of the frame, he clicked off the television. The eager, young reporters wouldn't tell him anything he didn't already know. Shantel, on the other hand, would be able to fill in a lot of blanks. How to coax it out of her remained the only unknown. She'd gotten testy lately, or at least whenever she talked with him. Her drivel about the finality of the divorce and getting on with their separate lives annoyed him, but if he planned to make any ground with her, he'd mask his true feelings. Her insider info about the investigation could make all the difference. In fact, with it, he could turn this whole unfortunate incident to his advantage.

There it was again, his innate brilliance combined with the preternatural enhancements that put him far ahead of everyone else. He'd never been sorry about what befell him in Tibet. Rather than diminish him, it made him better, and he'd always be grateful for that.

A buzzing inside him started as he stared out the office window at the waning light. He should take this time to be careful and keep his house in order. He never liked the word should.

CHAPTER THREE

Her glass of wine set down and forgotten, Johnnie picked up her cell phone. Not quite five. Rick would still have his phone on. His schedule wasn't even close to a set nine-to-five, and given what they'd found, he could be there half the night. She hit "call" and waited. He picked up on the first ring.

"You must be psychic. I was just going to phone you."

"What?" She momentarily forgot why she'd contacted him. Typically, she didn't hear from Rick after a search unless he needed a report faster than the normal twenty-four-hour window.

"Need you and Cougar tomorrow again, if you can make it."

Her mind whirled, and for a few seconds she said nothing. "Ah, yeah. I can make it work." Her hours were totally flexible. It didn't matter when she got her work done, as long as she made her contract deadlines. Right now, her middle-school history textbook neared completion. Another few days of tweaking, and it would be ready to go. Some might think her job writing textbooks a boring task. She didn't see it that way at all. The effort it took to pull together a work like that made her happy. To walk into a school and see one of her books helping young minds see the world gave her a high nothing else could match.

"Great. Meet me at the office at eight."

"Okay. We'll be there."

"See you then."

"Wait!" She caught him before he punched off the call. "I called you, remember."

"Huh. I guess you did. What's up?"

"Teeth marks."

"Say what?"

"On the bones. That's what caught my attention earlier. I didn't figure out why until I started to give Cougar a bone. It hit me then. The marks of his teeth on his bone were just like what I saw on the remains out there. Clear striations."

"Interesting." She could almost see Rick thinking it through. His eyes would narrow and his forehead furrow.

"I thought so too. Why would someone bury remains after some animal chewed on them? Doesn't make a whole lot of sense."

"Like this kind of killer makes any sense at all."

"True."

"Look. We got the new doc out here studying them. She'll work with Fred, and they'll figure it out. Pretty smart in that arena."

"Dr. Kind?"

"That's her. Know her?"

She'd heard about Dr. Kind, though she'd never seen her. Her arrival at EWU was a real coup, given her reputation, and Rick gave her kudos on bones discovered at a construction site some months back. The lady knew her stuff. "Haven't met her yet. Her reputation precedes."

"That it does."

"I just wanted to give you the heads-up when it hit me."

"Appreciate it. I'll pass it along. See you in the a.m."

She clicked off the phone, set it on the counter, and then picked up the wineglass once more, turning it in her hands as she studied it. Without taking even a sip, she put it back down. Instead of relaxing, she went back out to her truck and began to organize her gear for tomorrow's search.

❖

Fred, or Doc, as Shantel liked to call him, went back to his work, which equated to ignoring her. His actions didn't offend because she understood he and the forensic techs focused totally on the critical excavation, laying out a precise grid, taking careful measurements, and photographing the site a second time.

Her fingers twitched as the techs brushed away the dirt, revealing more and more bone. A mystery unfolded in front of her, and she wanted to solve it.

Not her role today and she left the scene to return to her car, mentally making a list of what to do first thing in the morning. They wouldn't finish here before midnight. Might as well go home, grade a few papers, and email her students. No classes for her tomorrow. She'd be in downtown Spokane all day. Hopefully, Erin could do the instructing while Shantel focused on the sleuthing.

Once home, she put on the kettle and then walked over to the tropical fish tank while waiting for the water to boil. "Hello, Stephen King. Hello, Anne Rice. Hello, John Carpenter. How are my beauties today?" She smiled as she sprinkled food into the water. The tank and the colorful fish that called it their ocean always brightened her mood. With her schedule, a dog or a cat wouldn't be the best pets. Companionship of the much more independent kind suited her lifestyle.

The kettle's whistle returned her attention to the cup of tea she desperately needed. It helped her focus. Now to get her thoughts down before she met Fred tomorrow. Her go-to Earl Grey smelled heavenly and tasted as good. No sugar, no cream, just straight up. Some folks liked a cocktail to relax, but a beautiful loose-leaf tea ordered direct did it for her. Used to drive Daniel batty that she refused to drink the prepackaged version sold in the local grocery stores with their paper filters and little strings. Some weren't bad and, in a pinch, would do. No pinch here.

The fragrant tea in hand, she sat at the table and frowned, thinking of her ex-husband and the sugary-sweet card delivered to her office earlier. He refused to give it up, and her brutal honesty didn't seem to penetrate his armor of denial. She'd been teaching a long time and had encountered denial in all its various forms. By rights, she should be an expert at dealing with people who didn't want to face reality, but nothing had prepared her for the battle when she left Daniel.

No doubt, she could have handled it all better. She usually tried to be strong and honest, except when it came to her closely held desires. She'd denied her true feelings for most of her life, until she couldn't anymore. She simply didn't love him and probably never had.

Good girls always did what was expected, and what a good girl she'd been. Until that night. The next day, she found an attorney and, five days later, filed for divorce. He'd ignored her then. He ignored her now, and her patience ran its course.

Better to ignore the unwanted tokens left in her office and focus on the job she'd face tomorrow. It's what she had trained for. More than that, it represented her passion since the seventh grade and Mrs. Hadron's science class. Her teacher would be proud of the doctor who'd found her calling in that classroom with the hard plastic chairs and vintage chalkboard. Did the school still stand, the chalkboard still a canvas for wanna-be taggers? She hoped so.

Her tea gone and her notes made, she went into her bedroom and sat on the edges of the bed. Intending to take a shower, she laid her cell on the nightstand and stared at the voice-mail icon. She knew who left it and that it would be smart to erase it. She touched play anyway. Morbid curiosity.

"Hey, baby. Saw you on the news tonight. We'll talk later and you can fill me in…" So much for curiosity. She deleted the message before it finished.

❖

Daniel didn't even try to resist. No point. No one would catch on. They were too narrow-minded and unimaginative, and way too convinced the rational world was the only reality.

He'd thought that way too when he'd taken off on that fateful journey. Like many young people, he had worlds to explore and oats to sow. So many oats. He'd thought it would be a routine college-grad, backpacking trip to Europe, an opportunity to see the world before he returned to real life and law school. It started that way and ended with his mind blown. Unlike many who undertook the coming-of-age adventure, he hadn't been satisfied with London or Madrid or Paris. He'd needed more, and thus his journey had taken him east to Asia. To Tibet.

Tonight wasn't a lot different from all those years ago. Older, of course, no getting around that. Still as full of it as he had been back then. Maybe even more because he'd learned much over the years. He'd grown wiser and more powerful. He'd always loved to learn, which was why law school beckoned him. Besides, most in his family ended up going, even if they'd set their sights on something else. For a brief time, he thought about becoming a doctor like little bro ended up doing. Then he decided that he would prefer the less touchy-feely profession of law. One where ruthlessness was viewed as an asset.

He got up close and personal with people on a regular basis, just not in the way doctors did. And he didn't have to worry about reviews on the internet after he touched them. In fact, he didn't have to worry about them at all. That one-and-done kind of contact was fun and satisfying for him, although not so much for them. So many perks to the life he'd created.

Just thinking about it brought a smile to his lips, at least until he drove by the convergence of vehicles that blocked the path to what he considered his ground. How dare they disturb his special place? Was nothing sacred anymore? Perhaps he didn't own it in terms of title. He certainly possessed it by rights of spirit.

To not draw unwanted attention, he continued by without slowing or stopping. People might call him many names, but stupid wasn't one of them. He passed the lights and the uniforms and continued into Cheney proper. Just for the fun of it, he drove through the Eastern Washington campus. His influence and connections were responsible for Shantel's tenure here, though she would never admit that truth. He'd meant to keep that fact to himself, at least until the night she declared that their marriage was over. Such garbage meant he'd needed to wield the truth.

How she still clung to the idea she'd attained the position and the tenure based upon her own merits was a mystery. Without him she'd still be trying to climb the academic ladder. No Ivy League education, no family of substance, no friends in high places. He, alone, took her to the top. She owed him, and one way or the other, he'd collect.

As he drove by the building that housed Shantel's campus office, he pushed the travesty unfolding at Fish Lake to the back of his mind. He'd deal with that fallout later. Besides, an idea began to take shape, and he'd expound upon it later. A twitch at the corner of his eye started. That it had taken him this long to come up with such a brilliant plan irritated him only marginally less than the activity in his sacred grounds.

Now, he focused on the Shantel issue and how to bring her around once and for all. This lesbian crap was complete nonsense. If she were inclined that way, he'd easily pick up on it. No chance that he'd fall for someone not one hundred percent hetero. He had an excellent sense of people. All he really needed was strategy. A good lawyer always prepared a good strategy.

He pulled into a spot with a two-hour meter down the street from her building, and after feeding the meter, he walked onto the campus. Brick paths, green grass, and tall lights were designed to facilitate the flow of students moving from building to building. Given the hour, only a few people meandered through the commons. She wouldn't be here either. In fact, he banked on her being gone. Just walking her hallways would help him strategize. It's how he worked. In his practice, he often used the get-in-the-mind-of-the-killer psychology. Insider knowledge about how a killer thought gave him the tools he needed for a solid defense. Guilt or innocence never figured into it.

Tonight, the gods smiled on him. Someone leaving as he approached gave him access to the otherwise locked building. They paid little attention to him as he caught the door before it clicked shut. Halfway down the hall he caught sight of a pretty young woman with long black hair. Native American, if he guessed right, and he always did. Not unusual in this region, where several tribes were indigenous to the area. Spokane, perhaps, or maybe Kalispel. Tribal affiliation wasn't the important factor. Attractive and young were the two things that really captured his attention. That and the fact that she'd just come out of Shantel's office, locking it behind her. An assistant. Perfect. His plan began to formulate like a well-laid-out spreadsheet.

She didn't notice when he followed her out of the building, his steps silent, another little perk of his special nature. Neither did she pay attention as she drove out of the staff lot, and he pulled from his curbside parking spot right behind her. She took the highway toward I90, and he allowed a couple of cars to get in between them. Everyone who headed into Spokane took this route, and the chances that she'd think it odd another car from campus also drove this way were zero. He believed in the old adage better safe than sorry, and continued to stay back enough not to become obvious.

When she drove into Browne's Addition, he smiled. Things were getting better and better. The icing on the cake came after she parked and walked into the Elk, a popular and excellent bar/restaurant just a couple blocks from his office. The stars had just aligned in his favor. Indeed, his plan had come together with the perfection that defined his practice and, indeed, his life. He parked behind her car, not worried now that she might see him. Coincidences happened all the time, but honestly, this was divine intervention. Things often occurred that way for him. He ran his fingers through his wavy hair, a little long for his father's conservative leanings. Perfect for a man with a palate such as his. Shantel told him on their first date what a Hollywood aura it gave him, and she hadn't been wrong. Had he been so inclined, he'd have been successful in the entertainment industry. Wasn't his thing. He liked the law, even if he often felt as though he'd been dragged into it. Once he got a taste of the criminal side of it, his resistance about becoming an attorney took a one-eighty. Competitiveness pulsed through his veins like lava.

He stepped through the door of the Elk, and there she sat on a tall stool at one of the buddy bars, several texts spread out in front of her as though she was prepared to do a little cramming. The air smelled of hops and good food, and the murmur of animated voices gave it a welcoming atmosphere. A waiter approached her and put down a dark brew on a paper coaster. She smiled at the curly haired man with the long black apron tied at his waist. Her white smile was beautiful against her dark skin, and just a hint of cleavage showed as she leaned forward on her arms. His blood ran hot. This had all the hallmarks of a thrilling evening. He walked to her table and stopped, smiling. "Hi. Is this seat taken?"

CHAPTER FOUR

Johnnie opened the truck's back door, and Cougar jumped in. She hooked the seat belt into the harness before she crawled into the driver's seat and turned the key. In her childhood, their dogs always rode loose, whether it be in the backseat of the car or the bed of her dad's pickup truck. It was just the way things were done back then. Times had changed a lot. A real example of doing better when she knew better. She was doing more than better. Maya Angelou would be proud.

Thinking of her dad made her smile. He'd been gone a long time now, the victim of a life-long dedication to road construction. For forty years he sat atop heavy equipment and breathed in diesel fumes and dust while he built the roads and freeways she traveled on now. His love of dogs had rubbed off on her, and though he hadn't lived long enough to see her search-and-recovery work, he'd be proud. Boy, how would he have loved Cougar. She reached back and rubbed his head.

They arrived at the location Rick texted to her last night. A glance at the temperature display on the dash told her she'd want to put on a jacket. Instead of the blue coat with "Search and Rescue K9 Unit" emblazoned on the back in reflective lettering, from behind her seat she grabbed an all-black jacket with no markings at all. There were times to be open and others to be covert.

Rick's car, along with the command-post trailer, was already there when she and Cougar put the truck in park. The trailer's presence signaled that they expected more of what they'd discovered yesterday. For a moment she sat there and took deep breaths, thinking that once again a serial killer set siege to her beloved hometown. How could an area so gorgeous allow evil to take root over and over? Was it something in the water? In the air? It didn't make sense, yet reality slapped her in the face. Breathe in. Breathe out. Repeat.

Her soul buoyed by the breathing ritual, she finally stepped out of the truck, grabbed her GPS from the back, and headed to the trailer. Inside, a low buzz of activity filled the narrow, cramped space. Rick nodded as she handed him the device, no chitchat required on either side. She signed in and walked back out into the crisp morning air. Inside the trailer they had their work to do, and outside, she had hers. First things, first. Cougar would get a break while Rick and his crew laid out the search areas.

"You ready?" Rick stepped out of the command post twenty minutes later, her trusty GPS in his hand.

Johnnie took it from him, studied the areas he'd loaded, and started mentally planning in her head. The map showed her terrain features and elevation. The wind on her face told her direction. It all came into play when she made a plan. "Okay," she said after a moment. "I'm ready."

That turned out to be a lie. Even if someone had told her what they'd encounter, she'd have never been ready for this. Cougar did his job like a champion. She wouldn't have expected any less from him, and he never let her down regardless of whether they were involved in a mission or a training session. His work ethic deserved a gold star.

After this session, she possessed a new appreciation for disaster dogs. Multiple finds were not the norm for her and Cougar, at all. They had located three separate locations for the techs to excavate today, making seven recoveries in all. A lump the size of a boulder sat in the pit of her stomach, and in Cougar's eyes shone a sadness she'd never seen before.

"We can take it from here." Rick's face mirrored the exhaustion that engulfed her entire body. He'd been with them every step of the way out there, quietly assisting and supporting them as they worked. He marked each spot where Cougar indicated the odor of human decomposition with flagging tape and delineated the perimeter with police tape. The techs would come behind them to lay out the grids and most likely expand the secure area with their own bright crime-scene tape.

Back at the command post, Johnnie once again handed Rick her GPS. "I'll come by and pick this up tomorrow." Usually, she waited while they downloaded her and Cougar's tracks. After they returned it, she would clear everything, make sure the batteries were charged, and then put it in the harness again so it would be ready for the next search. Not today. Wiped out didn't even begin to describe the drag on her mind and body.

"Understood." He took it from her as he opened the door and stepped inside the trailer, the tone of his voice echoing hers. The gravity of the finds affected all of them—mind, body, and spirit. It would kick the tar out of any decent human being.

On the clipboard outside the command-post door, she signed out, then headed to her truck. Cougar jumped into the back, and as soon as she had his harness clipped into the seat belt, he lay down. His eyes closed immediately, and she rubbed the smooth, dark hair on his head. "I understand, buddy. This just sucked."

As soon as they got home, she fed Cougar and then jumped into the shower. Having the warm water wash away the dust of the search should have helped her relax. Unfortunately, it didn't. She was as keyed up as when she left the search. Not surprising. Anybody who could wash away something as awful as what they'd found today had no heart or conscience. She'd never suffered from that problem, which was probably why the moniker of psychopath would never be applied to her. That's exactly what the person who did this had to be.

Dinner consisted of cold pizza and a rich, malty ale—perfect for the dark mood that hung on. After a brief run in the backyard, Cougar came in and fell asleep in his favorite spot on the sofa. No places were off-limits in her house. As hard as he worked, if Cougar wanted to sleep on the sofa or her bed, go for it. He was, after all, family. She took her pizza and beer to the chair across from him and put her feet up on the wide ottoman. With the remote, she clicked the television on, and the low murmur of voices filled the room with a comforting white noise.

It wasn't clear why being alone bothered her now. She'd been alone, except for her dogs, for years. She'd gotten close to marriage once, and while not consciously avoiding further entanglements, she had. Something in the back of her brain must have decided dogs were better companions than women. Or men. She'd gone down that path too, wanting to explore all options before landing firmly on the side of women. No one in her family had been overly surprised either. As her mother liked to tell it, they'd all figured it out long before she made a public declaration.

Halfway through the pizza, she put it down. Not because it was bad. A question had popped spontaneously into her head. She reached for her cell. "Tell me what they found."

Rick sounded as tired as she felt. "Hello to you too."

Point taken. That was rude. "Sorry. Hi. What have they found?"

"Nothing yet. They're still working."

"Come on. You were there for at least part of it. Or are you still there?"

"Left an hour ago."

"So?"

"I don't have anything yet."

"You know what I'm asking." She got that he couldn't give her details. That wasn't what she was after.

"Yeah." He said it on a long breath.

A tingle at the back of her neck made her shoulders tense. "Damn it. I knew it. What is going on around here?"

For fifteen plus years Shantel had been both teaching and working in the field of forensic anthropology. All that dandy knowledge didn't mean much today because she had no experience with what she'd seen at Fish Lake yesterday or right now. Her laborious and heartbreaking work in some of the war-torn countries should have prepared her for any conceivable situation. It didn't. She'd never encountered anything like this, and sure as hell not in her own backyard.

It was even more awful because of the condition of the long bones recovered from each grave. Every one of them showed signs of having been gnawed on. No other way to explain the condition. Back in the ME's office, the victims had been laid out as best they could, given not all the bones were present, and they proceeded to document the same finding over and over. She and Doc stood side by side staring at the remains and trying to make sense of it, except they both failed.

They'd locked eyes at one point, and she'd thrown out the elephant in the room. "Cannibalism?" A long shot, but she wanted to know where Doc stood given his lack of input on the subject yesterday.

His head shake told her everything. "No. Doesn't look quite right. Doesn't have the right feel either." In their field, they relied on solid science. She had yet to meet a peer who didn't also give credence to gut instinct.

Time to toss up the second elephant in the room. "Canine." Not exactly a legitimate question, given she'd seen similar marks before. Anyone who worked in her field viewed them, as animal intervention routinely happened when bodies were left in the open or buried in shallow graves.

His nod sent the mystery a lot deeper because animals did not take bones, chew them, and then come back and bury them in tidy, deep graves. "A really big canine."

Her hands on her hips, she leaned in close. "Really big."

She was still thinking about it an hour later as she pulled into her driveway. The how and the why weren't syncing up for her. Given Doc's uncharacteristic silence when she left the ME's office, it apparently wasn't syncing up for him either. He'd quickly become her favorite partially because they were so often on the same wavelength.

Given today's work, the probability of a good night's sleep ran quite low. Instead of spending a lot of useless time tossing and turning, she bypassed the bed and opted for research instead. She didn't hold out a lot of hope that she could uncover cases that might be even remotely similar to what they were seeing. That didn't mean she wouldn't try.

At least she didn't have any additional unwanted presents today. After yesterday, she figured a spate of cards, flowers, and gifts would be on the agenda for the immediate future. That's the way Daniel worked. He'd get all fired up and besiege her with anything and everything he could think of. Undoubtedly, he considered it romantic. Right now, she didn't have the energy to deal with him, and the empty porch she saw when she got home made her hope this round of obsession would be brief.

In the kitchen, she'd just poured the water into her tea kettle when her cell rang. She glanced at the display before she picked up. It wasn't Daniel. Good. "Hey, Rick. I don't have anything for you yet." Turnabout was fair play. She'd bugged him last night when he had nothing to give her, and now he came to her for more than she had to share.

"Did Doc tell you what we found today?"

"No." Not the question she expected. There couldn't be more, could there? "He was in his office on the phone when I left."

"Yeah, well, three more."

She sank to one of the stools at the island. The temperature in the room seemed to have dropped. "Damn it."

"No shit. Not what I was hoping for."

"What is going on around here? I thought this was a safe area. How many serial killers can one region give birth to?" Though she hadn't grown up here, she'd been schooled on the legacy of evil that several former residents visited upon the city.

"I hate to break it to you, but safety is an illusion. Evil exists everywhere. As to your other question, I wish I knew the answer."

Not quite a revelation for Shantel. When she chose this specialty, evil walked hand in hand with it. Particularly when she gave of her services in countries that experienced horrors most people couldn't imagine. Sure, she got that evil often showed up in the most beautiful of places. But a girl could hope to live in a place where the shadows didn't conceal menace.

"Not a news flash."

"Nope. Here's the deal. We had crews out there earlier and wrapped up for the day a little while ago. One grave done, two to go. We'd like to impose upon you again tomorrow to help out in the field. I'm bringing in Johnnie and Cougar, as well as another dog team to try to cover the remaining ground out there. We want them to search additional areas, and it would be nice to have you on standby."

She rested her head on her hand and closed her eyes. "I've got three classes tomorrow."

"You've got some grad students who can step in, right?"

"Erin has already covered a lot for me." It wasn't fair to Erin to throw all these classes at her. Usually, if she had to be gone for an extended period, they had time to prepare together. That wasn't the case here, and she didn't want to call her to just say, "Hey, take my classes again because I have a more interesting option."

"I wouldn't ask if it wasn't important."

She ran a hand through her hair and nodded, even though no one could see her. Rick didn't impose without good reason. "I know you wouldn't. Let me make some calls, and I'll get back to you."

When she couldn't reach Erin, worry ticked at the back of her brain. It wasn't like Erin to not pick up when Shantel called. She always carried her cell, and even if she didn't answer a call, she responded to a text. Shantel was just about to phone the department chair when Erin got in touch.

"Hey."

"Sorry, Shantel. I was sleeping." The grogginess in her voice attested to the truth of her statement.

Shantel looked at the clock and frowned. "Really?"

"Haven't felt like myself today. Was hoping I could sleep it off."

Now she really started to question whether she could impose on Erin again. It wouldn't be right to expect her to carry this load if she was ill. "Are you feeling any better?"

"Somewhat. Kind of weird, if I'm being honest. I guess I stayed out later than I should have last night. Met an interesting guy and... ah, you know how it goes. Usually, I bounce back quicker. I guess I'm getting old."

Relief flooded her like a shot of aged bourbon. Just a little too much fun on a weeknight. Relatable. "I've been there myself a time or two." Not for a long time, though she'd keep the details of her boring nightlife close for the time being anyway. Her life had become sad when excavating the remains of presumed murder victims became a highlight.

"What's up?" Erin's voice regained a bit of life. She must be shaking off the cobwebs of her nap. Good. Made it easier to impose.

Shantel gave her a quick rundown, or at least as much as she could share. She and Doc were required to keep some disturbing details confidential. Bottom line, she needed Erin to teach her three classes tomorrow.

"No problem. I can cover for you."

"Are you sure?" As much as she wanted her to step in, something in her voice bothered Shantel. Might be better to decline for tomorrow.

Erin didn't give her a chance to back out. "I'm sure. I'll be right as rain in the morning, and I'll be happy to put the students through their paces. Good practice for after I join the doctoral club and you cut me loose."

Her shoulders relaxed. "You know, I'll never totally cut you loose. You're stuck with me forever."

Erin laughed and sounded more like herself. "I'm banking on it. Now, don't worry. I've got your back. Go do your thing and help them catch this son of a bitch."

"Appreciate it."

"No worries."

Except worry lingered after she ended the call. Not enough to call Erin back and tell her to forget it, that she'd teach her own classes tomorrow. The intrigue out in the field called to her. Besides, like Erin said, she'd get a good night's sleep and be her old self in the morning. Grad students were accustomed to insane schedules and little sleep. She'd lived off coffee and protein bars while she worked on her doctorate, and she'd survived. So would Erin.

The next and last call Shantel made went to Rick. He sounded relieved when she told him she'd be available. Only then did she put the phone on the counter and turn to the forgotten tea. Long after she'd first intended, she turned on the tea kettle.

Next on the agenda, comfortable clothes. Yoga pants and a sweatshirt were exactly what the doctor ordered—that doctor, of course, being her. All her ducks were in a row and signaled time to buckle down for some quality research. The glamorous life of a smart, single anthropologist.

Daniel showed up at Erin's house just as the sun began to drop behind the mountains to the west. The colors of the sunsets here couldn't be beat. Crimson and gold, they slashed across the sky as though they flowed from the palette of Frederic Edwin Church. He'd always loved Church's paintings, though even a master couldn't beat the real thing.

He rapped his knuckles against the wooden door. She'd sense him and thus no need for a dramatic announcement. A light tap would do. She opened the door. To most people, the shadows beneath Erin's eyes might not have been anything much beyond weariness. To him, they were beautiful. They told him his plan progressed as he hoped. It always started this way—a weariness that hours of sleep couldn't shake and physical changes that made others do a double take. He smiled. "Hey."

"Danny? What are you doing here?"

Her surprise at finding him on her front porch wasn't faked. After the night they'd shared, she shouldn't be shocked. Unless she believed him to be the kind of guy who would fuck her brains out and then disappear. Not that he hadn't been known to do that a time or twelve, but with the special ones, not his style. She wouldn't be able to grasp his plans for her right now. Soon enough she would, and with him as her alpha, she'd comply. They all did, sooner or later.

His bent toward a solitary existence resonated strong within him. It didn't mean he couldn't be flexible. Like all of the lupus variety, he was a pack creature by default. At times, he surrendered to that part of his nature and built a pack, at least as long as it suited his needs, and at the moment, he could use the help. Once he got what he wanted, he'd have no further need for Erin, or anyone else he might recruit for the mini war he had in mind.

"Couldn't stay away." He gave her his best smile. It worked for him over and over, and it would now as well.

She ran a hand through her hair, which further highlighted her weary features. He'd have thought she'd be a little tougher. After all, in the big picture she was still a kid, and he hadn't kept her up that late. Maybe he did, but at her age and given what he'd shared with her, she should bounce back faster.

Her weary eyes met his. A flicker of something exciting almost pushed past the fatigue. "While I appreciate you not dropping me like a hot rock, I'm not up to anything tonight."

The smile that stayed on his face typically melted even the most hesitant. He could turn up the wattage when needed. "I get it. I just wanted to check up on you. Kind of crazy last night."

"It was, and after teaching my advisor's classes today, I'm beat. Thanks for stopping by." She started to close the door.

He put a hand out to stop it, while keeping the neon smile. "I like you." Direct tended to work better with those whose intelligence came at an above-average level. It wasn't a lie. He did like her. Use her, absolutely. The two were not mutually exclusive.

The spark in her eyes brightened. "I like you too, Danny. I'm exhausted though, and I have a ton of work to get ready for tomorrow."

"You're in luck. I came prepared." He presented the bag he'd been holding behind his back. "I bring you sustenance. How do you feel about prime rib?"

That offer piqued her interest and the hunger sure to engulf her. "Tell me it's at least medium rare. If it's well-done, I'm closing the door."

"Now you're talking my language." He had her. "Rare to medium. I was hoping you'd like it my style." He winked.

She pulled the door open wider. "Tempting."

"Trust me," he said as he stepped closer. "By the time you finish eating tonight, you'll feel like a new woman. I promise."

"I don't know if that's true, but I am hungry, and you said the magic word."

"Prime rib?"

"Damn straight." She finally smiled.

"How about we just spend a little time together. We don't have to talk. We don't have to do anything. Let's just sit together and enjoy some good food."

A mere flicker of hesitation, and in that moment, he had her. "Okay. Let's just sit together for a while and eat." She stepped back and opened the door wider.

He kissed the side of her head as he walked inside. "I'll be as quiet as a church mouse." What he planned for tonight didn't require a lot of words anyway. It might have been a while since he'd done this, it didn't mean he'd forgotten how it would go down. Not a single element slipped from his memory. A mind like a steel trap, as Senior liked to say.

Unlike most who made the transition from humanity to lycanthropy, his choice of solidarity over belonging to a pack came with risks. His existence became more dangerous, yet he wouldn't trade it for anything. The phrase lone wolf mostly referred to those who functioned in solitude for a reason. Besides, he couldn't discount the power it gave him. Even if those around him were unaware of his capabilities, it did not diminish its importance to him. If anything, it made it all more enjoyable. Watching them try to figure out the secret to his success entertained him to no end.

Of course, one person continued to ignore it all. For now, anyway. He planned to change that oversight. She would pay attention and see him fully for the first time. No longer would she be able to deny either his superiority or their unbreakable bond. The unnecessary separation would be over.

On some occasions he had second-guessed his decision to keep his secret from her. Perhaps if she'd known all along what he was and what he was capable of, all this wouldn't be necessary. Perhaps if he'd chosen for her to cross over, she'd be in her rightful place now. Perhaps. Perhaps. Perhaps.

He shook off the uncertainty that surrounded his previous decisions. Had he decided to become one with a pack, he would have made different choices, and the others would have forced his hand when it came to her. Another reason for the path he'd ultimately taken. He allowed no one to have that kind of hold on him, and so he would deal with the ramifications himself. She'd come back to him, and this time he'd bring her all the way in.

That attitude would take him to even more magnificent heights than he'd already achieved. His mood blossomed as he stepped into Erin's kitchen and began to unpack the meal she'd find appealing. With his fingers, he wiped up the blood spilled as he opened the containers, the heady scent making his smile grow. Licking the blood from his fingers, he sighed.

CHAPTER FIVE

Johnnie woke up thinking about the damn bones. Even worse, she'd dreamed about them too. Lots and lots of bones, all with the distinct marks of canine teeth. Like the beef bones she gave Cougar and that were now scattered throughout her house waiting to be kicked with a bare foot.

Except not. Unlike what she routinely bought for Cougar, the bones they'd found over the last several days didn't come from a cow. She'd completed enough training on identification to know the difference between human and animal. Those were most definitely human bones. Besides, like her visual training, Cougar could distinguish by scent between the two. Had they been animal, he would have ignored them. He didn't.

Since she'd been handling dogs for search and recovery, she'd been called out on some odd cases. Weird places and out-of-the-way locations that left her puzzled were all part of the job. This one topped them all on every front—odd, weird, and puzzling.

First things first. Without her morning latte, no one in their right mind could expect her complete attention. Mug in hand, she went to the living room and studied the vinyl lined up in alphabetical order on the shelf next to the turntable that once upon a time belonged to her grandmother. Grandma had been a wicked clarinet player and passed her love of music along to Johnnie. Her clarinet too, and it currently occupied a place on honor on the piano. When she got really stumped, she'd sit down and play. Unlike Grandma, a master of jazz, she preferred to play the classics. Mozart, Beethoven, Rachmaninoff. It cleared her mind and soothed her emotions.

Nothing from the classics this morning. Something a little harder. From the stack of vinyl, she chose what she liked to think of as mood music—the original 1975 Aerosmith *Toys in the Attic*. Between her grandmother and her mother, she possessed an impressive collection of albums. This was one of her favorites, and as soon as the music began to play, her shoulders relaxed, and her foot began to tap. She loved rock and roll.

Between the latte and the music, she refocused and prepared. A good pair of cargo pants, a pullover fleece, her favorite pair of boots, and she was ready to go. Cougar waited at the back door. The clothes and the energy she gave off were all he needed to understand the schedule of the day. It didn't matter to him how many days in a row; he was always ready to go. They loaded up and drove away from the farm.

Her focus escalated to the laser stage by the time she pulled in and parked next to the sheriff's unmarked cruiser. The uneasiness that brought her awake, gone. Curiosity about the condition of the bones hadn't left her mind; she'd just found a way to compartmentalize it enough to get out here and do the job for the third day. God only knew what they'd find today. It would be nice to find nothing. Not very hopeful on that front.

She opened the driver's door and got out. "You wait," she told Cougar. "I'll be back in a few." Some might find it odd that she explained herself to a dog. She didn't. She'd been talking to them since she was a little girl, and that wasn't about to change. People, she didn't always get. Dogs, she did.

After she slipped into her chest harness and checked her radio, she walked over to where Rick stood with a small crowd of people. Several familiar faces from previous searches and an unfamiliar one. The mystery woman had long black hair, braided and hanging down her back to her waist. A new addition to the sheriff's department? Over the last couple of years Rick brought up retirement now and again, so maybe she was training as his replacement. He'd been heading the county's search-and-rescue program for more than a decade, and one of these days, he'd leave. She didn't look forward to that day.

Rick turned as she got closer and nodded as he motioned her over. "Good morning. Ready for this again?"

She grimaced and answered with her trademark honesty. "Nope."

He barked out a laugh that held no humor. "No shit. Me either." Another reason she'd miss him when he decided to turn in his badge. He never failed to return honesty with honesty.

The mystery woman turned, and Johnnie's heart did a little flip. Now that was fucking strange. She rarely reacted to strangers. Practicing caution to a fault defined her. The walls she put up were there for a reason. Ghosts couldn't get through them. Neither did the living, breathing variety either.

Not the time to go there. Instead, she focused on Rick's introductions. "Johnnie, this is Dr. Shantel Kind."

Aha. Now she knew the face that went with the name. Not what she'd call beautiful. Arresting, with intelligence clear in her dark eyes. Beautiful, in Johnnie's book, was a dime a dozen. What this woman possessed, just on the surface, wasn't anything she encountered on a daily basis. Intriguing, as was her reputation. Given what Johnnie and Cougar did, their finds were sent routinely to bone doctors in their area. EWU had been lucky to grab someone with Dr. Kind's background, and now, here she stood at long last.

"So nice to meet you, Dr. Kind." She held out her hand. The dark eyes met hers straight on, and again, that little thrill raced through her again. Wow, just wow.

A firm grip when she accepted Johnnie's outstretched hand. "Shantel. Please call me Shantel."

More points. That she didn't stand on formality was a nice change. Her predecessor would have never tolerated a mere dog handler calling him by his given name. Fortunately, they'd rarely had to work together in the field. Usually, Johnnie and Cougar came out, marked a location in those instances where they were positive for the odor of human decomposition, and turned it over to law enforcement. At that point, their job was complete.

What they were doing today didn't follow the usual pattern, and that alone frightened her. Compound that with the presence of an anthropologist in the field, and it sent the weirdness meter off the charts. The day had all the hallmarks of being intensely interesting and, most likely, grueling.

"Nice to meet you, Shantel."

"Okay, okay, introductions done. Let's get to our search plan." Rick held out a clipboard with a small stack of papers on it.

Johnnie shifted her focus away from the good doctor and to Rick. Time to get this party started.

❖

Shantel shouldn't have been surprised when she met the dog handler Rick told her about. It wouldn't be the first time she'd worked with and around cadaver dogs…correction, human-remains-detection dogs. Though most people were familiar with the term "cadaver dog," they didn't just find bodies. These fascinating animals were trained to detect the odor of human decomposition, which included her particular specialty, bones. Amazingly, these animals could detect the presence of human bones buried deep in the earth. Watching them work never got old.

This particular dog, Cougar, had a reputation, even though she'd never met him or his handler, Johnnie Lancaster. When Rick asked her to join them this morning, she hadn't been sure what she'd expected. Not a tall woman with short brown hair that framed a face she'd bet could easily grace the cover of *Vogue*. Not drop-dead gorgeous but striking in an exotic way that the trendy magazine excelled in. Definitely cover-model potential.

Even in cargo pants and a black cap, she looked great. More than that, she also appeared competent, which counted for a lot more in her book. Something in her bearing and intense gaze as she listened to the deputy sheriff lay out his plan for today's search radiated competence. She asked a few pointed questions before nodding and turning to walk back toward her vehicle.

"She's good, isn't she?" Shantel cut her gaze to Rick.

"Honestly, she's one of the best, and we're lucky to have her here. With the flexibility her career provides, I can call her day or night. Trust me, that's not something I take for granted or abuse, which I'm bordering on now."

"What is her career?"

"You'd never guess it by looking at her."

Shantel waited a beat, thinking he'd continue. "And…"

"She writes textbooks. Specifically, history textbooks. Schools all over the country use her books as mandatory curriculum."

No. She never would have guessed non-fiction author. "Can't judge a book by its cover."

"Good one, Doc."

Honestly, it wasn't all in jest. The cover on that book definitely did not read history buff—or writer. She'd have gone more for consultant or advisor. The woman had an air about her that exuded the kind of confidence one found with people in those professions. Writers worked in such a solitary world, and someone who chose history took solitary to a whole other level. They preferred back rooms of libraries, old journals, family histories, and hours upon hours of sifting through it all to arrive at the truth. Once, only the winner wrote history. These days, truth was beginning to take more of a center stage, which meant a whole lot of work getting to it. She planned to peek at the books this very interesting woman had written.

Not now. And not in the foreseeable future, given what had been found over the last few days. Shantel had been working night and day helping to put all the pieces to this puzzle together. Thank God for Erin agreeing to cover her classes...again. She didn't like dropping out of sight for her students, but the contract she had with the county gave them the right to call upon her in instances like this. She hadn't come here only for the position at the university. The chance to work on interesting cases throughout a very large and diverse geographic area cemented her decision.

She always suspected Daniel and his family had put some pressure on both factions to get her here, and while she could be bitter about that tactic, she wasn't. The implosion of her marriage would have happened whether they came here or not, so at least she found herself in a dream position when the relationship crumbled beyond repair. All the king's horses and all the king's men would never put it back together again... regardless of what Daniel might still be thinking.

It would have been a completely different dynamic if they'd been someplace else when she finally walked away. He had his family as well as the family business, and she had work that let her use her knowledge and expertise. A win for both of them on that front. That he had fallen in love with a woman who managed to bury her true nature was unfortunate. It kept her in the relationship far longer than she should have stayed. Courage sometimes took most of a lifetime to develop. Very true in her case. Despite his pressure, she didn't plan to take a step back. She'd fought too hard to get here to let it go.

Who would want to anyway? The freedom that came with embracing courage was priceless. Not to mention that she now saw the world in a completely different way. Some days were bad, most days good.

This day gave her a little of both. She didn't like why they were out here. The implications of the findings over the last few days gave her chills. Over the course of her career, she'd been in some dark places. Nothing quite as dark as these finds hinted at.

On the upside, today she would work with a beautiful, fascinating woman. That took a little of the edge off the job and made her want to get going right away. To watch this woman and her dog work the field fascinated her. To use her own skills to assist law enforcement find out what happened in what appeared to be a massive killing field made it worth stepping into the darkness once more.

"Okay." Johnnie returned with a gorgeous German shepherd walking right next to her. Lean and powerful, and ready to work, yet he stayed next to Johnnie in a way that spoke volumes about their close relationship. "I've got my plan."

Johnnie laid out her search strategy, and Shantel paid close attention. While she'd worked with dogs on searches, this was the most detailed briefing she'd ever been involved with. Her initial impression of Johnnie jumped up on the respect meter.

From the Fish Lake parking lot, closed to the public since the first remains were found, they began a grid search to the southwest. A familiar trail given Shantel biked it at least once a month since moving here. Not too far from the Cheney campus, it provided an outlet for fresh air when it became necessary to clear her mind. Yet all the times she'd cycled this trail, she'd never imagined it might be a serial killer's personal burial grounds. What rational person would think of something like that?

Except it should have occurred to her. In her training, she'd been taught to expect the unexpected. Remains could be found anywhere. Not everyone received the privilege of a tidy grave in a cemetery or inurnment in a beautiful container. How many bodies could be found in unmarked graves along the perimeter of historical cemeteries, their families too poor to afford them a proper burial? Wanting them to rest in hallowed ground, the well-meaning family members covertly buried them as close as possible to the elaborate headstones.

"Ready?" Johnnie's voice brought her back to the here and now.

"I'm ready."

Rick handed the GPS to the man he'd earlier introduced her to as Damon. He would be handling the navigation, keeping everyone on track with the grid search designed to ensure they covered the entire area. They started walking as a group, following Damon as he led them to the starting point Johnnie had pointed out on the map.

The moment they stepped off the asphalt trail so lovely to ride a bike on, a shiver raced down her spine.

Daniel stretched his arms over his head and smiled. What a night. He'd forgotten how much fun having another person around could be. Since the misunderstanding with Shantel, he'd mostly stayed by himself—the sad son of one of the city's most prominent members mourning the loss of a marriage. And he played his part well. So much sympathy came his way, and he lapped it up. Especially the touchy-feely kind offered to him from those of the female persuasion.

Little did anyone know that the sadness he showed on the outside masked the fury boiling on the inside. He didn't get sad. Even before his transformation, sadness didn't resonate for him. His only two true emotions were happiness and rage. Who needed more than two solid emotions anyway?

He rolled over and kissed Erin on the side of her neck. "Wakey, wakey."

Her eyes fluttered open, and for a few seconds, confusion clouded them. Then she popped up, fully awake. "What time is it? I've got a class at ten."

He smiled and ran a finger down her arm. "Plenty of time. It's only a little after seven."

She swung her legs over the side of the bed and stood. "Seven, damn it. I've got prep to do and Jesus…"

"You have to learn how to relax." He leaned his head on his hand and laughed. What was it about highly educated women? In his experience, they were all wound a little too tight.

"You have to go," she said while heading toward the bathroom

"Come on." He flopped on his back and stared at the ceiling.

"Now. Go. Not all of us have the old family business to fall back on." She stood in the bathroom doorway, hands on hips. A beautiful, naked woman. What a way to start the morning.

"Ouch." But he was laughing. Her words weren't untrue, and it was the one bit of truth he'd shared with her even if he'd omitted some of the finer details of his life, like the actual identity of his family. It didn't bother him that he'd enjoyed privilege his entire life, opportunities and experiences most of his friends and acquaintances never had. Some were simply born better than others, and who was he to fight that? His personal philosophy had always been to enjoy whatever came his way, however it came.

"All right, grumpy. I'm out of here. Dinner tonight?"

"No."

"Want to think about it?"

"No. I've already lost two nights. You're cute and all, but you're not that cute."

He put a hand to his chest. "Now that hurts."

"Get over it."

Rolling out of the bed, he reached for his jeans and then grabbed his shirt from where he'd tossed it on the chair. "I'll call you." He caught her before she closed the bathroom door and kissed her. She didn't pull away. Atta girl. Dressed, he left the house whistling.

A small bell rang when he opened the front door to the law-firm offices. Their reception clerk, a young woman of about twenty with a pretty face, pink hair, and a name he could never remember, handed him a stack of messages. While each of them had voicemail, the old man insisted that a real, live person take the calls. The numerous messages proved that he was one fine lawyer in high demand.

He smiled as he strolled down the hall toward his office, reading through the slips and making a mental note of those he needed to attend to right away. Those with familiar names and who were attached to bank accounts substantial enough to support his fees went to the top of the list. Those he would have to investigate were tucked behind the priority calls. Two went to the bottom. The names on those were memorable, as was their lack of adequate resources to support his billing. They'd go in the trash as soon as he reached his office.

His father stood at the end of the hallway, his arms crossed over his chest and not a trace of a smile on his face. A cloud of darkness never appeared to be far away from good old Dad. He could probably count on one hand the times he'd seen him smile. If he had to guess, he'd say the old man might be afraid that if he did, his face would crack and destroy the chiseled good looks he was so proud of. Daniel did like the custom-tailored Italian suit he wore, although he thought it would probably complement his physique better.

"Inside."

Someone was in a mood. "Good morning to you too, Pops."

The frown deepened right before Daniel senior spun on his heel and disappeared into his corner office. He stopped just inside the doorway and studied the room. For as long as Daniel could remember, this office remained exactly the same. Dark mahogany furniture with a desk big enough to pitch a tent on top of, and floor-to-ceiling windows that not only let in tons of natural light, but also provided an unobstructed view of the neighborhood. Only the true power brokers had a view like Senior's. Of course, only the truly well-to-do could afford to own a place like this. It hadn't come cheap when purchased several generations back, and its value increased every year. Particularly now, given that the historical neighborhood enjoyed a resurgence of prestige. Urban renewal at its finest.

"Okay, Father. What's up?" Best not to poke the bear too much, even if the game might be one of his favorites. He'd suspected for years that Senior hated him, which made the sport all the more fun.

"You missed dinner last night."

He shrugged. "I had a date." Always something with him. Dinner with the parents. Cocktails with the elite. Appearances at strategic fund-raisers. All designed to keep the family name golden. It would be unreasonable to expect him to make them all. Not that being reasonable ever played into Senior's expectations.

"Indeed, you did." His gaze stayed stony on Daniel's face, his arms crossed.

He could stare the old man down. Been doing it for years, yet suddenly, he blinked. "No…" It hit him. "Shit."

"None of that in my office."

Pops didn't care for vulgar language, which always made him want to roar with laughter. So high and mighty for all the world to see. Except, junior here knew his secrets. Like the girlfriend he bought a tidy little house for conveniently far away from Mommy. Or the parties he and his buddies liked to throw out at the cabin, or that's what they liked to call the five-thousand-square-foot place on Lake Coeur d'Alene, where the booze and drugs flowed freely, and the young women were a plenty.

"I'll call Mother."

"You will do better than call her. You will go up and apologize, and you will take flowers."

He'd send her a big bunch of red roses and call her right away. Unlike his father, his mother forgave him his faults. She had a lot of practice after all the years of a painful marriage. Mother wasn't stupid. Though she'd never said anything, Daniel believed she understood his father one hundred percent. She chose to turn the other cheek. "Done."

"Don't disappoint her again."

He gave him a nod as he left and headed to the quiet of his own office. His father took the family standing in this part of the country heart-attack serious, and thus, the parties his mother planned to perfection were events to be respected. He hated them. That's why it had been so easy to put this one out of his mind last night when something more interesting lay on the horizon. Though he'd never tell his mother, a party to celebrate her appointment to the Governor's Clean Energy Council couldn't hold a candle to Erin, particularly now.

He sat down behind his desk and picked up his phone. First the flowers and then his mother. As he knew she would, she forgave him. He promised not to do it again, a lie they both ignored, and ended the call after giving her his love. That part wasn't too much of a lie. He did love her, in a way. Not like he loved Shantel. Nonetheless, she was his mother and deserved some bit of affection. He simply saved the bulk of his love for his one and only.

Now, he studied the spread-out messages, arranged in order of importance. The calls themselves would take much, much longer, which is why he allowed himself time to close his eyes and think over last night's adventures. The hard-on it gave him took a few more minutes to deal with before he could concentrate on returning calls.

CHAPTER SIX

It never bothered Johnnie, or Cougar, when people followed along as they searched. The moment they started working, her focus narrowed to the search itself. Everything else became background noise easy to filter out. A little different today. She was acutely aware of the anthropologist. Shantel didn't do anything distracting—didn't talk or get out in front of Johnnie, which commonly occurred for those unfamiliar with a working dog team. She did everything correctly. Obviously, not her first time out.

None of it made a difference. Cougar did his job without misstep, while Johnnie felt like Shantel's eyes were on her back the whole time. Odd. She sure hoped Rick didn't pick up on the weird emotions coming off her. She always aimed to be the consummate professional and didn't want to be seen as less than that just because an interesting woman joined the team. While search-and-rescue work might be all volunteer, the skill level and dedication didn't drop. Required to perform thousands of hours of training every year and earn multiple certifications in the various search disciplines, the term unpaid professional accurately represented what they did. Nothing amateur in this county or on her team.

With effort, she managed to shake off the weirdness and keep her attention on the work. Thank God for muscle memory. Ten minutes in and her focus returned. She blocked out everything else, Shantel included. She had a job to do and a dog to watch. Good to know she hadn't lost her edge.

Two hours in and they identified two more sites. Strain showed in Cougar's eyes, so she put him in a down to rest. Sure, he'd trained for exactly the job he'd just done, but nobody, human or canine, could do this and not be overwhelmed. People who said dogs didn't feel were out of their freaking minds. After three days of this level of effort, Cougar needed and deserved a little R & R. Hell, she needed and deserved a little R & R.

"We're done." She had to call it, and while Rick would most likely want her to keep going, her first loyalty lay with Cougar. Besides, according to her GPS track log, they'd covered it all. Enough was enough for both canine and human.

He didn't argue, and she stared at him, her eyes narrowed.

"We'll get to work on what Cougar found," he said as he turned and began to walk toward the parking area and the command-post trailer. Damon, their navigator today, had marked each area on his GPS, while Rick used flagging tape as a backup. Shantel and the techs would know exactly where to start. Of course, the tech team hadn't quite finished from yesterday. Rick would most likely send in deputies to watch the sites until they could begin the new excavations.

"I'd like to go back and photograph the areas." This was the first thing Shantel had said since they started the search. Despite the rocky start, Johnnie had almost forgotten she'd been following them.

Rick shook his head. "You don't need to do that. We'll take care of it."

"I do understand and respect that fact. What I want to do is for my review only. Helps me put everything into perspective. Please."

This time he shrugged. "As long as you stay back from the flagging, I'm okay with it. We'll go together." His face said he didn't want to. The cop in him would do it anyway.

"I'll walk with you too." Curiosity overrode her fatigue. Besides, a walk with nothing more to do than watch wouldn't be a bad thing. "Give me a couple minutes to put Cougar up."

"No problem," Rick said. "We'll go when you're back."

Cougar jumped into the truck as soon as she opened the back door, and she poured fresh water into his no-tip bowl. "You did good, big man. I'm proud of you." He leaned his head into her, and she leaned into him. "I get it, buddy. I get it."

Before she rejoined the group, Johnnie shrugged out of her pack, though she did leave on the chest harness with her radio, compass, and note pads. Damon had taken her GPS to the deputy in the command post who would download their tracks. She wouldn't need it for this trek and could pick it up before she left for the day. She also wouldn't need anything from her pack, and to get the almost twenty pounds of gear off her back made her shoulders really happy.

Damon waved to her as he headed in the direction of his vehicle. Only the three of them would be retracing their earlier steps. "Ready," she said when she rejoined Shantel and Rick. Shantel now had a nice SLR camera hanging around her neck.

"Let's do this." Rick shifted from foot to foot. She didn't blame him for wanting to get on it. This could be the worst crime scene in the area's history, which included a serial killer very dedicated to his craft some years back. He'd kept the city in terror before he'd finally been stopped.

"I'll be quick." Shantel's expression mirrored the seriousness of her words. Johnnie supposed she'd had the same look on her face as she and Cougar got down to work. They hadn't been out for a relaxing walk in the woods.

When they reached the first flagged area, Shantel took a series of photos that encompassed a three-hundred-and-sixty-degree view. Pretty clear she'd done this a time or two. She repeated the pattern at the next marked location, though instead of moving on to finish up, she stopped and knelt close to the ground. She stilled and stared through her camera lens as if transfixed. Nothing jumped out at Johnnie that might account for Shantel's eerie stillness.

"What?" Even as anxious as he was to get back to the command post, Rick took notice too.

"That's not possible…" Soft and full of disbelief, Shantel's words sent a chill down Johnnie's spine.

Shantel narrowed her eyes and stiffened. Probably just a coincidence…yet she'd never really believed in them. She stared through the camera lens, fixated on the small object near the flag marking the spot where earlier Cougar indicated that odor existed. She believed him. From the remains collected over the last few days, the dog didn't make mistakes. Someone, or what remained of them, rested beneath the soil.

That part made sense. She expected to see one, if not more—based upon their earlier excavations—set of remains once they began to move away the earth. What didn't make sense? The small, round object almost hidden by the pine needles that covered the ground like carpet.

"What?" Rick asked for the second time.

Shantel lowered her camera and shook her head. "Sorry. It's just that there's a bead on the ground over there." She pointed.

Rick shrugged and started to turn away. "We're probably going to find all sorts of junk out here. Nature of the beast. Public land, public's trash. Not everyone who comes out here is a good steward."

"Agreed. But this is different."

He stopped and turned back around. "Why? What's up with a bead? People wear those artsy bracelets all the time. Wouldn't be uncommon for one to break while running or hiking out here and have beads go everywhere."

Hard to argue with his logic. Hard to argue with hers too, given what she knew to be true. "It's familiar."

"Doc, am I going to have to drag this out of you one word at a time?" The stress of the day sounded in his voice.

"Sorry," she said again. She *was* being weird and vague, except this kind of was weird and vague. She'd at least try to explain so they'd all be on the same page. "It's a Tibetan Mala prayer bead. You don't see these beads often, and definitely not out in the middle of the woods in good old Cheney, Washington."

"Okay." Rick nodded. "I agree, given that explanation, that finding one out here is pretty odd. How do you know what it is? Do you have some?"

"No."

"But? Spit it out. I don't have all day. You know, clandestine graves and all that."

"But my ex-husband always carries them and has as long as I've known him. He spent a great deal of time in Eastern Asia after college and used them on a daily basis."

"You think this is your husband's handiwork?" His face telegraphed his skepticism.

"God, no. He's an asshole, but a killer? He wouldn't get his manicured hands that dirty." In all their years together she'd never seen anything in him that resembled the kind of violence these sites suggested. Arrogant and entitled, certainly. Obsessive and clingy, absolutely. A killer? No.

"Could be a fluke. Most of what we recover from scenes like this is nothing more than debris. Still, good to know it's unique. All probability aside, I'd be foolish to rule out the possibility that it might be important." Rick wrote in the notebook he'd grabbed from his car before they came back out. "Duly noted."

After the distinctive bead, she had a hard time focusing on anything else. She hadn't told Rick and Johnnie it wasn't just like the beads Daniel carried. It was *exactly* like them. Easy to order prayer beads online, yet he didn't want those. Oh, no. Spoiled little Daniel demanded a particular bead that could be purchased only in Tibet. He made trips back there specifically to do his "pilgrimages" and to bring home new strands.

"You okay?" Johnnie put a hand on her shoulder, her gaze searching Shantel's face. So much for keeping her concerns to herself. Poker face wasn't a skill she possessed.

She nodded. "It just struck me odd to find this. They really are unique and quite jarring when it popped up in my camera lens."

"Think about it. We're in a college town, and you know how young people latch on to things like alternative religions and metaphysics."

Johnnie hit on a great point. She'd been that way as a young woman, and the same tendencies in many of her students was difficult to miss. Youth often gives way to exploration and self-discovery. She'd embraced Buddhism as a young woman, which, in turn, became a piece of the puzzle that brought her and Daniel together initially. Also explained why she quickly recognized that bead.

She kept her gaze on Johnnie's face. "You're right about that. I'm just startled."

Johnnie tipped her head. "I do understand, though, I'm leaning in Rick's direction. It'll more than likely turn out to be nothing. We come across some crazy things in the middle of nowhere all the time. Like the trout we found in the thick of the woods a long way from the lake."

"A trout?" That visual pulled her away from her obsessive thoughts of the offending bead and made the trembling in her hands start to fade.

Johnnie nodded and gave her a small smile. "When I first came across it, I thought, what on earth? Then I realized that most likely an osprey or eagle grabbed the trout from Long Lake and dropped it up in Riverside State Park as it soared over the forest. Weird things happen all the time that seemingly have no explanation. Yet when you look a little closer, they do. Like a trout in the middle of the woods."

She appreciated Johnnie's view of the situation. It still didn't completely banish her unease, but it sure helped. "A good way to make sense of it." With a step away from the tape, she said, "Come on. I think I have all I need here. Let's photograph the rest and let Rick get on his way." She willed her hands not to start shaking again if she came across any more of the beads.

Rick was putting his cell back into his pocket. "They're just about ready to head this way. Let's get your pics done, Doc, and then you can start the first excavation with the crew."

"I'll be done in less than ten. Then I can assist the forensic-unit folks."

"Great."

"Mind if I watch for a little while?" Johnnie's question made her pause. She figured she'd be ready to call it quits after so many days in a row of locating one body after another. It surprised her when Johnnie wanted to walk along while she took her pictures. That she wanted to stay during the excavations did too.

Rick nodded, nonplussed. "Okay by me. Just check with Beth."

Shantel liked Beth Angelo, the forensic-unit lead. They were soul sisters the first time they met. Like minds and all. She didn't think Beth would object to Johnnie's presence, even if it was an unusual request. The search-and-recovery folks rarely hung around after they completed their part.

Funny thing is, she really hoped Beth said yes.

❖

After he'd returned the important call to his mother, Daniel got up from his desk to close and lock his office door. With no risk of being interrupted, he sat on the plush carpet and unwound the beads from around his wrist. Though he would never let on to his father, their earlier conversation managed to kill a good bit of his most excellent buzz. He'd had a great night and topped it off by waking up next to a luscious woman. Good and good. Then the old man pitches a hissy fit because he missed a dinner with a bunch of people he couldn't care less about. None of them were his friends, not that he really had any.

Of course, he also understood the nature of their business, and a great part of the firm's lengthy success had to do with community outreach. Mother's appointment by the governor played right into the image of the family's importance as community leaders, which in turn reflected favorably on the family business. Fuck it. Let the old bastard do it. He loved the attention and took credit for the success, whether it belonged to him or not.

Not to say that Daniel didn't appreciate attention. The difference between him and the old man was the kind of attention. He preferred beautiful women who put their hands and their mouths in just the right places. Pops, he tended toward old-fashioned social events with cocktails and small talk. He kept women on the side that he fucked when it suited him and then ran home to his dutiful, faithful wife. Mother turned a blind eye, while his father let everyone believe his dedicated-family-man persona. He almost gagged.

His eyes closed, he took a deep breath and began to recite his favorite mantra over and over as he worked his way through the beads. By the time he reached the last one, his mojo returned. Relaxation flowed over him, and his mind cleared of any troubling thoughts. Now he could face the day and the old man again, if he had to. A better plan would be to stay out of his way and not risk the wet blanket he'd once more throw over his mood. The guy excelled at wet blankets. This apple didn't fall close to the tree. It didn't even fall in the same orchard.

With a fluid grace that most wouldn't expect for a guy his size, he rose from the carpet. He'd been practicing meditation since his first trip to Tibet, and it never failed to calm him. In fact, it did more than promote calm. It focused his mind and channeled the power out there floating around in the universe just waiting for a guy like him to grab it.

It shouldn't be a surprise that he'd come into what he considered to be a gift. The pack that took him in all those years ago had seen something in him and thus felt him worthy of joining their ranks. In many respects he hadn't disappointed them. He had, indeed, become special—so much so that by the time he'd left to return home, he'd destroyed all except his master, who, even to this day, had no idea he'd caused the demise of the pack. He'd come into the group a willing participant and eager learner. He'd left a king.

At the same time he unlocked the office door, he used the remote to turn on the television. The morning news annoyed him. His family would attest to the fact that he didn't share well. Never had, never would. That's why the dogged persistence of the sheriff's department to sweep every inch of the Fish Lake recreational area with cadaver dogs pissed him off. How he wanted to scream, "Leave my treasures alone." No one had the right to take what was his.

"It's terrible, isn't it?" Pam, his ever-efficient legal assistant, walked in less than a minute after he'd unlocked the door and dropped several files on his desk. "The Spark Family trust docs. They're coming in to sign off on them next Tuesday."

Easy, even if it was outside his preferred defense work. He could do trusts in his sleep. His clients appreciated his dedication, especially when he explained the complexity of their requests. They didn't need to know how effortless they really were for him and how little time he spent working on them. Let them think he had to labor late into the night to get them what they needed. That way they didn't blink at the billable hours that showed up on their invoices.

"Thanks." His attention stayed on the news broadcast. The story moved from local to national. Discovery of multiple remains had a way of doing that.

"Did you see what they've uncovered out there? Creepy. I mean, the hubby and I ride our bikes out there, for heaven's sake. Makes me want to hurl thinking about all those bodies." Her voice so close to him didn't startle him because the stench of her cheap perfume let him know she hadn't left his office.

He didn't move his gaze away from the television screen. "A travesty." Pretty certain he sounded sincere.

"Definitely messed up. You need me to do anything else for you?" She bought his performance.

What he needed from her? Get out of his office like right now. He started to tell her that, in a nice way, of course, and then stopped. Another thought occurred to him. Brilliant, really. "I've had a potential client reach out to me, and I'd like to know a bit of her background. Dig up what you can on a Johnnie Lancaster." The lie came out with his trademark smoothness.

"Will do, Boss. How fast do you need it?"

"ASAP." Not a lie there.

She gave him a little salute and left his office, a trail of the hideous perfume going with her. He resisted the urge to lock the door again.

CHAPTER SEVEN

Beth showed up less than half an hour after Shantel finished taking her round of photos and gave her permission for Johnnie to watch. The bead intrigued her, even though she'd backed up Rick and told Shantel it might be irrelevant. She had wanted to provide a little perspective and then asked to stay to satisfy her curiosity.

It took a bit of reassurance she hadn't forgotten her dog or his needs before she got the green light. Cougar would be fine in the truck with the sunroof open to allow in fresh air and his no-tip water bowl to keep him hydrated. The training she'd started with him as soon as she brought him home from the breeder included spending extended periods of time in the vehicle. Waiting was a big part of search work. Participants had to make search plans, create teams, and attend briefings before they ever stepped out into the field. To be successful, both handlers and canines learned patience. Cougar would settle in fine and be content to wait for her return without becoming stressed or concerned. He trusted her.

Despite having been in the areas earlier, Johnnie stood far back now and did exactly as instructed. If anyone were with her while she worked, they'd respect her requests as well. Quid pro quo.

With her official hat back on, Shantel took a lot more photographs, and both she and Beth sketched the area before they laid out a grid matrix about three feet by six feet. All very methodical and mathematical. She liked the way they worked in concert and also alone, particularly Shantel.

The real effort began as Shantel and Beth started to remove layers of soil. The first bones appeared after they'd removed about two to three feet of dirt. Cougar's nose was vindicated yet again, except she took no joy in that confirmation of his extraordinary abilities. Another life gone, and not because of nature and most certainly not through the grace of God. An evil that had taken up residence in her hometown destroyed another life. Tears pricked at her eyes. Maybe it hadn't been such a good idea to hang out and watch this part.

Shantel's head came up and her eyes met Johnnie's. She saw her own despair reflected in them. Sometimes a person could hope to be wrong, even if she knew she wouldn't be. Cougar didn't make that kind of false alert. He knew his job and did it well. In a dog's mind, it became quite simple—yes or no—nothing in between. He'd done a lot of "yes" over the last few days.

"Damn," she muttered as she crossed her arms across her chest.

Beth grimaced. "You don't see this every day."

Shantel shook her head. "Not if we're lucky."

"Not so lucky this week." Geez, she sounded like a little kid. What happened to her professionalism? Not a hard question. A serial killer had stomped on it like a bug.

"It's the same," Shantel whispered as she brushed dirt away from the bones.

At first the comment went over Johnnie's head. That's what emotional fatigue could do to a person. Then her brain kicked in. "Teeth marks?"

"Yes."

Correction to her earlier thought: a *twisted* serial killer had stomped on it like a bug. "Damn, again. Gotta get this son of a bitch."

After a great many excavations and exposure to travesties most of the world couldn't even imagine, Shantel would have thought she'd become immune to depravity. How wrong she'd been. The sight of yet another set of bones, chewed on and then buried, made her stomach roll. Early on in her career she might have hurled. At least now she could control her bodily reactions to horror and not embarrass herself or, worse, contaminate a crime scene.

At the same time, she caught the deep emotion rolling off Johnnie. Bless her heart, the woman spent so many hours training for the work she did with her beautiful dog, every single moment of it unpaid. The goodness in her along with the dedication toward serving her community made her special, and she didn't deserve the angst that darkened her face. "Why don't you let us finish this up, and I'll reach out after that."

"I'm okay." Johnnie's protest sounded weak.

Shantel rocked back on her heels and, keeping Johnnie's gaze, shook her head. Over the years, she'd been around plenty of people who watched the work. Johnnie might think she was all right, but she really wasn't. A little time away with some sunshine and fresh air would go a long way toward steadying her emotions. Johnnie would need it more than she realized. While Shantel hoped the discovery of today's sites would be the end of their work, she didn't have any real hope. The evil that seemed to fill the air as they brushed away more of the dirt spoke volumes. Someone with the heart of a demon really liked their work, and those people didn't stop.

"Do it for me." She took a chance the thread of connection she felt was shared.

Johnnie opened her mouth to say something and then must have changed her mind. She nodded, turned, and walked slowly toward the parking area. Within a minute, the trees swallowed her, leaving Beth and her alone next to the grave.

"This is shaking her up." Beth's head stayed down, her gaze focused on the work, her blue-gloved hand gently brushing dirt away from the bones.

"You saw it too?"

"I did. She's pretty tough, or at least that's my impression. This is freaky, and even the tough get rattled. Most people don't typically get up close and personal with the handiwork of monsters like you and I do. It can be soul crushing."

"I hear that." Like Beth, Shantel lowered her head, and once more she started the slow, careful job of freeing the dead from the grave they didn't deserve. While she still felt for Johnnie, she pushed aside everything but the work.

Hours later, they stopped for the day. Her knees and back ached from all the time she'd spent bent over brushing away dirt. Beth had to be even more exhausted. She'd been involved with bringing out the earlier remains, while this afternoon, they'd brought out one of the two Cougar led them to today. Darkness made it too hard to do the work with the level of detail required, and they quit. Deputies secured the location, while Shantel and Beth, along with the other techs sifting the dirt they removed from the gravesites, returned to the vehicles, slipped out of their jumpsuits, and went their separate ways. They'd finish tomorrow.

Shantel intended to leave Fish Lake and drive straight home to shower and put her feet up. Didn't quite work out that way. Using her sleuthing abilities, she located Johnnie's address before she ever pulled away from the scene. Good old Siri told her how to get there, and twenty minutes later, she pulled off the Palouse Highway onto Sands Road. Another quarter mile and she spied the gravel driveway with an interesting wrought-iron gate. A closed gate. She stopped, intending to call Rick to get Johnnie's phone number. Before she could even hit send, the gate started to swing open. Cool. She drove in and parked in front of a detached three-car garage.

While she'd told Johnnie earlier that she'd keep her posted, doing it with a personal visit probably wasn't on her radar. If an unexpected visitor annoyed her, it didn't show. Johnnie smiled as she stood in the doorway. "Hey."

"Hi." Wasn't that an expressive response for someone with a load of education?

Cougar's tail wagged as he stepped around Johnnie. "This is a pleasant surprise. How did you know where I live?"

An excellent question. She hurried to explain. If she didn't, Johnnie might think her a weirdo stalker. "I told you I'd fill you in on what happened after you left, and I found your address on a location search."

"Ah...I..."

"Sorry. I'll just talk to you tomorrow. I'm sorry." She turned and started to hurry down the steps of the massive deck.

"Wait, wait, wait." Johnnie stepped out to follow her.

She paused and turned back. "It was wrong of me to come. Very intrusive and I apologize."

Johnnie smiled. "No. Actually it's pretty nice. A little scary that my address is that easy to find, but what can't be uncovered these days? Especially for the big-brain types, like you. And I mean that in a nice way. Please stay. Come on in. You look about ready to drop anyway."

"I should go."

"Don't be silly. You made all the effort to get here, so come in and sit. Fill me in. I really am curious to find out what you uncovered. Afraid too, but curiosity wins."

❖

As much as Daniel wanted to go out again tonight, he resisted. To reel Erin in all the way took finesse. No valid reason to push it. As Senior loved to say, the die had been cast. For the moment that would be enough. He'd have to entertain himself in other ways.

In his pursuit of Erin, he'd neglected his studies. With a pale ale from the refrigerator, he sat down at his computer. First up, the news. While he'd had the television in his office tuned to his favorite local news station most of the day, bothersome work got in the way, which meant he hadn't been able to pay as close attention as required to get the full picture. The effort not to roll his eyes every few minutes almost wore him out during meetings with several of his clients.

Now, home and in his own space, he could enjoy his beer and find out what Shantel had been up to today. Busy little professor, from all reports. Unfortunately, not much in terms of video coverage. The press hadn't been allowed an up-close view of today's chess game. The camera person filmed only a parking lot full of law-enforcement vehicles. Pity. If he had to lose his treasures, he deserved to see their faces when they found them.

No surprise to him what they'd be thinking. An active serial killer. After all, he wouldn't be the first one around these parts. They'd be wrong, however, in that assessment. Those were his treasures, which he had buried with care. He'd never deny that particular fact. How they characterized him would be a big deviation from all their training. Their profiles would most certainly be wrong. Predator, yes. Serial killer, no. A big fundamental difference existed between the two. One similarity, on the other hand, did exist. Both took care to cover their tracks, literally and figuratively.

It bothered him that they were uncovering what he so carefully concealed. That it had taken them several decades to do so provided him a bit of comfort. His early treasures might give him some cause for worry. He'd been quite green at that point. Not so any longer. Twenty plus years of hands-on experience made him quite the expert. Not to mention his well-developed preternatural skills and abilities. Nature and nurture combined to make him soar above any other. Not bragging. Truth.

He pulled out his cell phone and entered a one-digit code: 1. She would always be number one. While he hoped she'd pick up, she didn't. The call went to voicemail, and he waited with a frown.

"Hello, I'm not able to take your call. Leave me a message at the tone, and I'll return it as soon as I'm available."

"Darling, I hope you didn't work yourself to the bone today. Such a horrible thing to have happen here. Get some rest, take care of yourself, and I'll reach out again tomorrow. Love you." He pushed end.

The beer was almost gone, and she wouldn't call him back. She never did. At least not since the final divorce decree. She believed that a piece of paper signed by a judge he didn't care for would end their relationship, that they didn't need to have contact any longer. Silly woman.

Another cold beer and he'd fix himself a nice, rare steak. He longed for something a bit fresher and more tender, but a guy sometimes had to make do. Food, libations, and sleep. He'd be well-rested and ready for the next stage in his plan set for tomorrow night. Erin would also need to be in top form for the fieldwork he intended to introduce her to, and he trusted she'd sleep well alone tonight. Once he reeled her all the way in, the rest would be easy. Shantel wouldn't even see it coming, and this little inconvenience that the cops he held in such disdain had perpetrated would go away too. He was nothing if not adaptable.

CHAPTER EIGHT

Johnnie hoped the shock didn't show on her face as she opened the door. That Shantel would drive all the way out here was both unexpected and pleasant. In a way, she'd have loved to stay out in the field with her earlier. In another way, she'd known it was time to get out of the way of the professionals. Not to mention, Shantel had been right-on about the way the sight of those bones affected her.

Once home, she'd showered, made a cup of coffee, and relaxed in her favorite chair. After the coffee was gone, she decided to divert her mind from the events of the last three days by sitting down at her computer and diving back into her latest book. The deadline loomed, and her publisher would expect it to be completed on time. Fiction authors weren't the only ones with hard deadlines, and her editor's patience when she pushed the dates went only so far.

The distraction worked. Once she got her head back into the Crimean War, she forgot about serial killers and buried bodies. Or at least the kind in her own backyard. Working at her desk positioned in front of the floor-to-ceiling windows with their magnificent view of Mt. Spokane soothed her. Two things accomplished: a full chapter of the book completed and her emotions calmed.

Her gate-camera alarm beeped just as she saved and closed the manuscript file. From her desk, she could also see the end of the driveway and the same car from the CP parking lot. Could be only one person. Curious. She pushed the button that remotely opened the gate. As they said on the game shows, "Shantel Kind, come on down."

Though unintentional, the less-than-cordial greeting she offered Shantel almost sent her running back to her car. Bad Johnnie. Her mother would not be impressed with her manners. No defense really, even if the last person she expected at her gate was the interesting anthropologist. Perhaps she needed to have more people over. Then she wouldn't act like a total ass when someone showed up out of the blue.

"Get in here," she said when Shantel hesitated again.

This time she was rewarded with a smile. "All right."

"You can catch me up on what happened after I left and then tell me all about your mad detective skills for tracking me down. I'm impressed. It's not like I live on the beaten path."

"Don't be impressed with my meager skills." Shantel laughed as she laid her jacket over a chair. "It had less to do with me and more to do with a magical thing called Siri. From there, I took an educated guess that J.P. Lancaster was one Johnnie Lancaster and her amazing companion, Cougar."

"Brilliant."

"It was something, all right, though brilliant isn't the word I'd choose." Shantel sat. "This is a nice room. This is a nice place, period. You take care of all of it by yourself?"

Johnnie looked around the big, open room and smiled. She liked it too. Warm colors, comfortable furniture, and a plush area rug over real hardwood floors. It suited her. On the cold days, a fire in the natural-rock fireplace kept the room toasty. Cougar liked it too, and the big dog bed positioned right in front of the fireplace declared it his domain.

"Thank you. My parents built the place about forty years ago, and I took it over after my dad passed away. It's a special place for me, and I'm honored to carry on the family tradition here."

"I'm impressed."

"Don't be too impressed. If it wasn't for some awesome neighbors, I'd never be able to maintain it all. They are the best and help me keep it looking as awesome as when Dad worked it."

"Protestations aside, still impressed."

Johnnie felt a flutter. Silly to have such a reaction because one woman gave her a compliment. "What happened after I left?" Time for a subject change. She bonded with dogs easier than people primarily because she'd never been comfortable with having the focus on her.

A shadow crossed Shantel's face and chased away the small smile. "Horror."

"That's not news." Maybe that remark came across as a little snippy. "Sorry. That sounded bitchy. I mean, after the last two days, finding a couple more confirms everything we've seen so far. Some sick son of a bitch has been out there killing people and getting away with it for a while now."

Shantel nodded. "You know, I've been around the world and have been part of recoveries that have tested my soul. At some moments I have truly hated the human race."

Johnnie leaned forward, putting her elbows on her knees. "I get that." She cut her eyes to Cougar snoozing on his bed. At least he could relax. "Go on." Something beneath Shantel's words left her a little twitchy.

Shantel blew out a long breath. "I'm uneasy about these finds. You've seen what I have."

"Some, yes." Johnnie related to a certain degree. That Shantel had been in the ME's office studying the recoveries meant that she'd seen a lot more than Johnnie.

"Enough to recognize, I have no doubt." Shantel's words were soft yet powerful.

Johnnie began to buzz all over. "I've seen the marks, and it's as though the bones were chewed on."

Shantel's eyes met hers, and the buzz turned into a storm. "Exactly."

For whatever reason, it came easy, the confiding in Johnnie. That sense of having known her for years wrapped around Shantel—a comfort that develops after spending time together and sharing experiences. Communication unspoken and yet shared. She barely knew the woman. There it was just the same. She was glad she'd come.

In the welcoming living room with large windows the full length of the room and a massive stone fireplace that put out soothing warmth, she settled into the comfortable chair. Johnnie brought her a fragrant cup of tea, and now she stared out the windows at the shadows of the pines that swayed as a mild wind stirred them. It would be easy to stay here and forget all the ugliness revealed over the last few days.

Instead of forgetting, she pulled her focus from the beauty outside the windows and returned to the reason she'd come here. "Each victim we've brought out of the earth is the same. The marks are undeniable."

Johnnie set her own mug aside and leaned forward with her arms resting on her legs. A pained expression crossed her face. "Cannibalism?"

Sharp. She'd picked up on what might not be obvious to others. "My first thought too, but no. I don't believe that's the case here. It appears more animal-inflicted. More canine. Like animals had been allowed to chew on the bones before they were gathered up and buried."

There, she'd said it out loud. It would have gone into her final report on each of the victims, though she hadn't verbalized it to anyone except Fred, and that's because they were working together. She'd wanted to pick up the phone to call Dr. Soule and share with him the strange circumstances and didn't. She trusted him, so that wasn't what held Shantel back. She'd kept her opinion to herself for reasons she didn't quite get. Everything felt off in some really obscene way, and until she could make sense of this situation, she'd keep it close. Even from Dr. Soule.

Johnnie leaned back into her chair and put her feet up on the ottoman. She reached over and picked up her tea as she appeared to mull over what Shantel shared. Granted, it did seem far-fetched. What would be the point of allowing animals to desecrate remains and then take the time to gather them back up to bury? If the killer cared so little about the victims that they left them, at least temporarily, exposed to scavenging animals, then going back to tidy up didn't make sense in any possible scenario. To expect rational from a killer would be foolish. But this went beyond irrational.

Johnnie looked over at her. "That's what I told Rick."

"Excuse me?"

Johnnie dropped her feet and scooted forward until she sat on the edge of her chair. "Here's the thing. I called Rick on day one because what I'd seen when the first set of bones was exposed bothered me. Familiar, and once it hit me, I gave him a call."

"You've seen similar remains?" Shantel would have expected someone to have mentioned that detail earlier.

Johnnie shook her head. "No. That's not what I mean. Let me show you, and it'll make more sense."

She got up and went to Cougar's bed, leaned down, and picked up something before she walked it over to Shantel. In her palm lay a bone about six inches long and three inches in diameter. A beef soup bone.

"You see it?"

The lightbulb went on and Shantel nodded. She definitely appreciated this woman's keen observation. "The marks are identical."

"Yeah, like a dog chewed those bones before they were buried."

Daniel stood on the deck and watched the sky darken. Nothing special tonight. A normal, uneventful evening in the great Pacific Northwest. He would prefer to live on the coast, where the city teemed with life and excitement, the rain forests lush and beautiful, and the hunting grounds massive. Not his luck to come from a family on the west side. The Rodgers patriarchs made their name and fortune on the east side, with its four distinct seasons. From a beauty standpoint, it all existed here. The city, a bit conservative for him, was nonetheless his home. He adjusted.

That, and he did have his secrets buried here. Literally. No figurative language about it. That, more than anything, brought him home. Now, his wife had become part of the force destined to destroy his beautiful secrets. He didn't like that at all.

Above him the moon rose, and he tipped his head back to allow the light to wash over his face. The power that rolled off the massive golden orb fed his body and his soul. Even before the change, he'd been drawn to it, and many of his childhood sketches featured his vision of the moon. Once upon a time, he'd thought it might be because he wanted to be an astronaut. Only after that fateful trip did he comprehend the true origins of his fascination. Some things are, in fact, written in the stars or, in his case, the moon.

To gaze upon it filled him with power and longing. Tonight, it reflected waxing gibbous. All the phases were etched into his mind like stone carvings, and that knowledge resonated with him now. It told him to be patient, to train and use his recruit. Then, everything would come together on the approaching night, when the moon would rise full and spectacular. Finally.

He turned and went back into the house. The night air cooled, as it should this time of year. As much as he loved the milder weather of the coast, he also enjoyed the autumn on this side of the state. It could be warm and sunny, or cold and rainy. Soon enough the rain would give way to the snow that turned the ground white and the roads slick. The snow always created a challenge for him in terms of tidying up. It didn't stop him. He didn't mind creative problem-solving and never had. Made it all the more fun. As the health-club trainers liked to say, no pain, no gain. A little pain made the game even more delicious.

In his pocket, his cell phone buzzed. When he pulled it out and read the display, he smiled. "Miss me?"

"Shut up." Erin's voice, laced with equal parts irritation and amusement, sent a thrill racing to his groin.

He'd really believed she'd take the day to be alone, rest and recover. Without the magic of a full moon, progress slowed. With it, her transformation would have been immediate. As much as he wanted to push for more, he decided that exercising restraint would be his best choice. "Classes done for the day?"

"I have a few papers to grade."

His smile grew. "And?" He planned to make her say it. This wasn't his first rodeo.

"And I'll be done in an hour." Her words held a breathiness that told him everything.

"Hungry?" He licked his lips.

"Starving." She almost spit out the single word. Atta girl.

That thrill in his groin rippled down his legs. "I'll grab a couple of steaks and be there in an hour."

CHAPTER NINE

Even though Johnnie's specialty was search and recovery, she'd been required to take the same medical classes as those who specialized in live find. That meant she tuned in to the physical condition of people around her. In this case, the clear distress on Shantel's face. Fatigue and anguish rolled off her.

"Would you like something a little stronger than tea? Maybe a cup of coffee? I've even got that awful pumpkin-spice creamer. 'Tis the season, you know."

Shantel's smile was a little crooked and a lot enticing. "I'd actually love the coffee, but hold the creamer. That stuff gags me."

Johnnie laughed, not offended in the least. "You love it, or you hate it. One of those no in-between things."

"With you there, sister."

It took only a couple of minutes to brew the coffee. She dumped the tea, put the used mugs in the dishwasher, and grabbed a couple of clean ones for the dark-roast magic. Unlike Shantel, she poured a healthy dose of the offensive creamer into her own cup. As far as vices went, she didn't have many. Pumpkin-spice creamer fell into that category in her case. She handed the steaming mug of black coffee to Shantel.

Shantel sipped and sighed. "Oh, my. I didn't realize how much I needed that. I'm usually a tea drinker, but it just wasn't cutting it tonight. I feel like a giant boulder hit me. Coffee helps."

She held up her mug in a mock toast. "Nectar of the gods. Pumpkin spice and all."

"I might not always agree with that. But I sure do right now."

The coffee's kick boosted her too, though she'd had a lot more time to decompress. Not that the time away from the field didn't help when it came to disengaging. Johnnie kept puzzling over the gnawed bones. "What do you think is going on? I mean, I first thought cannibal, a mind-boggling possibility. Would take a seriously sick fuck, if you catch what I mean."

"You're not wrong, and I've seen my share of the handiwork of the very, very warped."

A shiver went down Johnnie's spine. Shantel, petite and scholarly, didn't look like a monster hunter, an interesting dichotomy. "I suppose you have, and thinking about it creeps me out."

"It also takes a sick fuck to let your dog chew the bones of a human being."

When the gracious Shantel echoed Johnnie's vulgar language, her head snapped up. Anyone who knew Johnnie expected profanity when she told a story. A different kind of thrill raced down her spine now.

"Yeah." All she could think of to say. A unique situation for someone seldom, if ever, at a loss for words.

She continued to watch Shantel—who perked up after imbibing in coffee—turn the mug around and around in her hands. Something else clearly weighed on her mind. They sat in comfortable silence. She'd wait all night if that's what it took.

Shantel sighed and looked over at her. "I can't dismiss that bead no matter how many rational explanations I run through my mind."

"The prayer bead." She should have guessed, given Shantel's earlier fixation. All their attempts to reassure her had obviously failed.

"Yes. I mean, how many people around here would have that particular bead? It's too weird to write off as run-of-the-mill trash regardless of how Rick tried to spin it."

Johnnie guessed where she headed. "You think your husband has something to do with this?"

Shantel winced. "Ex-husband."

Sore spot right there. "Right. Ex-husband." The sound *ex* appealed to her, though it also brought up questions. Why divorced? Infidelity? Incompatibility? Or something deeper? She hoped for the latter. Unlikely, of course, but hey, a woman could hope.

Stop it. Not the time or the place. Definitely not the time. Multiple murders. Mysterious forensic evidence. Focus on the here and now. Focus on the job, not the woman. Kind of hard to do when sitting in front of a fire with someone as alluring as Shantel. Beats out the job, hands down.

"I can't believe Daniel would have anything to do with any of this, yet that bead sticks in my head like one of those songs you hear and then hum for days on end."

She might hate herself later for asking, but what the hell? "Tell me about him."

Of all the questions Johnnie could have asked, to tell her about Daniel had to be the last one she'd expect. At the same time, Shantel wanted to tell Johnnie. With anyone else, she'd avoid the topic. Very few people knew the real reason behind the divorce, and she liked it that way. Most just assumed they grew apart, and that wasn't wrong. They had, in fact, grown far apart—just not in the way people believed.

Might as well start with the good. "He's brilliant really. Handsome, intelligent, incredibly successful." All the traits that fascinated her in the beginning.

Johnnie frowned, and the light in her eyes dimmed. "Sounds like a perfect catch."

For anyone else. In for a dime, in for a dollar. She wanted that light to come back. "He was…is…if it's a husband you want."

Johnnie's gaze snapped to Shantel's face. The frown vanished. "You didn't want a husband." Not a question.

She shook her head as she set her cup of coffee on the end table and dropped her gaze to her hands. To share all this for the first time had her digging deep. "No."

"Oh." The word came out a little breathy.

At last, she brought her head up and met Johnnie's eyes. She might be wrong about her, but she didn't think so. "I pretended as long as I could, and then one day, I couldn't do it one minute more." That night would always stand out in her memory—how she'd leaned against the sink, staring at herself in the mirror and crying. She hated who she'd become, the weight on her shoulders too much to bear.

Johnnie put her mug down and moved to the edge of the ottoman, close enough to take Shantel's hands. The contact sent tremors of warmth through her. "I understand. Trust me, I really do." Her words were soft and echoed with truth.

Shantel stayed there with Johnnie holding her hands, not wanting to pull away. How long had it been since she allowed anyone to give her comfort? Had she ever? Finally, she pulled her hands free to pick up the still-warm mug of coffee and take a sip. It gave her a moment to think before she spoke again. Amazing how that few minutes of comfort made all the difference.

She owed her the rest of the story. "In the beginning, Daniel and I bonded over our shared experience with Buddhism. When you're a Buddhist, you don't randomly meet someone who shares your faith often. Or ever."

Johnnie raised an eyebrow. "Sorry. Hard to relate, given I'm not on that sheet of music. I've always had a bit of a problem with organized religion."

Nothing offensive about that. "I get it, and it's one reason Buddhism appealed to me. I can connect to the meditations much easier than to the evangelical preachers my parents thought could heal me."

Johnnie's head tipped as she studied her. "You don't need healing."

Nice to hear those four words because they would never, ever pass the lips of her family. Most of them anyway. Her younger brother, Jamie, always had her back. "No. I don't. I'm okay just like I am." Wow, first time she'd ever said that out loud too. A night of firsts.

"Yes, you are." Johnnie's smile made her warm all over.

She kept her voice level so as not to give away that giddy feeling that wanted to burst out. Focus on the story. "Daniel came across as the perfect guy."

"There is no such beast."

This time she laughed. Hard not to like this woman, and talk about being in the same head space. "Definitely not the perfect guy for me. It became all about trying to fit in, and he seemed like a good piece to that puzzle. My parents adored him, and the push to have their daughter marry Mr. Perfect became an everyday thing."

"And you did."

She hated even thinking about the *wedding*. Lacking courage, she'd stayed when she'd wanted to run away. On her father's arm, a smile pasted on her face, she'd walked down the church aisle. "I did, and I lived the lie for longer than I should have. Over time, it became too difficult to pretend. Finally, I had to stand up for me. Let's just say when that day arrived, he didn't take it well."

"I don't know of any guy who would."

Another day she hated to remember. Daniel's loss of control had not been pretty. "I tried to let him down gently. I didn't mean to hurt him."

"No gentle way to do that."

"No, not at all. He didn't believe I preferred women to his manly physique and professional success." She'd never seen him that angry. The way his handsome features morphed into something very ugly still made her shiver.

"I'm sorry."

The empathy in Johnnie's eyes made her smile. "I'm not."

Johnnie's smile warmed her.

"Me either."

She quit smiling and frowned as she leaned forward. "Now, if I could make peace with that damned bead, I could get past this, get past him."

"Coincidence." Johnnie sounded confident.

"Let's hope." She didn't feel any.

"So, darling," he said as they lay naked and sweaty in bed. While Erin was no Shantel, he couldn't find fault with her enthusiasm. The power inside her grew with each passing night, and each time he touched her, it flowed from her. His control over her grew as well. Why he hadn't done this earlier, he'd never figure out. The obvious explanation—everything needed to happen in its own time, and now was the time for this.

"What?" she whispered. "I need sleep."

He ran his hand over her lovely black hair. No arguing about her beauty. Most would consider her far prettier than Shantel, and in some ways, they'd be right. Erin's attractiveness lay right on the surface. Her strong cheekbones and shiny, long hair. Her enticing figure, not too skinny, not too heavy. A shining example of what most men desired. Shantel's appeal came as a total of mind, body, and spirit, and no beauty queen could match that.

Erin brought much to the table that he appreciated. She didn't have to be the complete package like his wife because he needed only one Shantel. Erin had already begun to deliver what he needed from her. The sex invigorated him, her companionship empowered him, and her embrace of his gift gratified him. Soon, she'd begin her part in bringing Shantel back to him, and once that happened, they'd start over in a new place. The events of the last few days made that clear. He'd create a new garden of secrets.

The whole upcoming series of events played out in his mind and made him hard all over again. He rolled on top of Erin. She laughed.

"I swear, you are the horniest guy I've ever met. Not sure why you're not hooked up. How come a guy as awesome as you isn't taken?"

"Waiting for the right woman." He thrust.

"Oh, handsome." She moaned. "All the better for me."

Afterward, she slept, and he got up. Out on her patio, he raised his arms and let the cold air wash over his naked body. The folk legends got many things right about those like him. A full moon possessed a power unrivaled. What they got wrong? That only during a full moon could he change to embrace his true nature. He could call upon it at will.

In the distance, he easily heard the feet of small animals hitting the ground as they ran through the underbrush. His gift enhanced all his senses. Erin's place, while technically in the town of Cheney, was a mere block from open fields and undeveloped areas. Convenient for a night run or a quick hunt. He'd promised himself to lay low. Too much energy in him to keep that promise. Too many night smells that called to the beast inside. The night all but begged for him to come out and play. Who was he to deny the call of nature?

He turned his head and gazed into the dark, silent house. Erin would be in a deep sleep for hours, the result of his gift and the energetic sex. She needed to rest and recharge. The risk she'd awaken and attempt to find him? Nonexistent. Really, the risk of causing any issue ran very low. He returned his gaze to the beckoning night. A guy needed to do what a guy needed to do.

With his head tilted back and his arms still outstretched, he embraced the wild animal inside him. His howl echoed through the quiet night.

CHAPTER TEN

I need to go." Shantel set the empty coffee mug on the end table and stood.

Johnnie wanted to argue. Given she had nothing to argue with, she stayed silent. They'd been talking for over an hour and shared a second cup of coffee. Shantel's face looked much brighter than when she'd first stood on Johnnie's deck. A little bit of a win.

Wrong. Not a little, but a lot of a win, in her book. She'd learned so much more than she anticipated when Shantel first stepped inside her house. She'd been brought up to date on the excavations and received bonus points for learning why she remained single. A most interesting story, including the sad part about her family turning their back on her. Her own family had never missed a beat. They were a model for unconditional love, and she wished that could be the case for Shantel as well.

Overall, she wasn't sure what her revelation meant. Without question, she was attracted, yet she didn't have a clue if Shantel felt anything beyond friendship. A single word echoed in her head: patience.

Their time together here seemed to be wrapping up in a friendly, organic way. Not awkward or uncomfortable. Natural. Nice. Now, Shantel needed to go home and rest. Johnnie needed to get dinner ready for both her and Cougar, and get a little rest too. All of them needed time to recover after their draining work.

At least tomorrow, they could pretend the world remained normal. No searches, no forensic techs, no buried bodies. Not that they weren't still out there, but she didn't have to be. Rick had suspended any further searches while Shantel, Dr. Skelton, and the forensics unit completed their work. So much to investigate. It boggled the mind.

At the door, Johnnie leaned against the frame as Shantel walked to her car. Funny how a woman could package so much intelligence and power to affect the world around her in such a petite body. Much ado had been made about her when she came to EWU. She'd heard about the talented Dr. Kind and the references to an unnamed husband. Until tonight she hadn't known why she'd become the single and unattached Dr. Kind, and her casual interest from before had just morphed into something more intense. The media Dr. Kind didn't hold a candle to the woman in the flesh.

"Thank you," she said, for probably the fourth time. Criminy. She needed to take it down a notch. So not impressive.

Shantel smiled and waved as she slid in behind the wheel of her car. If Johnnie's blabbering bothered her, it didn't show. "We'll talk again soon."

"Counting on it."

In so many ways. But she didn't add that phrase. No sense looking like a smitten eighth-grader, even if that's how she felt. Not a bad sensation. She hadn't been taken with anybody in a long time, so she kind of liked the reaction even if the timing sucked. If she'd learned anything over the years, it was that she possessed zero control over things like this. Might as well roll with it. She'd just enjoy being around a woman who made her feel alive and engaged. It would be enough.

At the same time, the little issue of bodies buried out toward Cheney meant they'd see more of each other. The team she made with Cougar put them on a unique path to help their community. She didn't regret one single moment of the thousands of training hours. The failures. The successes. While she'd never imagined they'd encounter the horror of the last few days, she wouldn't change anything. What they could do made a difference, and that's what counted.

She saw the same in Shantel. No ego. No bragging. Nothing except calm professionalism. Sure, Shantel internalized what they'd discovered. The emotion had roiled right below the surface tonight. She'd felt the pain that made her hands tremble. If anything, she'd glimpsed the whole woman and found her all the more exciting.

That they both saw things in the same way made her want to work closer with Shantel. Johnnie had felt a little silly when she first called Rick about the teeth marks in the bones. Not anymore. Now she wanted all the gritty details, and Shantel could help her pursue that knowledge.

The driveway-gate sensor caught Shantel's car, and it began to swing open. She stood on the deck watching until the car turned onto Sands Road and disappeared from sight. Cougar pressed against her leg, his subtle reminder that his dinner had not yet been delivered.

"Yeah, buddy. I'll get your chow." Then she caught sight of the side-by-side buzzing down the road toward her gate. She smiled and leaned back in through the door to hit the button for the gate, stopping it from closing. It swung wide again to let the vehicle and its driver through.

"Hi, Johnnie. Wait until you try these. They are my best ever, truly ever. I hope you like them, and could you tell Mom if you do. She says they're expensive to bake and that they better be good, or they're a waste of money. I don't think that at all. They are good. Really, really good." Her fourteen-year-old Downs Syndrome neighbor loved to bring her magnificent baking creations for critique.

"Thank you, Polly. These look wonderful." She took the plate of chocolate-frosted drop cookies that did, indeed, look wonderful. She wouldn't be surprised if the girl someday worked in a bakery.

"Gotta go. Bye." She ran off the porch and back toward the side-by-side. Typical Polly, with her boundless energy. She wished she could bottle some of it for the days when she was dragging.

Halfway down the driveway, Polly stopped and yelled back at her. "Do you need a plate for your friend?"

"My friend?"

"Yup. Mom wouldn't let me come over when your friend was here, so I waited till she was gone. Maybe she'd like my cookies too."

Johnnie laughed and waved. "I'll save her a couple. How's that?"

"Okay!" She turned back around and drove toward the gate, turning left at the road as she headed back toward her own home. Anyone who said that those born with Downs Syndrome couldn't function in society had never been around the capable whirlwind named Polly. She loved that girl.

"You lose, buddy," she told Cougar as she put the cookies on the counter. "Plain old dog food for you."

❖

Shantel berated herself as she pulled into the garage. After everything they'd been through today, it would have been a very good idea to leave a light on in the house. A dark house didn't exactly instill peace and comfort. More a monsters-in-every-corner kind of atmosphere. It had been a long time since she'd been afraid of the dark, but she was right now. At least the fish tanks provided a tiny glow.

Stepping inside the kitchen door, she felt along the wall until she located the switch plate. The room flooded with light, and her shoulders relaxed. In the living room, she turned on a lamp before walking to the tank. As she sprinkled food into the water, she leaned down to peer inside. "All quiet on the western front?" Surely her watchdog fish had kept an eye on things.

The fish ignored her as they raced for the food. She had the same urge now that she'd made it home. Her stomach growled, and given the tense day, that surprised her. Most of the time when she encountered such bare, blatant evil, food became the last thing she craved. A good shower to wash away the stench of corruption became her first go-to in those situations.

In fact, now that she thought about it, a shower sounded perfect, and it felt perfect too. The scent of her handcrafted vanilla soap filled her senses with sweetness and pushed away the ugliness of the day. Ugly except for the time she spent with Johnnie. She liked that tall, lean, attractive woman even though they'd just met. She'd been impressed with how Johnnie moved through the field, always aware of her position yet always with an eye on her dog. The way the two were tuned into each other signaled a very special bond.

Her phone buzzed, and she resisted picking it up. At this time of night only one person would call her. Jamie lived on the Florida coast and would be in bed. It would not be her sleep-loving brother. If Erin needed her for anything, she would have called hours ago. Those two were pretty much the only ones likely to contact her at home.

Even though she'd been here several years now, she kept pretty much to herself. The divorce and coming out combined to send her into self-imposed isolation. Easier that way, at least for the time being. At some point she'd reach out. Had to be in her own time, though. Definitely on her own terms. It had taken far too long to get here, so a couple of years to make her way wasn't unreasonable.

That left only one person who would call her and the last person she wanted to talk to. Hindsight being what it was, she could now see all the signs she'd missed at the time. At first, she supposed, she chose to overlook them. Easier to do that than accept the mess she'd gotten herself into.

The beep told her he'd left a message on her phone when she refused to pick up the call. Never one to tolerate being ignored, Daniel would absolutely leave a voicemail. She deleted it unheard. She didn't need to listen because it would be the same. It always was. I miss you. We're destined to be together. We can overcome our differences. And, the most frightening one, until death do us part.

She didn't care to spoil the evening with any of that. Instead, she poured herself a small glass of brandy, grabbed a couple of crackers, and went into the living room to put her feet up. Her laptop sat on the end table right where she'd left it this morning. She picked it up and logged on. A few emails from students with questions, a few with easy answers, and a few with more that required some time and detail. Those she forwarded to Erin. The two emails from Daniel, she deleted, just like the voicemail.

The brandy went down warm and comforting as she sipped it, relaxing, and she welcomed the sensation. For at least ten minutes, she embraced the quiet time, which eased some of the strangeness of the day.

When the brandy was gone, she set the glass aside and turned back to her laptop. Done with anything official, she decided to do some more sleuthing. The researcher in her wanted more intel about Johnnie.

Her phone rang again, and this time she gave in to curiosity. Jamie. Alarm shot through her. "Dude, why are you up in the middle of the night?"

"Trouble in river city, sis."

She rested her forehead on her hand. "What?"

"Mom's had a heart attack."

In some ways that didn't surprise her. High blood pressure for years and way over her ideal weight, her mother thought exercise was stupid. She loved to bake and hadn't met a pound of butter or bag of sugar she didn't like. "I'm sorry."

"Come on, Tel. You can do better than that."

"What do you want from me, Jamie? She's the one who disowned me."

"Forgive her."

"It's not a matter of forgiveness. She made it perfectly clear what she thinks of me, that she never wants my sinner face around her again."

"You're better than this."

"I can handle only so much." The ugly words her mother said to her would be seared into her memory forever. Her mother tended toward the radical side, but she'd never believed she could lob such nastiness at her own child.

"You are the strongest person I know."

"And even the strongest have a breaking point."

Daniel went to work the next morning seething. He'd enjoyed a most excellent run, an almost satisfying meal of a wild rabbit, and several sessions of awesome sex with Erin. The bad mood had nothing to do with any of those things. What pissed him off was the radio silence from Shantel. He'd expected her to ignore his calls. That meant STOP for her. That she didn't call back after his voicemail and email sent him into a very bad mood. He expected better from her.

When he sat down at his desk, he reminded himself that in a few days, he would finally turn all this around. All the irritation of the past would become a distant memory.

Not to say that the last few days hadn't been fun. He'd like to think he could keep Erin around even after Shantel returned home. Her spirit intrigued him, and he fed off it. It would be a shame to have to let it go.

The more he thought about it, the more the idea held merit. His own little pack. Despite his consistent dedication to the lone-wolf mentality, establishing a special pack appealed to him. Perhaps he'd just needed to create the right one, and that's the point he'd missed earlier in his life.

Or not. For years it all worked for him with a beauty that defied description. He enjoyed his life, his love, his success, while his solitary pursuits provided him with a blanket of protection. It kept him off anyone's radar, and he reveled in the power and freedom that rolled his way. Perfection suited him. After Shantel left him, it had all started to falter, culminating in the desecration of his special burial grounds.

If only she'd stayed true to her vow, none of this would be happening. She liked women, or so she'd told him, and couldn't live a lie any longer. Not for a moment did he buy into that declaration. No way could he have picked the wrong mate. He didn't make mistakes like that.

He didn't claim to be perfect. Everyone, regardless of how intelligent and talented, made mistakes now and again. Case in point, the discovery of his special place near Cheney. He'd been able to keep it his secret for a very long time, and now it lay in ruins.

Right now, he'd take a little time to ponder his next steps. He continued to lean toward a new start in a new place, with fresh hunting grounds. He could go through several cycles and not give in to the urge to take a human. A bit of a lie really. He could always avoid taking a human. He just chose not to. When the temptation overwhelmed him with desire, he gave it free rein. No one had been the wiser until now, so why not?

The old ones who turned him warned against the dangers of taking human life. They wanted to protect centuries' worth of legacy, but he didn't give two shits about their legacy or hundreds of years of history. Nothing in the universe compared to indulging in the forbidden fruit.

To keep his secrets out there in his special place and walk among them anytime he wanted made it all even better. It wasn't necessary to see or touch them, just stand on the ground above them and remember. The wolf inside him howled each and every time.

Pam interrupted his lovely thoughts when she stepped a few feet into his office wearing some god-awful purple sweater that made her look like a giant grape. "You have a partners' meeting in thirty minutes."

Shit. "Fine," he said.

"Do you need anything for the meeting?"

He shook his head. It didn't take a rocket scientist to notice how infatuated she'd become with him. She'd been on the staff ten years before he came home to join the firm. His father had moved her into the position as his assistant, believing that her experience would make her a good match for him. In that respect, Senior hadn't been wrong. She had brains and ability and probably should have gone on to law school.

The problem didn't reside with her professional abilities. It came down to her puppy-dog devotion to him and outfits like the purple monstrosity. Soon enough he'd have to make a change, because he didn't quite trust her to keep it in the office. The last thing he needed was someone who showed up unannounced on his doorstep. Or, even worse, if she started following him. She had that kind of stalker-like air.

"No," he said, as he glanced out the window. "I have everything I need for the meeting."

The expression on her face radiated disappointment. "All right, but if you do need anything, let me know." She patted her hair and tried for a bright smile.

"Of course. Will you shut the door, please?" Nobody could accuse him of not being polite, even when he felt like shouting for her to get the fuck out of his face.

Alone again, he pressed his lips together, swiveled in his chair, and stared out the window. He picked up his phone and punched number one. Right to voicemail. Again. Next, he called Erin. His tone became bright. "Hey, beautiful."

"You're an asshole."

"What? Me?" He smiled because she'd hit it on the head. He was an asshole. Most who achieved the kind of success he had tended to be that way. It wasn't an insult.

"You didn't even leave a note."

"Sorry, love. Had a meeting with the old man so had to jet." Not technically a lie. He did have a meeting with Senior and the rest of the partners, as Pam had just reminded him.

"Terrible excuse."

"Yet a valid one just the same."

She laughed. "Okay, asshole. What's up?"

How he could charm them all. "I need to talk to Dr. Kind, but she's not answering. Do you know where I might be able to find her today?"

For a second, he thought asking about Shantel made her angry. "You need to talk to Dr. Kind? I wasn't aware you two were acquainted."

"It's for a case I'm working on. Her name came up, and I realized you work with her. Makes my job of tracking her down a whole lot easier."

"Gotcha. Actually," she said, sounding fine. He could convince anyone of anything. "This serial-killer thing has her tied up like a Christmas package. I'm handling her classes for the foreseeable future while she works with the cops and the medical examiner."

"Darn. I really hoped to talk with her. I assume they're out searching for bodies again today. I've been following a bit on the news."

"Don't think so. I believe, at least this morning, she'll be at the ME's office working on the bones."

"What's she say about them?"

"She doesn't say anything. That would be unprofessional."

He laughed. "Of course, but since you work so closely together, I figured she'd share with you."

"You figured wrong."

"Can't blame me for asking. It is pretty bizarre. Everybody would love to know more."

"I have nothing." Her words were firm. She was loyal to her boss.

"Darling, you have a lot." He kept his own words light.

"Get your mind out of the gutter." The stiffness in her voice eased off as he joked.

"Tonight?" He'd get what he wanted from her one way or the other.

"Maybe. I'll call you. I have a lot to do."

"Sure. Just call me later." He smiled as he put the phone back into his pocket. She would call.

CHAPTER ELEVEN

Trying to get some sleep last night had turned into a real challenge for Johnnie. Shantel's unexpected visit to her casa had been surreal enough to keep her mind buzzing for hours. From the moment they'd been introduced, she'd liked her. Some people had that unseen aura that screamed trust, and Shantel definitely exuded that. Her resume alone instilled trust. The flesh-and-blood version put the paper to shame.

More than that, Shantel gave a new meaning to the term interesting woman. She'd never met anyone quite like her. Two words came to mind: relatable and approachable. Her students had to love her.

A few hours of sleep finally under her belt, she now sat down at her desk with a cup of coffee and logged onto her computer intending to wrap up this latest history textbook. After ten minutes of staring at the manuscript, she closed it. She hadn't written a single word.

At her bookshelf, she lifted a pile that consisted of three books: *The Complete Guide to Witches, Werewolves, and Vampires, The Encyclopedia of Preternatural Folklore, and Hereditary Witchcraft.* She also grabbed two spiral notebooks containing research notes on the same subjects. Guilty pleasure for a writer of nonfiction. Back at her desk, she flipped open the thickest of the three books, whose author was dedicated to finding the truth beneath the stories passed from generation to generation. Some of her counterparts might disagree. They could be such snobs.

At first glance, the complete guide seemed like a lightweight compilation of the creatures of gothic fiction. It did include those creatures, who had their place. It also included a comprehensive history of folklore, and that's what she was drawn to now.

It had come to her in a dream last night. Or, to be more accurate, it triggered a memory. What led her to the books? The burials.

The condition of the bones displayed a distinct and unique condition—big-animal intervention, which took her thoughts right to wolves. They were showing up more and more in the Pacific Northwest, although technically north of where the gravesites were discovered. Still, it wouldn't be impossible to find a wolf in this area. Could explain the marks on the bones. Did nothing to explain the burials.

That left one other possibility, which she'd keep to herself for the time being, as she didn't care to have people believe she'd gone crazy. Enough found her a little out there already because she preferred dogs to humans and worked most of her career all alone. Throw in thoughts about preternatural creatures, and they'd lobby for some professional help.

It was a mere theory anyway. No one could argue that sometimes it helped to think outside the box. Even writing nonfiction, she liked to let her mind expand, and that's what she planned to do now. A great many of the legends had a basis in fact, and perhaps something would speak to her this morning.

As she read through passages on night creatures, she conjured up all sorts of images that sent little shivers through her. Good and evil definitely existed. The work she and Cougar did too often put them in the path of evil. She'd seen it firsthand and knew it was real. As evil showed its face, so too did the good all around them. Many of those she worked with volunteered strictly from the goodness of their hearts. They didn't get paid, and it cost them thousands of dollars and hundreds of hours every single year. Yet, they always showed up. They came in the middle of the night to find a lost child. They left their Thanksgiving dinners to save a depressed, suicidal soul who didn't believe anyone cared. They demonstrated to them that strangers cared enough to come search for them. Yes, good and evil existed.

She couldn't help going down a path that started for her decades ago. A young girl, standing in the dark, in the forest, seeing something she couldn't explain. The wolf had been too big to be real. Her twelve-year-old mind zipped right to werewolf, and that's where it had stayed.

It's what fueled her on-going intrigue with folklore. She tapped the pages of the book, the eighteenth-century drawing of a snarling beast triggering memories. She had no definitive proof that werewolves existed then or now. No one would take her seriously. They hadn't all those years ago when she'd tried to make her case, and they wouldn't today. Some things didn't change.

That didn't stop her from reading about them in all the books and taking notes of bits and pieces of information that caught her interest. It seemed reasonable that if something like that did exist, they could and would do exactly what they'd uncovered during the searches.

She sat back and stared at the pages of notes she'd made this morning. What should she do with them? Let them percolate maybe? That made the most sense. Get back to her bill-paying work and let all that she'd read sit there percolating until she could make sense of it. Attach it to the real world, and in a way that might help them.

When her phone rang, she jumped. Too much time reading about the world of the supernatural, she supposed. She glanced at the display and frowned. "Hey, Rick. Don't tell me you need us again today."

"No. Techs are still processing the scenes out there. Should have it all wrapped up today though."

"And?" He didn't typically call her unless they needed her and Cougar.

"And that means we do need you tomorrow. I realize we're imposing on you, and I apologize. You and I both know Cougar's the best dog we have, and with something like this, we need him. And you."

So, they did need them. "This is crazy."

"Sister, you aren't kidding."

She didn't have to think twice about it, even though it creeped her out to learn they still had unrecovered remains. "We'll be there."

"Great. I really appreciate you doing this. I'm fully aware it's cutting into your life pretty heavy."

"It's what we train for."

"Nobody trains for this."

She frowned. "No, we really haven't trained for *this*." No team in the world trained for a serial killer.

"None of us have. See you at eight?"

"Same CP?"

"Same CP."

"Tomorrow."

She hung up the phone and could think of nothing except that, tomorrow, she'd spend time with Shantel again.

❖

Shantel stared at her phone for a long time. She needed to get out the front door and to the field. Her brother Jamie's call had gotten to her despite her harsh words to him about their mother. Her parents turned their backs on her in what she considered a very unchristian-like way. If she did the same thing, what did that say about her? The answer didn't make her comfortable, and that pissed her off. She didn't want to take the high road after everything she'd been through.

Finally, she picked up the phone and punched in the number Jamie had made her write down last night. It rang three times before her mother picked up. "Hello?" She wouldn't catch Shantel's number because she hadn't called her in a very long time and thus her greeting was warm and friendly. Most likely she thought it a church friend calling to check on her.

"Mom."

"Why are you calling me?" Her question was filled with ice, all traces of her warm greeting evaporated.

"Jamie told me you had a heart attack. I'm calling to check on you."

"Did you come to your senses and go back to Daniel?" Still nothing except disdain.

"No."

"Don't call me again. You don't exist for me." The call ended.

Slowly, Shantel put the phone back down on the counter, tapped it with her fingers, and took a few deep breaths. It surprised her the rejection still hurt. If nothing else, her mother remained steadfast in her black-and-white morality. Some people were capable of change. Her mother wasn't one of those people.

She rocked back on her feet and wiped her forehead with her arm. Then straightened her shoulders, grabbed her phone, and headed out to the car. Nothing like excavating a body to take her mind off things like a holier-than-thou mother.

Four hours later, she set down her tools and looked at Beth. "We're done here."

Beth stood and stretched her arms over her head. "Thank the good Lord."

She stood also and studied the disturbed earth surrounded by beautiful trees and green foliage. "This makes me so sad."

Across from her, Beth began to pack her tools. "I have to shut down the emotion, or I couldn't do this job. Some of the things I've seen would turn your hair white."

"Me too, except this feels different. More personal."

"Backyard," Beth said simply.

She began to put away her own tools. "I suppose. I've done some excavations that were nothing short of flat-out horror and made it through without losing it. They were in different parts of the world, a long way from home, and maybe that's why they didn't hurt my heart like these are doing. I want to sit down and cry, and that's not like me." She could be honest with Beth without worrying about being judged.

Beth stopped packing up. "How many of those brought up remains that looked as though somebody'd made a meal out of them?"

The bizarre element that none of them could ignore. "Out of all of the retrievals I've worked on, precisely none."

Beth nodded. "New one for me too, and it almost makes me want to go vegan."

She got that. This work had a way of changing everything about a person, including their eating habits. "Back at you."

A couple hours later as she stood next to Fred staring down at the bones of each recovered victim laid out tidy and precise, the chills kept coming. Most consisted of only skeletal remains. A few were more recent. None gave them much to work with. That didn't deter her and never had. She saw a key part of her job as bringing the lost home no matter how long they'd been gone. This wasn't a dead end, more like a challenge, and she was up to it. Each and every set of remains would have a name before they were done. She promised.

"Fred, this is messed up."

His arms folded across his chest, he shook his head. "Haven't seen anything quite like this before, that's for certain, and I've been doing this a long time."

"What is going on around here? Is someone killing these people and letting their dog enjoy the spoils of the hunt? That is wrong on every level."

"It looks that way to me, but honestly, Shantel, I'm at a loss. At this point, I can't definitively determine the cause or manner of death. Nothing about this is dropping into place."

"Okay, so we've got a solid case of undetermined."

"At this moment, yes."

"We need more."

"We do."

"Tomorrow?"

"How about we start early. Say, seven?"

She nodded as she continued to stare down at the mystery. "I'll be here with bells on."

He smiled slightly. "Haven't heard that phrase for a long time."

"You can thank my grandmother. She had a million of those little sayings. I always thought they were corny when she said them, and now that she's gone, I miss them like crazy."

Shantel was still thinking about the bones when she pulled up in her driveway an hour later.

For a long time, Daniel stared into the unlocked desk drawer. The bone resting in the padded jewelry box like a precious diamond held special significance for him. His first human from a long-ago hunt thousands of miles from here. The little box went with him everywhere. Since moving back to Spokane, he'd kept it in the top drawer of his home desk, where he could look at it, touch it, smell it anytime he needed, like right now.

Through the years, conversations with friends often centered around the road not taken. This little box reminded him of the opposite: the road taken. He didn't care about the regrets of his friends or their bemoaning of all the what-ifs. The universe opened up to him an unparalleled path to enlightenment, and he'd embraced it completely. Not a single what-if to bemoan.

He picked up the bone, worn smooth through the years, and it all returned as though it were happening in real time. His head tipped back, he closed his eyes, breathed in the scent, and remembered.

The wolf roared and ran through the woods where the trees were massive, with a thick carpet of green foliage beneath. The scent of Himalayan pine heavy in the air and the sounds of antelope, monkey, and gazelle infused him with energy, and he ran even faster.

The strength and body of the wolf combined with the mind of the man, euphoric. Never could he have imagined something this glorious. Never could he imagine not being this masterful being.

He followed the others as they raced through and around the trees. He could stay this way forever, never be human again. The scent caught him as he flew over the downed branches and fallen leaves. Was he wolf or eagle? The others were far ahead when he stopped, pawing the uneven earth, the twigs, the dampness.

The chants of the lone woman were soft and didn't change as he padded in near silence closer to the clearing. He'd come to this place for the same reason as the woman—to find himself, to embrace inner peace, to achieve clarity. He'd sat in just such a clearing, working through the prayer beads that now lay discarded on his hotel bed.

As he inhaled, his nose lifted. Nerves tingled. The hair rose on his back. His front legs stretched out, and he bowed forward. With the pack it might have been considered a sign of play, and in a sense, it still was. Play for him. Death for her.

He opened his eyes, the memory giving him such joy, he needed nothing else. He placed the bone back into the box and then slipped the box in his pocket. Time to share. His talisman since that wonderful night, it would keep true to the magic it always seemed to bring, he hoped. As he walked out to the garage, his cell rang. Erin. He touched ignore and got into his car. He'd call her back later. After.

CHAPTER TWELVE

After one day's rest, Johnnie and Cougar were back at it, for another two days. The first day they located two more gravesites. Today, thank God, nothing. Rick called the search and said there would be no more tomorrow. They were done, and she was grateful. Five out of six days of searching went way beyond anything she could have imagined in her own region. When she'd committed to search-and-recovery work, this kind of scenario never entered her mind. She hoped it wouldn't again.

At home, she fed Cougar and then sank to the sofa, where she put her head on a pillow and her feet, shoes still on, up on the arm. The cushions were soft, and the throw she grabbed and pulled over her warmed and comforted her. For a few minutes she wanted to lie here and think about nothing except how nice it felt to be home, where no secrets were buried beneath beautiful trees. No death to spoil the beauty of the forest floor. For just a minute.

Shantel took her hand. She smiled and leaned toward her. The moon overhead shone bright and full, the forest around them bathed in the buttery light. The hoot of an owl floating through the air made her think of a symphony. Romantic. Thrilling.

They walked hand in hand, the night wrapping around them. How had she gotten so lucky to find a woman like her. Alone for more years than she cared to admit, now she strolled through the forest on a moonlit night with a beautiful woman who made her breath catch. Not only her beauty beckoned to Johnnie, but her intelligence made her want to spend every minute with her. Talk with her into the wee hours of morning. Wake up to her when the sun rose again.

They could be together for hours without saying a single word. Silence with Shantel filled her with comfort, and she didn't want their time together to end. And it didn't seem to. They walked and walked and walked. She held Shantel's hand tighter and smiled as she stumbled on a downed branch. Her smile faded when she gazed at the ground.

"Look." Shantel's voice held a note of wonder.

Shantel let go of her hand and knelt. One by one she picked up the beads scattered over the ground near the branch that had made Johnnie stumble. "Daniel's beads. Why on earth are they here?"

Johnnie sat up. "What the fuck was that?"

Cougar ran over and nudged her hand. His dark, intense eyes studied her. The caretaker part of his nature wanted to make sure she was okay. Another thing she loved about the breed and why she'd shared her home with German shepherds for a lot of years.

"I'm okay, buddy." She rubbed his head between the ears. His expressive eyes signaled he didn't quite buy her reassurance. "Really." She pleaded her case to her dog. "I'm fine."

Except the dream left her uneasy. The beginning had been a dream, the last bit, a nightmare. Those beads were identical to the one Shantel discovered when she'd put her camera to her eye, and somehow her subconscious found a way to tell her they needed to discover more.

Of course, dreams weren't reliable, and the most rational explanation would be random synapsis activity. Or not.

Shantel woke up early. When she'd stretched out in bed last night at a little after one, she'd figured her eyes would snap open at dawn. It made perfect sense: get to bed late, get up early. Her circadian rhythms might as well be as wonky as the rest of the world. She skipped her morning tea and went right for the hard stuff: Dr. Pepper. With a mother born and raised in Texas, it had been a staple in their house growing up, and now her comfort drink. Used to drive Daniel nuts when she'd pop open a can at six in the morning. Helped her think—something quite useful at the present.

She ran her hands through her hair and closed her eyes. A slight pounding started behind her right eye, typically the first sign of a migraine she didn't have time for today. Normally, Saturday would be a day to enjoy a long run before grading a few papers. For her, even with the work she'd still have to do, the weekend promised time to relax. The Centennial Trail traversed the city and county, going all the way across the state line to Coeur d'Alene. She loved getting out and running that beautiful trail, waving to her fellow runners and enjoying the comradery of a region full of outdoor enthusiasts. Today, she wouldn't have time, damn it anyway.

Might as well get on with it. Between a hot shower and the cold Dr. Pepper, she felt much more alert and ready for the day by the time she dropped a pile of books on the kitchen table. Energized despite her lack of sleep, she popped a second can and flipped open the first book. Round one consisted of staring at the photographs, and it yielded the expected results. The sugary goodness that was Dr. Pepper tasted like ambrosia as she took a big drink and studied each photo.

She tagged about half a dozen with Post-it notes, intending to come back to them later. The colorful little flags attached to the book pages created a rainbow. Leaning back in her chair, she pondered what she'd seen and what she'd read. Back in her school days, they studied all different scenarios repeatedly. To be a good scientist, she had to be well-versed on what could and would happen both out in the field and in the lab.

The lessons were worthwhile, and she had, indeed, encountered a great many of the scenarios she'd been assigned to study. Her mentor at Texas State, Dr. Soule, delighted in pushing her to consider everything, seen and unseen. She fell back on those lessons now and tried to consider things from every single angle. Uneasiness wrapped around her until she finally picked up the phone. Eight her time made it ten in the Lone Star State. Not too early to hear from a former student. Right?

He picked up on the first ring. That was the kind of man he'd always been. Available, knowledgeable, and most important, kind. He expected the very best from his students, and each knew of the high bar set for them without ever being told. Under his tutelage, no one got away with anything less than their best, which was why she thanked the gods he'd mentored her. Always grateful for everything he taught her and encouraged her to do, she continued to become a better scientist because of him.

"Shantel, my dear, I had a feeling you'd be calling." He sounded cheerful.

"You've been watching the news." To expect anything different from him would be a mistake. He kept an eye not just on his own area, but the world. She'd learned early on that one had to get up early to get a jump on the impressive Dr. Soule.

"What's a retired man have to do except follow current events?"

"Relax?"

"My dear, it is relaxing when I am assured that capable people are handling the important tasks this kind of news requires. I know that because I watch said news, and there is my brilliant former student doing precisely that."

"I appreciate your confidence."

"Nothing you haven't earned. You continue to fill me with pride."

Another thing she loved about him—he didn't pull punches. And he didn't give compliments freely. They had to be earned. An urge to make him proud had driven her all the way through her program. He'd been the one who'd handed her the degree she'd worked hard to achieve and the first one to address her as Dr. Kind. His faith in her abilities buoyed her. "I need to run some things by you. Confidential things."

"Shoot."

After she finished briefing him, he said simply, "That's interesting."

"That's it?" Her letdown no doubt echoed in her voice.

He chuckled, even though the subject matter was far from humorous. The chuckle was for her and about nothing else. "Let me tell you a few things I don't share in my classes."

That statement stopped her. She'd spent years studying under and working with this man. By her estimation, she'd absorbed all he had to offer. From the tone of his voice, quite a mistaken belief. "Tell me, Professor."

He turned serious. "It's time you call me Ed."

What? Like her world wasn't getting strange enough. Call the man, the doctor, she revered, Ed? "Okay…Ed, tell me." It felt super strange to call him by his given name, almost disrespectful.

"You sitting down?"

"Yes…" The whole Ed thing dropped her right into a chair before he asked.

"Good. Now you're going to want to take notes."

Her hand trembled as she picked up a pen and flipped to a clean page in her notebook "I'm ready."

"What do you know about werewolves?"

❖

It almost killed him to backtrack and go home unfulfilled. Shantel wasn't home yet again, and she should have been there.

The gift he'd brought was far too precious to risk leaving on her porch for who knew how long. Lately, she'd been shaking up her schedule, and he didn't like what it signaled. Her deviation from her regular routine thwarted his plan once more, and it didn't set well with him. He preferred order and reliability when it came to his woman. He'd even given serious thought to calling Erin again, but that hadn't placated him either.

Once home, he'd put the precious bone back in its normal spot in the desk drawer and gone to bed. That should have been the end of it, except his failed attempt had been eating at him. That he'd tried and failed again this past night with the same result irritated the shit out of him. This time when he returned home, he headed to the kitchen, where a twelve-year-old bottle of scotch took some of the sting off his rage. The first night, he'd been disappointed. Last night he'd been full-on pissed off. By the time he'd dropped into his king-size bed, he'd had a righteous buzz going.

The headache he woke up with reminded him why he rarely over-indulged in alcohol. Only when he sat alone in his home did he allow himself the very infrequent luxury of getting drunk. He couldn't afford a lapse in judgment brought on by the loose lips that booze promoted, and the Buddhism he'd studied so intensely frowned on drinking to intoxication. Last night, alone and angry, he could do as he pleased. No harm. No foul.

Except for the fucking headache. A double shot of espresso helped on that front. So did four ibuprofens. By the time he reached his office, the pounding dulled enough to tolerate Senior and his ever-so-helpful assistant. He really would have liked for them to leave him alone. No such luck. After all, he had the nine o'clock with the most successful developer in Eastern Washington, and Daddy would be eternally—and publicly—disappointed if he bailed on that, even if it was a Saturday the asshole intruded on. The client was simply too busy to take time during the week to meet with his attorneys. Instead, everyone had to cater to him. Fucker.

He didn't bail despite the almost overwhelming urge to leave them all hanging and imagining the fury that would cause Senior's face to glow red. Like the good son he was, he put a big smile on his face, shook the asshole's hand, and sat down across from him at the shiny walnut conference table. They talked for an hour and a half about contracts and plans for future developments. Truthfully, he couldn't stand the guy and hated people like him who took perfectly beautiful land and stripped away all that made it special and unique. They put up cookie-cutter houses or strip malls, displacing wildlife and cutting down trees that had been there when the first settlers to the region came through. They did it all without blinking an eye about the destruction to the natural world and, once they finished, would leave without another thought. They had no concern for the environmental destruction, the traffic impact, or the stress put on school systems already overloaded.

The hatred roiled inside as he sat at that table and smiled, nodding when appropriate and promising contracts to be delivered on time. All the while, he thought about what it would be like to chase this arrogant jerk through the very woods he wanted to cut down, to sink his teeth into the soft flesh of his neck and feel the blood flow. Not today. Too much scrutiny to risk it, regardless of the intense satisfaction he'd achieve. Down the road a bit? If he had a little black book of names, Mr. Developer's would be right at the top.

He kind of liked that idea. A book of names would give the game a new pop. Not that it ever got old for him. The hunt never disappointed. With Erin now in the mix, the next one or two would be quite exciting. He'd enjoy it for as long as it lasted.

"I'm out of here," he said as he passed his father's office.

"We should talk about the contracts." His father, dressed even on a Saturday in an expensive suit and tie, came to the door with the expectation of unquestioned obedience clear in his face. Too bad, Daddy. He had other, more exciting plans.

"Not today. Besides, I'm a defense attorney, not a contract guy. Get one of your underlings to do it." He didn't look back.

"Now."

"No." He went out the door and still didn't look back. The no-eye-contact strategy worked best with the old man. If he so much as faltered, he'd have him here the rest of the day and then tell him to come in tomorrow as well. Fuck that shit. He'd had enough for a Saturday. Fun beckoned out there, and he intended to grab it with both hands. Besides, his head still hurt like a motherfucker.

Outside, he pulled his cell phone from his pocket at the same time he hit the remote for his car. "What are you doing?"

"Just finished talking to Shantel about classes next week," Erin told him.

"Oh? She coming back? I still need to talk with her. My client issue."

"Doesn't sound like it. I'll probably end up covering the classes next week too. Hope your client isn't in a hurry. Or you can always hit up Dr. Santoro over at Washington State."

Nope. Dr. Santoro wouldn't do at all. "I might do that if the client pushes." He lied. "How do you feel about dinner tonight?"

He could hear the smile in her voice. "What time?"

CHAPTER THIRTEEN

Johnnie got dressed, took Cougar for a run, and wandered by the local espresso shop on the way home. A latte for her and a cookie from the barista for Cougar, which he devoured in about ten seconds, or maybe less. As a puppy he'd discovered that any place with a drive-up window pretty much guaranteed a treat for him. If she drove through one on the way home from training or a mission, he could be sound asleep in the back and then pop up like a bottle rocket the second he heard the slide of the stand's window. The baristas all loved him, and he rewarded them with excited yips and a wildly wagging tail.

The latte gave her a nice little pick-me-up as they walked back toward the house. Her legs were pleasantly fatigued, and the benefits of the endorphin release would carry her through the day. Every time she came out like this, she wondered why she didn't make it more of a priority. Right after that thought, she'd justify not running every day by telling herself that her work with Cougar filled in the gaps. Wasn't the same, even if the two of them covered many miles in both their training and the missions. She made it work in her head, though, and not much guilt made it through.

Showered and dressed, she wandered through the house. Not like her to be so disconnected. Usually, a to-do list waited for her, and while she did have one, none of the items appealed to her. Her thoughts kept rolling back to the idea of the wolf and, as much as she tried not to go there, werewolf. That dream hadn't helped either. She couldn't shake it even after the run and the latte. More than anything, she wanted to share it with Shantel. A bit of a risk, given she'd likely think Johnnie was losing her grip on reality. She was inclined to take the risk.

Most likely she'd be savoring her own peaceful Saturday, so calling Shantel would be rude. However, they'd both been working for days on this unique case, so her call would be natural rather than intrusive. If she wanted to do something bad enough, she could rationalize anything.

Because of the dream, her research, and her natural curiosity, she picked up her phone. When Shantel didn't answer by the fourth ring, she let her finger hover over the "end call" icon. Instead of tapping it, she dropped her hand. A message composed in her head, she waited. It took her a second to absorb that a real live voice greeted her and not the recorded voicemail intro she expected.

"Good morning, Johnnie." Nice. Shantel had picked up.

"Good morning to you too. How did you know it was me?"

"I put you in my contacts." Of course she had. The organized, detail-oriented scientist would do that.

Johnnie had been able to read people well forever, and Shantel's tone made her pay close attention. "Is everything all right?"

The pause before she responded didn't jibe with her answer. "Yes. All fine."

"Not buying fine. Talk to me." Might be a bit of a reach, given they hadn't spent a ton of time with each other to date. She couldn't help it. She heard what she heard and not her style to ignore anyone hurting.

"What are you doing this morning?"

The abrupt question took her off guard. "Ah…"

"Sorry. That came out of left field, but if you don't have anything super pressing, would you like to meet for coffee?"

"Of course." Maybe the answer was a little fast. Like lightning fast. Shantel didn't seem to notice. "Great. Meet me at Midnight Espresso Café. Do you know where it is?"

She had to think for a second. "On Northwest Boulevard."

"That's the one. At ten?"

"See you then."

It didn't matter that she'd already made an espresso stop this morning. If Shantel wanted to meet for coffee, or in her case, more coffee, she was all over it. And, if she'd been curious before about what she'd found, that curiosity ratcheted up about a thousand-fold now.

She put her phone down on the counter and shot a glance at Cougar. "I've got a date." He cocked his head and studied her. "Okay, not really a date, but it's as close to one as I've had in a long time." He blinked and walked away.

❖

Shantel picked a spot outside on the coffee shop's red-brick patio. The small table with the striped umbrella had a friendly if not intimate ambiance.

After the week they'd had, the cleansing sensation of sunshine rocked. Pure and bright, it dispelled the gloom of what they'd been working with and, she hoped, would give her a clearer vision of the remarkable story Dr. Soule shared with her.

How she loved that man who'd become her friend. She valued his brilliance in the field of anthropology, but beyond that, he had a rare combination of genius and common sense. That's what made his remarks disturbing on many levels. If he put merit in it, then what was she to think? Could she take it seriously? And, if she did…what in the holy hell were they dealing with? Talking about upsetting the apple cart.

Her world to date consisted of science and facts, even if she'd spent years ignoring some of the facts of her own reality by marrying Daniel. Dr. Soule's theory went way out of her wheelhouse and tossed science right out the window. The jury was still deliberating on the facts part of it. She'd have to do her own research before she weighed in on that one.

"Hey." Johnnie walked to the table and smiled down at her, her face lighting up. Beautiful. Her legs were a mile long in a pair of slim jeans, and the sleeves of her shirt were pushed up enough to allow a peek of the tats on her arms. Wow.

"Good morning." At least that greeting didn't come out too breathy.

"Your call surprised me," Johnnie said.

"Not in a bad way, I hope. I mean, we've met under less-than-wonderful circumstances, but I feel like we're becoming friends in spite of it all." She needed to slow down. Rambling didn't add to the credibility she hoped for and would need before she finished her story.

Johnnie sat down across from her. "We are friends." She smiled. "For me, search and rescue is probably where I meet most people. I mean, I work from home, I train nonstop, and I go out on missions. Doesn't leave a lot of room for making acquaintances."

Shantel nodded and appreciated the sentiment. "I deal with a lot of people between eighteen and twenty-five, so it's always a pleasure to spend time with someone my own age."

"Cheers to that. Speaking of which, let me run in and get a coffee. You need anything?"

Shantel touched her cup. "I'm good. Thanks."

Despite what she wanted to bounce off Johnnie, warmth spread through her the moment she showed up. Between the sun and the woman, the day felt a little better than it had when she'd completed her call with Dr. Soule. The thought of her mentor threw a bit of cold water onto her mood. How to bring up the unbelievable with Johnnie and not sound like an idiot weighed on her.

It took five minutes for Johnnie to get her coffee and return. Her smile still lit up her face, and it occurred to Shantel it would be super easy to get used to that every day. Crazy thoughts. The morning had been riddled with crazy, so this idea fit right in. Might as well go with it.

With her hands wrapped around a bright-red ceramic mug, no wasteful paper cup there, Johnnie looked over at her and held her gaze. "Tell me."

Now that the moment had arrived, Shantel wasn't sure she could do this. She liked Johnnie, and talking about her conversation with Dr. Soule would most likely cause the woman to flee post haste. She didn't want her to run away. Quite the opposite. Would it be worth the risk?

"How are you with folk legends?"

"Excuse me?"

"You know, things like lycanthropy. Lycans."

"You mean, like werewolves?" Johnnie had put down her coffee and leaned back in her chair, an unreadable expression on her face. Putting a little distance between them? Damn, going south after the first couple of sentences. She pushed up the sleeves of her shirt, revealing more of the enticing ink.

Shantel pulled her gaze away from the tats and back to Johnnie's face. "I mean like werewolves." Might as jump into the deep end.

Johnnie stared at her for a moment, and then a light came into her eyes. "No fucking way."

❖

While Daniel's exciting plans for tonight were laid out in his mind, the rest of the day stretched out dull and boring. The meeting at the office done, he had some time to kill. That thought made him smile. For most, that might just be a turn of phrase. Not in his case. Most of what he said was literal; it went over the heads of the majority of people. Their loss and his gain.

At home, he pulled the little box from the desk drawer again. Perhaps this afternoon would be the time. More than anything, he wanted to hand it to her in person, to relish the moment as recognition dawned. He imagined how it would be or, rather, what he wanted it to be. He didn't quite trust her yet. He'd kept his secret during their time together for a reason. As much as he'd loved her, at some level he'd also understood her. She'd have found it impossible to reconcile his true nature with her science. He'd kept his secret intact, waiting for the right moment to share everything.

Her little girl-on-girl adventure threw all his plans into turmoil. To say he hated it would be an understatement. Downright stupid, and while he'd allowed her time to regain her senses, his patience waned. She continued to barrel down her delusional track of believing herself to be a lesbian. Even thinking of the word made him furious. For a smart woman, she could be downright oblivious.

His mission was to help her see the light. That's what he'd been doing since she'd managed to get a decree signed. His objections aside, damned if she hadn't gotten her way. At least that day. Her stubborn resistance to his attempts at reconciliation hadn't deterred him. Man's laws simply couldn't break some bonds, and that said a lot for a man with a big fat law diploma hanging on his wall. Laws were fine for lesser people. They didn't apply to him.

With the box on the passenger seat, he drove to her house. She'd used the settlement he'd been compelled to pay her to buy a much smaller house. Their home far surpassed the mediocre choice she'd made on her own. He didn't understand at the time, and he didn't understand now, why she'd choose something so insignificant. No matter. Once she returned to her real home, they'd dump this one in a New York minute. He smiled, thinking through all the marvelous plans for the near future.

The smile faded. She wasn't home yet again. Probably working, either at the university or helping out the county. She was like that. A workaholic. People talked about the incredible hours attorneys worked. They had nothing on professors who also contracted as consultants. Talk about putting in those sixty- and seventy-hour weeks. Shantel could do it without blinking and be the first one to put up her hand to volunteer more. He'd believed at first her willingness to serve had to do with her dedication to her profession. The reality behind it: she used it as an excuse to put distance between them.

Disappointed by her absence, he nonetheless, got out of the car and walked around the house to the backyard. She'd been the one to landscape the acre plus of grass that flowed right to the edge of the undeveloped wilderness—state land—which had been one reason she'd purchased the house. That remained the only feature that made sense to him. At the far edge, the landscaping featured a four-foot-urn fountain, the water flowing into the decorative rock surrounding it.

For a good ten minutes he stood and focused on the sound of the water as it rose through the top and then flowed down the side of the urn into the rocks. Truly lovely, and he'd give her kudos for a job well done. The good professor had many talents.

As much as he hated it, it would be best for him to leave. Shantel would not be pleased to find him in the backyard. She'd become very territorial since she started living alone. Pity. He'd like to stay here a little longer and give full rein to his imagination. A better and more prudent idea, to leave without conflict or her becoming aware that he'd been here relaxing in her private oasis.

Of course, he hated to make a trip without accomplishing anything. He smiled as he unzipped his pants and proceeded to mark the urn. He shook off before zipping his pants back up. Now, he was ready to leave.

CHAPTER FOURTEEN

Johnnie couldn't help it. She sat up straighter and leaned in toward Shantel. "You're going to think I'm insane."

"After what I just said to you?"

True enough. She would have to say something truly outrageous for Shantel to consider her loony. She tapped her fingers on the side of her empty coffee mug. "Hear me out, and then you judge."

"Shoot."

Johnnie took a breath. Probably shouldn't go where she intended to, but nothing ventured, nothing gained. Shantel brought it up first. "I'm pretty sure I've seen a werewolf."

"Come again?" Wide eyes that screamed obvious disbelief.

Johnnie threw up her hands. "I know. I know. It sounds crazy, and my friends definitely thought I'd gone around the bend." Her buddies made fun of her for years. She still hadn't lived down that "one time at scout camp" with a certain group of friends.

Shantel rested her elbows on the table. "Where? When? How?"

She half expected Shantel to get up and leave and was gratified that she came closer instead of fleeing. She also couldn't believe she'd said it out loud. When it happened all those years ago, she'd been scared shitless and expected support from her friends. It hadn't happened, and from that day forward, she'd kept her lips shut about it. As impossible as it seemed, she'd never doubted what she'd witnessed. "Camp Sky-Lo. I was twelve and heading to the bathroom at midnight. Pitch-black with a full moon."

"You went alone?"

"Sure. Hey, I was a skilled Girl Scout. I didn't need anyone. My roommates were asleep in their bunks, and I headed up the little hill to where the bathroom and showers were. We all did that because it was a safe place. You didn't have to be scared out there."

"What did you see?" Shantel's eyes were bright.

Johnnie found herself leaning in closer too. "At first I thought it was one of the counselors. I could make her out in the moonlight, and it took a second to hit me she was naked. Shocked my little preteen self, let me tell you. Then a howl that scared me so much I ducked behind a tree. That's when I saw the impossible."

"Saw what?"

"She changed. One minute, human as clear as could be. The next, a wolf."

"Wow."

"Wow is definitely it. I ran back to the cabin and woke them all up, but nobody believed me. Our cabin counselor told me I'd been dreaming."

"It wasn't a dream."

"No. It wasn't. I knew what I'd seen, and nothing has changed my mind in the years since. I'm still just as convinced today I saw a werewolf. It's one reason, albeit an unspoken reason, I work with dogs and search out in the wilderness. In the back of my mind, I'm wondering if I'll finally run across another one and be able to prove I was right."

"Never would have guessed it to look at you."

"What? That I'm crazy?" She didn't want Shantel to think that. Quite the opposite really.

Shantel shook her head and leaned back in her chair. "No. That you have a very open mind."

She wasn't sure if she should be relieved or insulted but decided to go with relieved. "Until that night, I was a pretty normal kid. I did all the stuff others my age did, and it was all good. After that night, I grew up. The wonder in the world sort of disappeared because I no longer took things at face value. I've been searching for the unseen ever since, and I suppose that's why I moved toward human-remains detection. It combines my love of dogs and finding what others may try to hide."

"I'd call that noble."

"Naw. More like my way of making sure I'm really not crazy."

❖

Shantel had been around the world and seen enough to convince her things existed that had no explanation. She believed, with all her being, that good and evil were very real. She'd met people who were truly saints in the flesh and witnessed the handiwork of devils who walked the earth. No theory about it. Reality showed her the unvarnished truth, and during the last week it all hit home again. No one in their right mind could argue that whoever buried those people out near Cheney could be anything except evil.

Her conversation with Dr. Soule and now listening to Johnnie confirmed her belief in things unseen. They were all on the same wavelength, at least in terms of dark forces. A little like Daniel, who loved everything paranormal. Books, movies, television shows—the darker the better for him. She'd considered his choice in entertainment to be creepy and, though she never told him, didn't much enjoy it. He'd played enough werewolf movies during their time together that, had she paid more attention, she'd have a much better foundation in the folklore Johnnie referenced. Of course, movies and books didn't quite stay true to the old legends. From what she could glean, the creators of the popular media Daniel liked to binge on used a lot of creative license.

"All right. I don't believe you're crazy at all. I also think my doctoral advisor is far from certifiable."

Johnnie appeared confused. "Your advisor? I'm not following."

"No reason you should. I said werewolf, and we sort of took a detour."

"Sorry. I guess I've wanted to tell someone my story so long that when you said werewolf, bam, I was off and running. And it felt good."

"Totally understandable." She knew a lot about the weight of secrets.

"Tell me what you'd planned to before I hijacked the conversation. What about your advisor?"

Shantel smiled and nodded. She too wanted to share. "Here's the thing. Dr. Soule was the absolute best to work under as a doctoral student. He's been my rock since the day I walked into his classroom. No shock to you that what we've uncovered has disturbed me. Really unusual. I needed to bounce it off someone I trust, so I called him to consult. It's not the first time I've picked his brain on a particularly difficult case."

"He came up with werewolves?"

"Not exactly. He recommended keeping an open mind and told me about the legends from Eastern Europe and East Asia. He also mentioned things he came across during his travels that didn't make sense in our particular field of science."

"Like human bones that look like they have canine teeth marks?"

"Not look like…do have."

"Oh, crap. He's seen it before?"

She nodded and thought about the pictures he sent her after their call. Too similar to what they'd pulled from the ground around here to leave her feeling warm and fuzzy. His words haunted her. "A number of them in Eastern Europe and Asia."

"No shit." Johnnie leaned back in her chair and ran both her hands through her short hair. For a second, Shantel's breath stopped. How she wanted to pull those shirt sleeves away and run her fingers over the art that peeked from beneath the fabric.

She refocused on their conversation. "He sent me pictures." Might be a good time to share and she handed Johnnie her phone. She watched as she scrolled through them.

Shaking her head, Johnnie handed the phone back. "Seriously freaky. Now fill me in on his theory. I have a feeling it's pretty wild."

Wild might not be the word she'd use. Frightening sounded more appropriate. "He picked up stories from the locals during his travels. The consummate researcher, he's kept notes on everything. He even recorded some of the people he interviewed."

"Locals have all kinds of insider knowledge."

"The stories didn't make sense, though, and at the same time, they did. Everything people told him lined up with the physical evidence we're pulling out of those graves."

"Except, I'm guessing, the part about werewolves being responsible for what happened."

"Except for that. When people got comfortable with Dr. Soule, which he makes easy, they shared the unwritten legends—stories of men who morphed into wolves that terrorized the forests and killed both animals and humans."

Johnnie once again leaned forward. "Where did your professor friend land on all of this?" Shantel saw the same intrigue in her eyes that she felt earlier when talking with her mentor.

She took a deep breath. The words she'd heard from the man she so admired still didn't quite sit right with her. "On the side of the stories."

"He thinks it's werewolves."

"He does."

It probably wasn't Daniel's best idea to visit Shantel's garden and leave his little marking gift, even if she'd never be aware of it. His time there today unsettled him, though usually it calmed him. More than once, he'd relaxed in the space she'd lovingly created. Only, of course, when she was away. It didn't make sense for the visit to disturb him like this.

Or maybe it did. Too many of his secrets were now emerging. As careful as he'd been all these years, the unthinkable happened. He hated these discoveries, even if they represented only the tip of the iceberg. He also didn't like that she played an intimate part in the travesty.

Let it go. Out of his control. He must accept reality and focus instead on gathering information. After he made sure nothing could lead back to him, it would be business as usual. Then, and only then, could he take his adventures a little further afield or maybe start over somewhere completely new. He'd grown comfortable after coming home, and comfort could, and often did, lead to mistakes. He'd seen it too many times with the people he represented.

Today's contract work for his father's special client wasn't his specialty. He did it only to appease Senior and keep him off his back. His heart was and always had been in criminal law. Many of his colleagues saw the field as a way to help those wrongly accused or the ones whose potential punishment didn't fit the crime. Not him. He breathed it all in—the lies, the danger, the depravity—and it filled his soul. To get these people off made him a king, a result he couldn't have achieved in any other area of the law.

His musings about his profession planted the seed of a most excellent idea. He could put the multitude of files he kept locked inside his mind to good use. His mood instantly rose, and he knew exactly how to fill the rest of his day. Someone would pay for his loss, and at the same time, no one would get close to him.

He began to whistle as he drove back to the house to refine his plans. By the time he reached Erin's for dinner and a run, his world would once more be righted. God, he was a genius.

Chapter Fifteen

A ll right." Johnnie sat back, her coffee cup empty, her mind full. "He's not on meds, is he?"

Shantel shook her head. "Most brilliant and sane man I have ever met. I was his teaching assistant while I completed my doctorate, and it's fair to say I've spent a great deal of time with him. We became close, and I began to travel with him on cases. Rational and logical are the two words that best describe him."

"Okay, I mean, I am the one who said I saw a werewolf, so I guess it's not very charitable of me to ask if he might be...well, you know what I mean."

"I'd be more concerned about you if you didn't ask."

What was Shantel thinking about Johnnie's own admission? She'd gone out on limb. The compulsion to blurt out her secret strong enough that she'd done it, but...

Being in limbo didn't work for her. Might as well put it out there. "How crazy do you think I am?" Now that she'd asked, Johnnie didn't really want the answer and needed it all at the same time. She dropped her gaze to the floor. The truth in Shantel's eyes hurt.

"On a scale of one to ten, I must say...zero."

Johnnie's head snapped up, and she stared at her. She couldn't have heard that right. "Seriously?"

Shantel's smile lit up her face. "Seriously."

"But I told you I'm always on the lookout for werewolves."

"And now we may very well have found them. Your persistence paid off." Shantel spread her hands.

"It doesn't seem real." All those years of searching in every shadow and staring up at the full moon waiting for something to happen crashed down on her. Gazing at Shantel steadied her. Their amazing connection gave her strength.

"I'm not sure it is."

"You just said we found them…"

"It's definitely a theory bolstered by the old folktales, which might help us make sense of the evidence we've brought up from those cold graves. At the very least it's a place to start."

Johnnie hadn't thought about it like that. Her young mind had latched on to werewolf and never left room for anything in between. She started nodding. "Folktales are rooted in reality."

"That's it. Now we have to find out what that reality is, and then we'll discover who's doing these horrible things."

She stopped nodding. "Maybe." She drew the word out as her mind raced. Shantel's scientific brain put her on the path of the just-the-facts journey. Johnnie, while certainly dealing in the real world, favored more of a blend of the rational and the not-so-rational. That youngster in her didn't want to forget that night and what she'd witnessed beneath the light of a full moon. Her mother would call her stubborn. She preferred focused.

"We will." Shantel took her hand. "We'll figure this out, together."

Johnnie didn't pull away. Too nice to let her go. She held Shantel's gaze. "I believe we can discover who's responsible. The thing is…" The path they were on differed slightly.

"The thing is what?" Shantel appeared genuinely interested in her thoughts.

She squeezed her hand. The mojo flowed back in. "I think that, just maybe, whoever's doing this isn't completely human."

No question as to how strongly Johnnie felt about the werewolf theory. Like Dr. Soule, something strange and unusual touched her, and she'd spent years searching for answers alone. Given her scientific background, Shantel leaned toward solid facts. To her mind, that's where they would find the truth.

She couldn't dismiss what she'd seen both in the field and on the tables, any more than she could deny the legends that cropped up all over the world. She also couldn't dismiss the young Johnnie's traumatic encounter at camp. How could the similarities exist throughout the world if they didn't share some basic truth? Surely a common thread would lead her to the answers. A good researcher looked at everything, regardless of how the mind might be trying to frame the event within a context of the known. The mind had to stay open and receptive.

"All right." She tipped her head up to meet Johnnie's eyes. The intelligence that shone out of them drew her in. To solve this mystery, with this woman as a partner, was a new and exciting prospect. Sure, she worked closely with many people, Erin being her right hand these days. No argument that Erin was fantastic. Smart and driven, she would be a shining star in her Native American community, or any community, which is why she considered it a privilege that Erin asked her to be her mentor. A quick yes followed that request. Dr. Soule had given her the gift of his brilliant guidance, and she paid it forward with Erin. She only hoped she could be a fraction as good as Dr. Soule.

So, yeah, a fair number of people inhabited her circle. None whose mere presence captured her attention quite like Johnnie. And don't even get her started on Cougar. That dog astounded her, and she'd been around her fair share of search dogs. Like Johnnie, he was special.

"All right..." She kind of got lost in her own thoughts. "Say I buy in to the theory you and Dr. Soule put out here and admit that preternatural creatures really do roam undetected among us mere humans."

Johnnie tapped her fingers against each other. "I say it's a plausible theory."

"If I grant the plausibility of it all, where does that leave us?"

Johnnie tilted her head. "Good question, to which I have no answer."

Talk about being on the same page. Neither did she. "I haven't exactly spent a lot of time investigating the preternatural world."

"I have to admit that I have, and I still have nothing concrete to offer. You know what?" Johnnie winked. "I say let's do it. You call your doc back and pick his brain some more, and I'll make some of my own calls. I might write nonfiction, but I have plenty of friends who work in the paranormal field. I'll also pick some brains."

Shantel smiled. "I like the way you think."

"What are you doing for dinner?"

Warmth flooded through her, and it had nothing to do with the golden sunshine. "Cooking with you?"

"I'll pick the wine."

Daniel hadn't bothered to make calls. No need. The addresses he kept in his mind were as sharp as if he'd written them down with a big black marker. He'd made the visits up close and personal. Besides, he didn't want to risk that anything he said could be tracked. That meant cold and personal calls.

He just needed one, maybe two, and the duo he selected would have no issues doing his bidding. He'd kept them free men, and they'd do as he asked now simply because he asked. Yet that wasn't all of it. They would deliver on his command because it ran deep in their blood. They loved it, and that he summoned them to do what spoke to their souls meant the word no wasn't in the cards.

By the time he reached Erin's house, all the pieces were in play. Perfect plan. Perfect execution. He arrived at her front door with a bag of steaks. The only thing that would have made the night better? A full moon. Impatience tickled the back of his mind. He could accomplish so much more if only they had lunar power. Soon enough. He could, and would, be patient.

"Hey." Erin opened the door, her smile bright and her long, dark hair framing her face. No question about the level of her beauty. Smart too, and that had its own special appeal. No wonder Shantel selected her for one of the coveted graduate-assistant positions. Shantel would surround herself only with the best and the brightest. He doubted Erin really understood her luck. He'd always been proud of Shantel's brilliance. It reflected well on him that he'd selected someone with such a shining future to share his life.

"Hey." He held up the bag. "I come bearing gifts." The scent of warm beef wafted into the air.

"They say a way to a man's heart is through his stomach. It works pretty damn well for a woman too." She took the bag, inhaled deeply, and turned toward the kitchen.

He returned her smile. "No one can accuse me of not feeding my women."

She stopped, her expression darkening. "Women?"

With a shrug, he said, "Figure of speech, my darling. You should know you're the only one for me these days."

"Do I?" She didn't sound convinced.

He put on his perfected innocent expression. Combine that with his soft eyes and hair falling over his forehead, and she didn't stand a chance. No one could stay mad at him. Correction, no one except Shantel could stay mad at him. "I'm quite single."

"Sure, I get that, but how would I know about anyone else? Single doesn't mean exclusive. You're a smart guy, and semantics are well within your abilities."

"A good point. Consider this, however. When would I have time? It's been you and me since that night at the Elk. I go to work. I see you. Period. I'm that kind of single."

Her smile grew a little brighter. "You do have a point."

God, he was good. "Of course, I do. I'm an experienced trial attorney."

"Anyone ever tell you that you're kind of full of yourself?" She turned away and took the bag of food to the kitchen.

He stopped in the kitchen doorway and watched her pull the contents from the bag. "Every damn day."

She laughed and walked over to give him a hug. All had been righted with her world. "Let's eat."

CHAPTER SIXTEEN

It's your fault." Johnnie handed Shantel a glass of iced tea. "Seriously, all your fault."

Shantel took the offered glass, tilted her head, and studied her. "What exactly is my fault?"

"I got zippo done today on my bill-paying job. Instead, I spent the whole day researching werewolves and vampires and ghosts, oh my."

"Isn't that part of your job?"

"Sure. I research every day. Love it, and you're right in that it's a big part of my process when I write textbooks. That said, I don't typically research preternatural creatures and their origins. As much as I'd love to prove my werewolf theory, the schools would dump my books in a heartbeat if I included that kind of information."

"Would make them more interesting."

"Hey! You saying my work is boring?"

The smile on Shantel's face made her breath catch. "No…"

Johnnie laughed. "You got me there. Textbooks aren't exactly the 'keep you on the edge of your seat' kind of reading."

"They're important though."

"They are, and I do try to make them as interesting as I can. I remember what it was like for me in school, and I started writing textbooks because I wanted to make the experience better for others. I feel like I've done a pretty good job. I hope to keep them from falling over in their chairs, even if I can't keep them on the edge of their seats."

"My impression is you've achieved your goal."

"It's a living, and so far, it's been a pretty good one. Can't complain. The work is interesting, and the hours are great." Most people were intrigued when they learned she was a published writer, and then when they learned what she published, they became politely disinterested. Shantel's genuine curiosity sent warmth all through her.

Shantel held her tea between her hands. "Tell me about today's information dig."

She grabbed her own glass of tea and sat across from Shantel, a plate of veggies and cheese between them. Even werewolf hunters needed nourishment. "First, I have to 'fess up that I have spent a fair amount of time delving into the stories about werewolves. I've tried to make sense of what I saw that night at camp, and ever since I've read what I can find."

"I would too if I'd experienced the same. This is good, by the way." Shantel held up part of a slice of smoked gouda before popping it into her mouth.

She appreciated the sentiment about the research and the compliment on the cheese. "The information you shared with me from your convo with Dr. Soule sent me in a different direction, and it turned out to be pretty interesting. Ever hear of an oborot?"

Shantel shook her head at the same time she picked up a carrot stick from the plate and popped it into her mouth. If she kept doing that, Johnnie would have a hard time concentrating on anything else.

"No," she answered after she finished chewing the carrot.

"Russian folklore says that an oborot is someone who can transform into a werewolf at will. They go into a forest, stab a tree with a copper knife, and voila, they are a werewolf, off and running through the wilderness."

"I suspect similar stories exist throughout the world."

She'd had the same thought and found many stories throughout the world minus the knives. She picked up one of the carrots and rolled it between her fingers. "True enough. Lots of stories with variations. The thing is, I zeroed in on that one because of everything we found in the woods. For lack of a better description, it felt right. Vibes and all."

Actually, when the words left her mouth, her comment sounded kind of stupid. Vibes? Really, that's how she explained it to a scientist? Shantel had to think she was an idiot. Yet getting that out of the way right from the start might not be a bad idea. If she still hung around after hearing how idiotic some of her thoughts were, well, who knew where it could go from there.

"Right back at you."

"What?" She hadn't expected that response. The carrot fell to the table.

Shantel threw out her hands and shrugged. "I got stuck on loup-garou."

She laughed. "The French version. Nice."

"The wolf-man has an interesting ring to it."

Johnnie stood up, picked up both glasses, and turned toward the sink. "Screw this iced tea. How do you feel about scotch?"

The first sip of the scotch Johnnie handed Shantel went down like velvet. Not the cheap or even mediocre versions. This was the kind that came in beautiful gilded boxes with hefty price tags. It hit all the right notes as she started talking about her day. "We got through several more sets of remains today."

"They were all the same, weren't they?" Johnnie sat back in a chair with her feet up on the ottoman.

Shantel nodded. Even without closing her eyes she could picture the distinct marks on the long bones. "Evidence of animal disturbance."

"Not unusual for bodies left out in the wilderness."

"Not at all. The thing that has everyone scratching their heads, however, is that animals don't bury the remains. No matter how we come at it, that is unexplainable."

"There's that."

"There's more to it than just the burial aspect."

Johnnie tipped her glass of scotch in her direction. "Do tell."

Shantel pursed her lips. "I shouldn't go into details."

"I'm part of this."

"True enough." Shantel didn't talk about the cases with anyone other than the ME, so to share with Johnnie would be way out of her normal procedure. She had to think about it for only a few seconds. The unique nature of it all made her throw out normal. Besides, Johnnie had a good point. She'd been involved right from the beginning, so it wasn't like she was blabbing to the general public or, God forbid, the press. Johnnie's work included confidentiality as much as hers did. This was a safe place, in more ways than one.

"We compared the marks on the bones to those made by standard canine teeth. They matched in some respects. Didn't in others."

"I'm not following. From what I saw, they were pretty consistent."

She understood Johnnie's frown. The same one had been on her own face most of the day. "The marks are absolutely consistent with canine, but they deviate in the size. We compared the marks to the largest canine teeth, and no match to any known samples."

"No shit."

"No shit."

"That's interesting and frightening at the same time." Johnnie took a slug of her scotch.

All day long Dr. Soule's hypothesis ran through her mind, and the more they studied the remains, the more it stuck with her. "I don't want to buy into the werewolf theory. Except, right now, it fits in a really warped way, while nothing else does."

Johnnie slapped the end table, and Shantel jumped. "I knew I'd seen a werewolf all those years ago. Sorry, that sounds callous, and I don't mean it that way. It's just that my twelve-year-old self wants to scream, 'told you so!'"

Shantel's phone buzzed and she glanced down. She swore as she pushed the ignore button.

"Everything okay?"

She blew out a breath. "My ex."

"You need to take it? I can give you privacy."

"Lord, no."

"You sure?"

"You have no idea how sure. He won't let it go. We've been divorced for a while now, and he just can't give up. Drives me insane. He's like a dog with a bone."

"Now that's bad." Johnnie couldn't stifle her laugh.

Shantel raised an eyebrow. "Maybe too soon."

Johnnie leaned in and touched her glass to Shantel's. "You are an interesting woman, Doc. Serious and dedicated, and then when you least expect it, humor. I like it. I like you."

"And I like you." Shantel hadn't said that in a long time. No need to, given she hadn't met anyone in forever that she felt this comfortable around. Most of the time, she kept up the walls she'd erected. Easier that way, and it wasn't like she was a kid longing for the throes of passion. Mature women could be content with friends and a fascinating career. It was enough.

Or not.

Sitting here with Johnnie, drinking her fabulous scotch and talking through theories, however wild they might be, brought up a longing for something more. A tickling in the back of her mind said friends and work alone weren't filling the void inside of her.

Johnnie's face lit up. "All right then. Now that we've established that no exes are allowed to intrude on our evening, let's do something wild."

Interesting. "I presume you have something in mind?"

"As a matter of fact, I do. Let's go on a woodland adventure and see if we can find any evidence of werewolves."

Perhaps the scotch was getting to Johnnie. They hadn't imbibed much at all, but alcohol did affect people differently. "Are you serious?"

Johnnie jumped up and held out her hand to Shantel, pulling her up. "As a heart attack."

❖

Riverside State Park off Government Way tended to be heavily used, yet he drove there anyway. An easy trip from Erin's, it also had great parking areas with plenty of space. He didn't care to have anyone park close enough to his car to risk door dings. His high standards of care extended to all aspects of his life, including his ride.

Once they walked a fair distance from the car, they could do whatever they wanted. The possibility always existed that they would encounter trail runners or cyclists, but at this time of night, that would be the exception. If they did run into said runners or cyclists, he'd behave himself, because now wasn't the time to make the authorities any more curious than they already were. He came to run, as a human. Period, as much as that pained him. Besides, he wasn't quite ready to take it all the way with Erin. Timing was everything.

Tonight would be all about the run and the sex—two out of three of his favorite things to do. It would be enough to keep him happy and sated. He had a particular route in mind that he'd been on many times. Convenient and beautiful. One of the things he appreciated about his hometown. Not many cities offered the convenience of a large metropolitan area with an abundance of nature accessible within a matter of minutes. Spokane did it right in that respect, and he'd been availing himself of the bounty since he'd returned, beautiful wife in tow. Actually, he'd availed himself of the convenience since he'd returned from his fateful trip after college.

Now, he'd take Erin on a run. It would get her ready for the full transformation coming up. She'd mentioned how much her running had improved since they'd begun working out together. After a week she'd been able to drop her per-mile time by two minutes. All he ever did was smile and nod. As of yet, no need to fully explain why. Let her think it occurred only because of the time they spent training. Soon enough, she'd be in the loop, and at least for a brief time, they'd be able to share the magic.

She also didn't need to know that it wouldn't last forever. At least not for her. Though he toyed with the idea of keeping her after his reconciliation with Shantel, in his heart of hearts he knew it wouldn't happen. When his use for her ended, so too would her time on this earth. Just the way things went.

In Asia, the secrets of their kind were shared with him. Another advantage to having come into his powers with the pack to support him. All that they'd known, they freely told him. All those he'd met to date embraced the share-and-share-alike mentality.

Nice for him, though he didn't necessarily subscribe to the same philosophy. Good old dad taught him an important lesson: always look out for number one. Growing up with a cold, narcissist father, coupled with a closet-alcoholic mother, meant that little Danny had a boatload of his own issues. No need for a psychologist. He totally got that he was fucked up. Not really a problem, in his opinion. He liked fucked up. It worked for him.

He let go of the little detour down memory lane and concentrated on the here and now. "Come on." The car parked near the historical military cemetery on the bluff overlooking the Spokane River, he held out his hand to Erin. The relatively small area with the old carved headstones remained green and well-tended, even a hundred plus years after it had been established. "A couple of hills here that may give your legs some burn, but I'm betting you can tackle those bitches like a rock star."

Erin laughed and took his hand. "A week ago, I'd have said you were nuts."

"Never, baby, never." He leaned in and kissed her.

"Come on, loser," she said as she kicked and started to run. For a few moments he did nothing except watch her. Those long, lovely legs. The black hair tied back and swinging in the breeze. Her breasts, tight and high in the snug shirt. A vision.

He ran and caught up to her in mere seconds. Though her long stride and sure footing had her covering ground like a pro, he needed to pull back to stay beside her. Running next to a beautiful woman always felt good. "Let's take the hill," he said.

"Yeah! I'll race you." She took off, and her speed made him smile. He followed, enjoying the sight of her toned legs and firm behind. Her enthusiasm, her physical prowess sent a clear message. The wolf grew strong inside her.

CHAPTER SEVENTEEN

Johnnie changed into tights and tied her favorite pair of running shoes. At the front door Cougar sat blocking it, and his intent quite clear: you're not going without me. Not a chance. Not that it was ever a question. She never ran alone, and even if Shantel went along, a big German shepherd made a world of difference in the safety department. "In a minute, buddy."

Cougar didn't abandon his post by the front door. "He's not taking any chances, is he?" Shantel had also changed into the running attire Johnnie found for her. Because they were nowhere near the same size, a pair of Johnnie's knee-length tights and a dry-fit shirt were as close as she could get to something that might fit the smaller woman. At least Shantel had her own shoes, the most important piece of running equipment besides good legs.

"He's a smart guy," Johnnie said.

"After watching him out in the field, I'd take him anywhere."

She smiled and rubbed his head. "I'm pretty proud of my buddy. He's been a joy to work with and a great housemate. A special guy."

"I have fish."

Johnnie stopped and stared. "Fish?" Who had fish? Sounded kind of snobby, but they weren't real pets. They were a hobby.

Shantel laughed. "Here's the thing. Fish are easy to care for, and with my job, easy is key. They're fascinating to watch and quite beautiful. It's the closest I can get to a pet and not do it a disservice."

Now she smiled and nodded. "I see what you're saying."

Shantel laughed even more. "I never heard that phrase until I came here. First time someone said that to me I thought it was crazy. Then I heard it again. And again. Finally made the connection to local vernacular. I stopped taking it literally."

"I guess it sounds kind of dumb, but around here, it's just what we say. Kind of like 'you guys.' Doesn't matter if you're male or female, if there's more than two of you, it's you guys."

"Yes. figured that one out after a couple months here too. My Texas roots come with the all-purpose ya'll."

"I haven't heard you say that."

"No." She smiled. "I weaned myself off that one once I went to college. Come on. Let's go run down a werewolf."

Johnnie put her hands on her hips. "Gotta say, it sounds a little like you're humoring me."

"Of course, I'm humoring you. I'm also giving free rein to my own curiosity and imagination."

All righty. "I can live with that. I plan to drive in toward Spokane Falls Community College. Some of the parking areas at the trailheads might be closed, as it's getting near sunset, and I know one that doesn't close. It'll get us into some of nicest parts of the park. We can run and search and, in general, enjoy nature."

"You think we'll find something?"

A wild-goose chase went through her head. Instead, she said, "Probably not."

"We're going to take a run anyway." Shantel didn't sound convinced her plan had merit.

She had a counterargument at the ready. "We're not accomplishing much sitting around here tonight, so what can it hurt?"

Shantel finished tying her shoe and stood straight. "Not a thing, and after being cooped up in the lab all day, running through the trails will feel wonderful."

"A good run to burn off the scotch, and then we can come back here for the stew I've had in the slow cooker all day."

"Deal. Let's roll."

It didn't take long to drive to the trailhead she had in mind, though the parking area she expected to be empty wasn't. Darn. She'd been hoping they'd have the place to themselves. A bit optimistic, considering the size of Riverside State Park and its popularity throughout the area. They wouldn't be the only ones who got out for an early evening run. What did surprise her was Shantel's exclamation.

"What the hell?"

If his car hadn't been there before they pulled in, Shantel would have sworn Daniel was following her. Enough of his shit already. Exactly why she'd ignored his call earlier. Now this? God almighty, would she ever be free of him? Like a bad penny, he just kept turning up! She wanted to grind that penny right into the dirt.

"What is it?" Alarm sounded in Johnnie's voice. She'd probably scared her when she went rabid bitch on her for no apparent reason.

She pointed to the only other vehicle in the gravel lot. "That's my ex-husband's car."

Her shoulders relaxed, a good sign she hadn't scared her off completely. "No way."

"Way."

Johnnie shifted in her seat. "How could he know where you'd be? You didn't know where you'd be."

She'd been wondering the same thing since they pulled in. Unless he'd been sneaking around, which wasn't out of the realm of possibility, he'd have no way to know they planned to come here. Still not all that plausible, given he'd have to use sophisticated listening equipment to be able to do that, and even he wouldn't go that far. Would he? Her answer to the unspoken question scared her. Yes. Yes, he absolutely would.

She shook her head. "He couldn't." Denial easier to accept than the belief he'd gone to extremes to stalk her.

"This is some kind of crazy. Look, we can go somewhere else."

She almost told Johnnie to do just that. Back out of the parking lot and drive all way across town. The last thing she wanted would be to pass Daniel on the trail. With Johnnie the muscle pain of the run was certain to disappear in a haze of companionship, and the sight of him would pour cold water all over her good mood. Just his face these days sent her into a funk. She wanted it...correction, him...to go away. If they'd had kids, or even a dog or cat, perhaps his inability to separate himself from her might be understandable. That wasn't the case with them. She didn't even get her fish until she was on her own. Nothing tied them to each other, and damn it, she wanted peace.

Not for the first time, she wondered if she might need to leave Spokane in order to get the space she desperately wanted. Needed more than wanted. To be forced to leave would be far from fair, considering she'd come here because of the professional opportunity it offered. To give up what she'd worked hard to achieve just because Daniel turned out to be a horse's ass wasn't right. Or perhaps he'd always been an ass and just now showed his hand. Either way, not fair.

She made her decision. "No. We're going to march right on with our plan. We're not changing anything because of that bastard. Screw him."

"Are you sure? Not a big deal to go to another open trailhead. I mean, really, despite my enthusiasm for the hunt, I'm pretty sure we're not going to actually find a werewolf."

"Are you certain about that? I mean, aren't you the one who said to keep an open mind?"

"Yeah…"

"Then let's do it. I'm ready to run, and then I'll be super ready for your stew. Screw my ex-husband. If we bump into him, we'll kiss and send him into cardiac failure."

A light flickered in Johnnie's eyes. Pretty sure the kiss comment put it there. "If you're certain?"

"I am."

She sounded confident, but she wasn't. If they bumped into Daniel out there, she didn't have a clue how she'd handle it. To date, she'd employed the "ignore him and he'll go away" tactic. That one wouldn't be very successful in a face-to-face meeting. Maybe she needed to suck it up and be a big girl. No reason she couldn't remain calm and collected. She'd introduce her friend and call it good. As much as the kiss in front of him scenario appealed to her, it would be fuel on a fire already raging. Better to make it short and sweet. They'd go their way. He'd go his.

Sounded great in theory, and on her side, she could make it work just like that, if she stuck to her guns. It wouldn't go that smoothly for

Daniel. He'd make a scene and say something assholey to embarrass her in front of Johnnie. Maybe she needed to rethink this going-forward idea. Or, the kiss.

Johnnie got out of the car before she could change her mind and tell her as much. She followed, and the fresh, cool air gave her the jolt she needed. The sun was dropping in the west, and the sky had turned gorgeous shades of gold and red. The beauty alone made her feet move. A few minutes in and thoughts of Daniel were pushed to the back of her mind. Instead, she focused on the long legs and easy stride of Johnnie, Cougar running easily beside her, a bright-orange long-line clipped to his harness.

They left the asphalt trail shortly after they started. The varied landscape made it an interesting spot to explore. As they traversed the ridge, the river running clear and strong below, the energy of it filled her with joy. Another reason why she hesitated to move away from the area even as Daniel became more and more of a pain in the ass. She didn't want to give this all up. And now she followed a fascinating woman and her beautiful dog. One more motivation to stay. A big one.

She also loved the university. Her growing reputation meant she could secure a position at bigger and more prestigious schools. Not a driving force for her as it was for the majority of her higher education counterparts. Here, she loved the smaller class sizes and the freedom the university gave her to pursue her work outside teaching. That it made the university look good too didn't escape her, and that was okay. It became a winning situation for both her and the school.

She wouldn't allow Daniel's obsession to drive her out of building a life that made her happy. Her job, this area, and the woman she ran with all enriched her world. Too many wasted years to give up what she'd found here.

The mysterious murders definitely did not make her happy. Their puzzling nature bothered her on a variety of levels. Talking with Dr. Soule bothered her. Johnnie's werewolf questions, on the other hand, should bother her and didn't. More like intrigued her. As she spent more time with Johnnie, she fascinated Shantel more and more. Anybody else might admit their search for a werewolf and come off as out of touch with reality. Somehow, coming from Johnnie, it not only didn't seem weird, but it also came off as probable. In what world would hunting for a werewolf be rational?

Yet here they were. For anyone who might glimpse them, two women out for a run. Only they knew that, as they ran, they scanned the woods for the unlikely. Her ten-year-old self would have loved such an adventure, and her much-older self wasn't having much trouble with it either. The freest she'd felt in decades.

They'd just crested a trail that overlooked an area called the Bowl and Pitcher, when a howl, deep and rich, came to them on the breeze. She stopped and stared in the direction of the sound.

"Did you hear that?"

Johnnie stopped and clapped her hands. "Ha! Who's crazy now? Definitely a wolf."

"A wolf wouldn't be totally unusual here." Several packs had been spotted in outlying areas, although she wasn't aware of any making their homes this close to the city.

"True enough, I'll give you that. How many wolves have a howl that echoes in the whole damn park? I'm telling you, Shantel, we're on to something. Your prof was too."

"Kind of a stretch." She wasn't quite ready to buy in all the way yet and could rationalize it as the normal course of the creatures of the wilderness.

"Not when you really think about it. What else could make the marks on those bones AND bury the bodies?"

For a few seconds, she paused. She could concoct all sorts of argument to the contrary, except she didn't want to. After everything she'd witnessed in the world, the evil that sent thousands to hidden graves, nothing came off the table. Slowly she brought her gaze up to meet Johnnie's eyes. "A werewolf."

Johnnie nodded, her hands on her hips. "Yeah. A werewolf."

Easing Erin in had been a really good idea. When Daniel stopped and let out the howl that had been building inside, she didn't even flinch. It would have scared someone lesser or, rather, more human.

Not his lovely partner. So far, so good. When the full moon hit in a few days, she'd be primed and ready.

The very intentional route he took them on gave him a bird's-eye view of his plan in action. He'd set it all in motion, and things were going as he hoped. Number one had been put into place, which made him almost giddy. Undoubtedly, his client also felt a great amount of joy. Between them, the seeds of doubt were planted, and by the time the week ended, the authorities around here would be in a world of hurt. They wouldn't be able to figure out the details behind the so-called crimes. Perfection, and as architect, he deserved full credit.

Back at the parking area, it wasn't shocking to find another car there. The trailheads were popular places. He preferred the dirt trails to asphalt, and plenty enough of those were around to make bumping into others the exception rather than the rule.

While the car didn't surprise him, the familiar scent did. Now, how did his lovely little Shantel know he'd be here? He walked around the other vehicle slowly, inhaling. The air held all her secrets. She'd arrived as the passenger, which made sense given this wasn't her car. He'd know if she'd purchased a vehicle, and she hadn't. A new little friend? His recent flush of excitement faded as fast as a flash burn. Shantel out here with a date? His hands curled into fists. If her claims were to be believed, she'd be here with a woman.

"Are you okay?"

He turned and faced Erin. "I'm fine," he said with a clenched jaw.

Her expression conveyed that she didn't believe him. "Really?"

Shake it off. He smiled even as his jaw ached from the effort. "Really."

She inclined her head toward the other vehicle. "You know that car?"

He didn't have to lie. "No."

"Okay..."

Give it up, he wanted to scream. "Interested only because it's unusual to see a car here this late."

"We're here." Stating the obvious didn't accomplish anything except to irritate him further.

He smiled, forcing into it the warmth that historically melted even the most resistant. "We are."

She smiled back. His charisma worked its magic. Oh, the effect on women. Worth its weight in gold. "I'm hungry." Her smile grew.

He laughed and didn't have to fake it. "Far be it from me to keep a woman from her food after a good workout."

"Thirsty too."

"How do you feel about merlot?"

"Deep, dark, and red. Perfect."

He walked away from the car that reeked of Shantel and got behind the wheel of his own. He liked the way Erin thought. A little food, a little wine, and a good screw would go a long way toward settling both his mind and his body. Once he achieved a more Zen-like state, he'd think about who Shantel's buddy might be. Maybe she'd find the little treasure he'd arranged for her out here. Wouldn't that be rich? Now, wouldn't that throw a whole pool full of cold water on a date?

That possibility buoyed his spirit. Fun could be found in the most surprising places. "Let's roll."

Erin reached over and put her hand on his crotch and echoed his words. "Let's roll."

Blood rushed to his groin, and his dick grew hard. He pushed the accelerator and didn't worry about the possibility of getting a ticket. He could fix it.

CHAPTER EIGHTEEN

Even in the darkness, Johnnie couldn't miss the strain on Shantel's face as they ran back to the car. The vehicle parked there when they arrived started to pull out onto Government Way, and the falter in Shantel's stride coincided with that sight.

"What is it?"

"It's him."

"Your ex?"

"Daniel's driving, I'd recognize him anywhere."

"And his car?"

"Absolutely. High-end luxury, all day, every day. The man has serious car issues. Drove me crazy when we were married. Why do you need a new car all the time, and the more expensive, the better? I've been driving the same one for six years."

"I'm with you there. I find what I like and drive the wheels off it. It's still bizarre that he came to the same place we did."

"Always a pain in the ass."

The expression on Shantel's face pulled at her. "What did he do to you?" The words were out of her mouth before her brain kicked in. Damn it, she hated when she did that.

Shantel leaned over and put her hands on her knees. "Obsessive, stalker, in denial. That about covers it."

"I'm sorry." Johnnie couldn't imagine what that might be like.

"Like I mentioned before, he didn't take it well when I left him. My coming out became a personal thing to him when it had absolutely nothing to do with him. Couldn't then, and still can't, convince him of that fact."

"That's got to be a pain in the ass."

"You have no idea. Finally understanding who I was and taking control of my life freed me in some respects."

"I get that."

Shantel stood up. "You do, don't you?"

Johnnie nodded. "I think I always knew about myself, but when everybody has expectations for you, darned if you don't try to live up to them even if it's not what's in your heart."

"Exactly."

"I figured it out in my late teens, and by the time I got to college, I knew who and what I was. No boyfriends or husbands to deal with. No muddy waters."

"Lucky you."

"Which is not to say I haven't experienced my own share of bad breakups. Nobody gets out alive, so to speak."

"Did any of them ever refuse to let you go?"

"Fortunately, no. Come on. Let's don't let him intrude on our night. We had a great run on a beautiful night. Now, we should go eat some dinner and talk about our failure to track down a werewolf." Johnnie wanted to cheer her up. For some reason she couldn't put into words, it mattered.

Shantel smiled, and the light came back into her eyes. "Not a bad idea."

Shantel thought about Daniel the entire way back to Johnnie's. A woman sitting in the passenger seat of his car made her wonder what game he was playing. Just like him to stalk her at the same time he screwed someone else. With only the back of the woman's head visible, no way to determine her identity. Truthfully, she didn't care who Daniel hung out with.

But why come here? He lived on the opposite side of the city, with plenty of nearby places more convenient. In fact, the trails off High Drive were magnificent. He could satisfy his preference to be in the woods there without having to drive all the way across the city. Like Daniel, running had become part of her life, and she would do it in town if she had to. She did prefer the quiet beauty of nature, though. It toned the body and nourished the soul.

Tonight's outing, with Johnnie, had been one of her best. It didn't matter that they set out to search for the impossible and came up short. It didn't matter that once more Daniel intruded. She wouldn't have traded the last hour for anything. The best time in ages, as strange as that sounded under the very odd circumstances.

Back at Johnnie's house, Cougar raced in for a drink and then dropped into a plush bed situated in front of the big living-room windows. Flopped over on his side, his legs stretched out stiff and straight, he didn't look particularly comfortable, yet his light snores sounded content. She smiled. Her fish didn't snore. Kind of made her wish they did.

"Here." Johnnie handed her a frosty mug, which she put to her nose.

Deep and dark, it smelled wonderful. "Local?"

Johnnie nodded. "A buddy of mine owns the brewery. Good stuff, and just the right drink post-run."

"Or to commiserate about a failed mission."

Johnnie took a sip and shook her head. "I prefer post-run refreshment."

"For someone who specializes in recovery, you have a surprisingly optimistic view on things."

Johnnie turned serious. "I honestly don't look at what we do as a negative. True, when they call us out, we assume that the person we're searching for has passed on. But we bring them home, and that's incredibly important."

"I get it. I went into my field for many of the same reasons. I knew I'd be working with all that remains of what was once a living, breathing person. That I would face things no one should have to hold as memories, and yet..." She closed her eyes.

"And yet, you too wanted to help bring them home to their families, to not let them disappear as if they didn't matter." Johnnie spoke softly and gently. She understood.

She nodded as her eyes opened and her gaze connected with Johnnie's. "Exactly, and that's why what we're doing now is important beyond explanation. We have to help find who, or what, is responsible for killing those people and hiding their bodies."

"I wouldn't give the monster the courtesy of calling them a who. This is a monster, and that falls under a what. Pretty black-and-white in my book."

Again, she nodded. "What as in monster, creature, devil. As Hamlet says, 'There are more things in heaven and earth, Horatio, than are dreamt of in your philosophy.'"

Johnnie slapped a hand to her chest. "Be still, my heart. You're quoting Shakespeare? My word, can you get any better?"

Shantel laughed. "You're good for my ego, and just for clarity, I did have to study a thing or two outside my major."

"Like Shakespeare."

Shantel put a hand to her chest. "You don't want to get me started on the great poets."

"Good God. I think I'm in love."

A shot of energy surged through her. She knew Johnnie joked, but her words filled her with warmth just the same. "Good to know all my studies weren't for naught."

"Definitely not. I also think a good liberal-arts background is essential when it comes time to think about everything and from different angles. I appreciate science in all its forms, but it can sometimes limit the path of enlightened thought. And this, my new friend, is not a time to limit anything."

Shantel didn't take offense. While she might be a scientist, it didn't mean she failed to appreciate what liberal arts brought to the table. Great thinkers, philosophers, and writers were important. Through the ages they forced people to think and to question. "Yes and no." They couldn't ignore the two sides here even if they wanted to. "We can't investigate these murders. Not really, anyway."

Johnnie tapped her mug. "Nope. Not our jobs. You and I are on the same page there."

Not the end of the story though. She was developing a pretty good sense for the way Johnnie thought. "We're going to anyway, aren't we?"

Johnnie stopped tapping and laughed. "Let's just say we're going to look at possibilities without getting in the way of the work our buddies in the sheriff's office need to do. Rick doesn't *have* to be brought in the loop on everything, if you follow me."

Shantel smiled back at Johnnie. She understood exactly what she meant. "Works for me." She held up her mug and touched it to Johnnie's. "Now, let's eat."

❖

After Daniel dropped Erin at her house, he went home and showered. Cleaned up, shaved, and with fresh clothes, he paced the house, his steps muffled by the thick rugs his housekeeper kept spotless. Sleep wasn't big on his list of things to do. Never was. He could function quite well on an hour or two here or there. He supposed the pull of the night and the power of the moon, regardless of the phase, played a big part in his insomnia. Even as a kid, he hadn't been a sleeper, much to his parents' horror. They preferred to do their own thing and never wanted to be bothered with a child who refused to lie down and stay out of their way. His avoidance of sleep made it all the more natural to become what he had. Another place where destiny came into play.

Tonight, he obsessed about that car in the parking lot at the trailhead and the strong scent of Shantel wafting from the passenger door. Impossible she'd be aware of his presence there despite his history of embracing exercise where lots of space, thick trees, and plenty of wildlife made it extra appealing. Tonight, of course, it held a special appeal for him that he hadn't wanted to forego. Everyone had weakness.

All of that aside, it still didn't track that she'd follow him. Her MO since the divorce had been to put as much space between them as possible. He, not Shantel, tried to minimize that space. If either of them was inclined to follow the other, it would be him. He'd undertaken that task on many occasions, not that she'd ever caught on to his stealthy observance.

His profession gave him access to individuals with particular skill sets not available to the regular Joe, one of those skills being surveillance. His favorite practitioner from the roster at his office provided him with a crash course on stealth when following and observing. The ex-undercover cop possessed some serious skills and didn't even ask why Daniel wanted to be schooled. A bit of flattery and a promise of defense if the occasion arose were all it had taken to secure the lesson.

His Shantel wasn't usually deceptive, except perhaps the little part about believing herself to be a lesbian. The deception theory still didn't resonate with him. She'd obviously lost her way, and that line of thinking worked much better for him. It also made more sense.

At his desk, he resisted the urge to take out his special box again. The need to share it with her neared the point of overwhelming. Still, he didn't pick it up from where it rested in the drawer. In the back of his mind the countdown ticked away, and soon enough he could present her with it as a token of his undying love.

Until this point, he'd been patient in allowing Shantel to come to her senses. He rationalized her adventures in the world of women would wear thin, and given a little time, she'd come home contrite and ready to resume their life together. Never harbored a doubt on that point. Thanks to the discovery of the bodies out at Fish Lake, things changed, and his patience came to an abrupt end. No more waiting. He'd push the issue because he had to.

Erin as a distraction worked beautifully to keep him grounded, and as a bonus, she kept him apprised of Shantel's movements. Tracking her that way was a whole lot easier than following her around. The opportunity to indulge in things like pleasure came as a decided perk. His hedonistic cravings rivaled those of any drug addict or alcoholic. That no one ever knew of his kinkier side made it all the more fun. That secret thing again. In his law practice he'd learned the best way to do what he wanted and not get caught: tell no one.

He closed the drawer containing his special box and headed to the basement. Not quite the time for the heartfelt gift. Instead, fixating on what he wished to do and couldn't, he went to the custom wine cellar and pulled out a bottle from a special rack. On their honeymoon to Tuscany, Shantel had fallen in love with many of the wines they enjoyed during their travels. Her favorite had been a Baraacca & Fassoldi chianti. The rapture on her face as she sipped it on the patio of the villa they rented for a month still lingered in his memory. He'd recently ordered a case of the chianti direct from the winery. Now this was the kind of message that would resonate with her without playing his hand. He took it with him to the car.

At her house where the windows were all dark—again—he employed another little trick taught to him by his buddy. Lock pick. He smiled at the telltale click. Nothing he couldn't master.

He slipped the small tools into his back pocket and picked up the bottle of wine he didn't care to leave sitting outside. Something this lovely shouldn't be left to the elements or, worse, porch thieves. It deserved to stay safe and sound on her kitchen counter. Given her love of the vintage, she would appreciate the caring gesture.

A few feet into the kitchen, he stopped and tilted his head. Nothing. Another deviation from her normal routine. Too late to still be out in the park running with her mystery partner. Where was she? His hunch didn't sit well with him. For her to get further wrapped up in the delusion she might be in love with a woman could turn out to complicate his plan. He had to keep her eyes on the truth, which was her life with him. Divorce didn't change that reality. Misguided notions about her sexuality didn't either.

He blew out a long breath and moved to the island. The kitchen hadn't changed since the last time he let himself in. Her police buddies had to have cautioned her about not having an alarm system in the house. Its absence testified that she didn't listen to them anymore than she listened to him. Made it easy for him to come and go as he pleased. It would shock her to find out how many times he'd been here. He'd memorized the location of every glass, cup, and plate in the dark-blue cabinets he hated and sighed at the sparse contents of her refrigerator. No wonder she'd lost at least fifteen pounds since they began living apart. Soon enough he would put meat and muscle back on her bones. She'd need it for the adventures they'd share.

Out of the cabinet next to the refrigerator, he took down two stemmed wineglasses. It surprised him when he'd discovered them on one of his previous reconnaissance missions. She'd made it clear she wanted a new start, so why hold onto the crystal glasses they'd purchased during that memorable trip to Tuscany? He thought he understood. In the back of her mind, she acknowledged they'd ultimately end up back together. On that day, these glasses would go back into the glass-fronted, cherrywood cabinets of their real home, right where they belonged.

On the island, he positioned the wine and the two glasses just so. Intimate and romantic, except it didn't quite hit the mark. He stood back and studied the presentation for a few moments. Pendulum lights hung over the island, and he moved to the far wall to flip the switch to turn them on. Still not right. They lit up the whole kitchen instead of creating a special ambiance. For a few seconds he studied the setup again, and then it hit him. Easy enough fix. He reached up and loosened the bulbs in all except the light directly over his gift. Now that was what he'd been going for. Perfect. A makeshift spotlight was exactly the kind of presentation she would be sure to appreciate.

Whistling, he left through the same door he came in.

CHAPTER NINETEEN

Johnnie couldn't sleep after Shantel left. It got late while they sat and talked about all the *whys*, the *what ifs*, and the *hows*. The werewolf theory couldn't be more out there, and yet Shantel, the consummate scientist, went at it like the intelligent professional she had shown herself to be. Every minute they spent together, Johnnie liked and admired her more. A nice feeling, really. It had been a long time since she'd met someone she connected to like this.

Cougar appeared to echo her feelings. Earlier, he'd jumped up on the sofa next to Shantel and curled up before promptly going to sleep. Socialization wasn't an issue with Cougar. He loved people and most other dogs. Even given his affinity for people, the level of relaxation and closeness he demonstrated with Shantel wasn't typically his style. Cougar really liked her. For Johnnie, this was an extra level of confirmation in her read of Dr. Kind. She trusted her dog when it came to people. He knew the good, the really good, and the bad. Obviously, Shantel was one of the really good.

Not a great idea to stand here and stare out the front window the rest of the night. With multiple searches taking up her time of late, her work needed more intense focus. The deadline for her latest book loomed large, and while time remained to get it all done, without some sleep, she'd put out crap. There was no other way to put it. If she turned in less than stellar work, it would come winging right back from her editor.

A warm shower helped with relaxation. In sweats and a T-shirt, sleep didn't appear to be so far away now. Her shoulders relaxed and her thoughts slowed. Cougar, already stretched out on the bed, snoozed with his head on a pillow. No matter how many times she told him no on that front, he refused to comply. One of these days she would have to give up even trying to change that habit.

Johnnie sat down on the edge of the bed as her cell phone rang. It both surprised and pleased her when Shantel's name popped up on the display. "Hey. What's up? You miss me already?"

"I shouldn't be calling you."

The seriousness in Shantel's voice concerned her. "Nonsense. You can call me anytime. What's wrong?"

"I shouldn't bother you with this."

"Just spit it out. No judgment here." Something had Shantel rattled. She sat up straighter, ready to jump into action.

"My ex-husband broke into my house while I was with you."

Now she did jump up at the same time she reached for her jeans. "What did he do?"

Her laugh held a brittle edge. "He left a bottle of my favorite wine on the counter and made sure it had a romantic spotlight on it."

She stopped moving and frowned. What a weird thing to do even for a weird guy. "That's fucked up."

"I'm so tired."

The sadness in her words pulled at Johnnie. She wished they were together and that she could take her hands. "Tell me."

"He won't let me go." The hitch in her voice hurt.

First things, first. "Do you feel safe at your house?"

"No."

Afraid that would be her answer, Johnnie readied a response. With her phone on speaker, she began to slide into her jeans. "Is your security system armed?"

"I don't have one."

What? Someone as bright and competent as Shantel who happened to have a nutso ex-husband had no alarm in her home? Not great. "Is he dangerous?"

The pause was significant. "I don't know. I don't think so."

She stopped dressing and changed course. "Not good enough. Come back here. Right now."

"I'll be all right."

"Of course, you will. You're smart and strong, and you have Rick's phone number in your cell. None of that shit matters. You come back here because he'll have no idea where you are. He can't get to you if he can't find you. And, until you have the locks changed and a security system up and running, you'll stay with me. Now, pack a bag and get back here."

"I…"

"No arguments. Don't make me send Cougar over to get you."

That last comment rewarded her with a small laugh, and the sound was music. "Thank you."

"Shut up and leave that place. You have five minutes to get your ass in your car."

Shantel acted on pure instinct when she'd punched in Johnnie's number. If she'd stopped to think about it, she might have called Erin first. Her graduate assistant had become a friend of sorts. Not close. More like coworkers who share a drink now and again. Close enough, however, that she would have felt comfortable calling her with this.

Yet, she didn't. Instead, she called Johnnie, someone she'd met mere days ago. Not her style at all. While she put together a bag with clothes enough for a couple of days in the allotted five minutes, it occurred to her that perhaps it might be time to change a few things. She'd been in denial about her security and her old style until tonight. More like she'd kept her head in the sand, thinking if she ignored him, Daniel would magically go away. Hard to deny the truth on her counter.

She'd told Johnnie that she'd pack a bag and come stay the night. Now, she stared at said bag and hesitated. If she did this, it would be a huge imposition. It wasn't like they were best friends with a long history together. What kind of person would do that to someone they only just met? Her mother would be unimpressed, except she didn't have to worry about what her mother would say. That rejection still stung and wasn't something she cared to let rise to the level of consciousness.

Letting that particular sore subject flutter at the edge of her thoughts spurred her into action. Her family, for the most part, wanted nothing to do with her, and thus, relying on a new kinder, gentler friend couldn't be all that bad. She appreciated the fact Johnnie accepted her for the genuine Shantel rather than the mold her family insisted she stay inside.

Her hesitation faded. She grabbed the bag and took it to the back door, where she dropped it. Before she could leave, she needed to feed her friends. The fish might not be dogs, but she'd miss them. She sprinkled the flakes over the top of the tank and watched for a few seconds as they swam to the surface and snatched them away.

One more thing to do even if it exceeded the five minutes mandated by Johnnie. In case Daniel decided to return before she could secure the house, she'd leave him a message he'd be certain to grasp. She picked up the bottle of wine and threw it into the sink. The glass shattered, and deep-red wine flowed out around the shards of glass before it flowed down the drain, leaving stains that resembled blood.

Less than half an hour later, she stood, bag in hand, on Johnnie's deck. She glanced down at her watch and grimaced. Midnight. Could she impose on Johnnie anymore? It would be way more polite to turn around and leave, although since Johnnie had opened the driveway gate when she'd pulled in, that might come off as rude.

"Come on." Johnnie stood in the doorway and held the door open for her. "It's cold out tonight, so get your ass in here."

All thoughts of making a hasty retreat flew out of her head. Johnnie rocked in sweats and a T-shirt, her dark hair curling around her face. Her breath caught. Once more she wondered how in the world she'd ever thought she could make a marriage to a man work. Every nerve in her body came alive. She refocused before she did something she might regret. "I feel like a bit of jerk imposing on you like this."

"I repeat, get your ass in here."

So, she did.

When her phone alarm went off at seven, Shantel jumped and experienced a moment of panic. After a couple of blinks that brought Johnnie's comfortable guest room into focus, it passed. She'd slept surprisingly well for being in a strange room and bed. That she could relax that much in Johnnie's house told her everything important. While Shantel might be a woman of science, she still valued her instinct immensely. Johnnie was the real deal, someone she could trust.

She could use that right now. Daniel's last stunt shook her up, and she suspected he'd breached her house before. Nothing concrete. More a sense of violation that whirled around her like a cloud. Last night, he'd apparently decided to discard his previous stealth and go for clear and loud. Just thinking about walking into that scene made her hands tremble. He'd taken asshole to new heights.

Sitting up with her legs over the side of the bed and her feet on the floor, she clasped her hands and took even, long breaths. Her hands stopped shaking. She slipped from the bed to the floor, crossed her legs, and folded her hands in her lap. Quietly, she meditated, letting the words work their magic.

Five minutes later, she raised her head and smiled. Much better. She stood and stretched her arms. Coffee. The sweet, sweet scent carried all the way to the guest room. Bless that woman. Since she slept in leggings and an oversized shirt, she didn't bother to put on real clothes. Instead, barefoot, she headed straight for the kitchen.

The happy greeting on the tip of her tongue died as she took in Johnnie's expression. "What's wrong?"

Johnnie held up her cell phone. "Rick just called. They found another body."

"Where?"

"Right off one of the trails we were running last night."

Daniel believed Shantel would call after she found his thoughtful gift. He woke up still pissed about how she'd blown him off. After the effort he expended to get the expensive wine for her, a call would have been the polite thing to do. Though why should he expect her to behave any different than she had over the last couple of years? Perpetually optimistic, he supposed. Another of his finest qualities. He preferred to seek the positive in every situation, particularly when it concerned him.

The old man's negative view on just about everything always grated on him. He tended toward a polar-opposite view because of it. Also, one of the reasons he preferred to practice criminal-defense law. He could take even the tiniest positive spin and blow it up until a jury saw only daylight and not darkness, even if his client's soul was ebony.

Prosecutors hated him, and he fed on their emotion. Pushed him to be even better despite an already established reputation as the best.

As if to punctuate that fact, his special cell rang. Good news, he hoped. "Yes."

"It's a bingo."

"They found her?"

"Dude, you doubt me?"

"Not for a second. Why do you think I called you for this?"

"I appreciate the confidence. I'd appreciate cash a bit more."

He'd expected this particular request. He'd been around good old Thane enough to understand how his mind worked. "How much?"

"Fifty grand should do it. I have expenses, man."

The little pisser would be back in the blink of an eye because that's about how long it would take him to blow through fifty k. He knew this guy inside and out. Part of his skill when defending the dregs, he could see into their souls. But he'd play along. "Not a problem. I can swing the cash."

"Tonight."

"That might be more difficult." He didn't want to make it sound too easy. The game called for a touch of finesse.

"Don't fuck with me, Counselor. You have a lot of scratch, and you can get your hands on it. Tonight, or I send pictures to the cops." He'd be well aware that Daniel kept that kind of money at the ready because he'd charged him twice that amount to get him off a manslaughter charge. It should have been a first-degree murder charge. There'd been no heat of the moment about the murder committed by this guy. Another example of Daniel's brilliance. He not only got the charge down to manslaughter, but he'd then gone on to get him acquitted.

The jerk remained an idiot despite all his careful grooming before and during the trial. He honestly believed Daniel didn't calculate all angles and arrive prepared for every scenario. He would most definitely fuck with him. "Meet me at the Seven Mile trailhead at nine."

"I don't know where that is."

It took effort not to snap. "Figure it out."

CHAPTER TWENTY

Johnnie didn't need to go with Shantel and, technically, hadn't been invited. The services she and Cougar provided weren't required. No need for a search team, only the expertise of recovery experts. It didn't matter. She went along for moral support anyway. What she'd seen on Shantel's face when she relayed the conversation with Rick stayed with her.

To come along represented more than just friendship. This situation made her head-to-toe twitchy. First, all the remains Cougar located for them were south of town. The location made a twisted sort of logic because of its proximity to EWU. Cheney, a college town, wouldn't be the first one to suffer through a serial killer who preyed on the young and unwise. She couldn't point fingers at the young people who put themselves into the path of danger either. Lord knows she'd been crazy enough during her college days. Those initial blips of freedom and the invincibility of youth too often combined to become lethal. At the time, pretty damn fun too. Thank goodness, she'd lived through those years without encountering trouble.

She also wanted to come along because it didn't feel right. Too coincidental, and she wasn't a big believer in coincidences. Maybe she'd been around too many cops, and it had rubbed off on her. In this instance, kind of a too-good-to-be-true type of scenario. They uncover a killer's burial grounds, and then lo and behold, a body is found on the other side of the county? Add the fact that the burial wasn't as clandestine as those Cougar found, and her bullshit meter started a deafening clang. Frankly, the whole thing smelled rotten.

Good intentions aside, the work she'd been planning to do today would have to wait. This took precedence. Shantel took precedence. She'd find a way to meet her deadline and provide moral support for Shantel.

They pulled in behind Rick's marked truck and parked. He didn't drive a cruiser because of the gear he carried. Like the search-and-rescue volunteers he supervised, he kept within easy reach all the items he'd need for any kind of search, whether urban, forest, mountain, or water.

He waved as Shantel parked, though his eyes narrowed when she got out. "Hey, Johnnie. Surprised to see you here. We don't need Cougar today."

"Cougar's at home. If he saw you, he'd go nuts, and if he didn't get to work, well, you know how bad that would be." Cougar knew the clothes, the boots, the gear, and, most definitely, the people. If he'd been in the back of her truck, or in this case, the backseat, and didn't eventually get the chance to participate, he wouldn't have been a happy pooch. Leaving him home had been the only option. Also, one big reason why they came in Shantel's car versus Johnnie's truck.

"Fair enough. You're going to have to stay here though, Cougar or no Cougar."

That didn't surprise her, even if she might have harbored a hope otherwise. Nor did the no-small-talk approach. Like Shantel, Rick had an edge to him this morning. His voice gave it away, as did his body. He probably wasn't buying the random appearance of this murder any more than she was. "I understand."

"I'm sorry." Shantel squeezed her hand. "I shouldn't have asked you to come. Not fair that you have to sit here and wait."

"Trust me, I'll be fine, and I'd have come even if you hadn't asked. Besides, I've spent half my life waiting at command posts. It'll be okay. I promise."

Shantel's expression cleared. "I suppose you have."

"Not even a little white lie. Truth." No one could possibly imagine how much time they spent waiting. Part and parcel of what search-and-rescue volunteers signed up for.

"I'm glad you came even if you have to wait in the car."

"I'll be fine. Go do your work, and I'll be here when you're done."

Shantel took her kit from the trunk, yet another reason she'd been the one to drive, and slipped into a jumpsuit before following Rick. They ducked under the yellow police tape, headed down the side of a hill, and disappeared from view. Nothing Johnnie could do and nothing she could see. She returned to the car and sat in the passenger seat.

Like out at Fish Lake, the parking area pulsed with activity. Moved and set up in the new location, the mobile command post buzzed as various people moved back and forth from the hillside to its door. A number of the officers and techs working the scene were familiar, though a few were new faces. No one stopped to acknowledge her presence except for a few nods in her direction. The mood outside had turned dark. The city was under siege, and the darkness that dropped over this beautiful stretch of nature affected them all. They had to stop this guy.

Johnnie stared down at her empty hands and shook her head. Definitely off her game because if she'd been thinking before they left the house earlier, she'd have brought her laptop. At least then she'd have been able to do a little work and get closer to meeting that deadline. Then it occurred to her that no computer didn't mean she couldn't do anything. Her phone had a full charge.

Shantel hated leaving Johnnie. Had it been up to her, Johnnie would have accompanied her. But it wasn't her scene. Johnnie wouldn't have been able to help much, even if she had been allowed to come out, but a lot could be said for someone's mere presence. She'd never needed or wanted that before. Her student assistants, sure. Her counterparts on recovery missions, absolutely. A partner, never.

Partner. An odd word to pop into her mind, particularly at this point. They barely knew each other. Friend would be a much better descriptor, and she'd need to keep that thought forefront in her mind.

Unlike the recoveries south of town, this body hadn't been left out in the wilderness long. The runner who found it quite literally stumbled on the soft, disturbed ground, tripped, and fell. When he put his hands down to push himself back up to his feet, they sank into the freshly dug earth and encountered the body. Talk about the kind of trauma that would haunt the poor man's sleep for months, if not years.

Normally, she'd get right to work. The forensic-unit folks, with Beth in the lead once again, were already here. The cooperation and coordination she enjoyed with the professionals here made the horror of the work easier to take. After this week and the time she'd spent one-on-one with Beth, they'd be best friends before it was all over. She'd worked with many throughout the years, and this group was by far her favorite. One more compelling reason not to leave the Spokane area.

She paused now, not because of any of the attending professionals, but because of the scene itself. "Am I totally off base here, or did someone do this intentionally?" The location under the tree clearly mimicked the earlier graves. The position of the remains was also eerily similar. The long bones, once recovered, would tell her if the trinity existed. She had no reason to believe they wouldn't

"It's murder," Rick said, his hands in the pockets of his light jacket with the word Sheriff stenciled in yellow on the back. "That's mighty intentional."

She shook her head as she kept her gaze on the site. "No. That's not what I mean."

Beth spoke up. "Someone wanted this found."

"Exactly." She knew she liked that woman. No big wonder why she led the entire forensic unit. The county had made a wise choice in hiring her.

"You think?" Rick didn't sound completely convinced. He knelt down on one knee. "Looks like the others to me, only more recent."

"All true enough. Here's the glitch. He or she went to a lot of effort to keep the other bodies undetectable. Why leave this one so easy to find? I don't like the way it feels. Too intentional."

"Playing with us?" Rick studied the grave before standing up.

She met his eyes. "Playing something." The hair on the back of her neck tingled, and the sensation creeped her out. Evil permeated everything here.

The body and the ground around it would tell them the tale, and the sooner they got to work, the sooner they would be able to put the story together. She zipped up her jumpsuit and slipped on her gloves before she moved any closer to the site. Rick stood and backed away, giving them plenty of room. He knew how it went and stood in silence, watching. With her mask on, she kneeled, and with Kay, a forensic tech, on the other side of the grave, they began the laborious, meticulous work of excavation.

This one didn't take nearly the time or effort as those near Cheney. The ME took control of the body, or rather the pieces of the body, after they moved aside the earth. Because she worked in concert with the ME, at the moment that responsibility fell to her. She didn't talk as she worked. Neither did Kay. Television shows got that wrong. The actors were always jabbering away and making their declarations about time of death, manner of death, and possible suspects. That wasn't her job, not at this point anyway. She focused entirely on uncovering the remains, and doing it with the precision required to preserve clues and evidence. Kay did the same, her skill and expertise evident, without either of them needing to speak.

Her thoughts on anything else except the excavation stayed inside her head. She would not steer the investigation one way or the other. They all had their jobs to do in these situations, and investigation wasn't hers, tempting as it might be.

Once back at the ME's office, she would put all the pieces together. Then, and only then, would she determine things like cause and manner of death, if she could. It wasn't always possible, but they did their best. Her job relied on facts, and that's what she'd do. She liked the field work, in spite of her extensive lab training, because what she could experience here helped put what she would discover in the lab into context. It provided her with a full picture, an invaluable part of her work.

The freshness of the site made the excavation go quickly. She didn't need days to complete it because of the freshly turned earth. No time for it to pack down and harden, so the soil brushed away easily. She and Kay finished their work in a little over three hours. The rest of the team took photographs at every stage and bagged evidence. They collected and retained everything in the nearby area whether they thought it came from the victim or the killer because they had no way of determining what might be important. While she worked, Shantel tuned out the techs with their bags and their cameras.

Unlike their previous recoveries, most of this body remained intact, except for the long bones of the left leg. Someone was playing games here. Her earlier reservations held true as she gazed down at the bones. An attempt to make them mirror the Cheney remains had failed. One word came to mind: copycat. Two thoughts followed that. The same killer had not perpetrated this murder, and how did he know about the long bones since that information had never been released to the press?

❖

The news Daniel read online quite pleased him. The body had been found, and if he were a betting man, he'd put down odds that his Shantel was already on site. They'd be certain to call her in, given the resemblance to the remains found earlier. So far, so good with his most excellent plan.

At the very least, it would pull their focus from the south county to the north side. It would be good to accomplish that goal, and it appeared he had. They hadn't discovered all his secrets yet, and he really didn't want them to. As the day progressed, he'd keep his eye on the news. Sometimes, the online news channel put out quick blips about what might be happening around the area.

The problem came with the lack of coverage after that. If the event didn't rise to high-enough interest level, the news channels didn't pick it up for the evening broadcasts. The online source rarely went into any significant amount of detail. It put the information out there, ranging from serious crimes like murder to fender benders throughout the region. It let other news sources cover the specifics. Given the high-profile investigation ramping up, little question existed about the coverage of this event. Reporters would converge soon enough to jockey for what they could capture about the latest body before their rival stations.

Part two of the plan would happen later tonight. Or, rather, parts two and three. He had planned one, while the other had presented itself, and he wasn't the kind to ignore a gift when it dropped into his lap. Before tonight, however, he had a little mission to accomplish. Erin would never catch on to her part in this plan, which made him smile. How easily people could be used. Erin was smarter than the average man or woman, yet with the right set of circumstances, even the brilliant doctoral student dumbed it down when a handsome man paid attention. When that attractive man shared a special gift with her, all the norms dropped right off the table.

He studied the ID badge with the tiny gold chip in the lower left corner and Erin's pretty face in the upper right corner before he slipped it into his pocket. By and large, he believed Erin's access mirrored Shantel's, and that's all he'd need to accomplish his goal. Erin had plans with friends today, and thus the chance that she'd even be looking for her badge were slim. Perfect for his purposes. Plenty of time to return it before she missed it.

At the university, he sat in his car for a few minutes, watching students mill about the campus. No matter when he came here, people were always about. He figured right now, the minimal activity would lessen the odds anyone would remember him. Even if they did recall his presence here today, it would be easy enough to explain it away. He just had to say he'd come to meet with Dr. Kind because he needed her services on a case. He never made a move without examining it from every single angle.

The pass easily opened the locked door to the building that housed Shantel's office. No one walked the hallways, though these days security cameras would track his path from the front door all the way to her office. That his presence in the building would be tracked didn't bother him. If someone walked with purpose and gave the impression that their visit was appropriate, no one paid attention. He projected all those qualities, keeping his stride steady and his face tilted slightly. Not up enough for a clear image of his face, and down enough not to draw suspicion.

At the door featuring a plaque with her name on it, he once more swiped the badge across the pad below her name, and voila, the click of the lock disengaging echoed in the empty hallway. He stepped inside and stopped. Now he did tilt his head up, breathing in deeply. It smelled like her. Despite the fact her fieldwork took her out into dirt, mud, and everything in between, she cleaned up quite nicely. Her unique scent that included the familiar sweet vanilla of the special shampoo she liked to use wafted over him. Too faint for a mere human, it swirled around him like a familiar blanket.

He opened his eyes. One might expect the surfaces to be covered with all manner of bones, papers, and notebooks. Not the case for his lovely. In keeping with her personality, clean and clear ruled. With an almost religious respect for the tools of her trade, everything was in its place. Though she used human bones as part of her curriculum, they were safe inside their cases, never on display outside of the active classroom. She consistently taught her students that the only thing people truly owned were their bodies, and thus treating their bones with anything but ultimate care was disrespectful.

Their personal codes didn't align in that regard. He'd never voiced his disagreement to Shantel, for that would be the time she grew angry. She rarely displayed temper, except when it mattered at that level. Rather than argue or question when she got up on her soapbox, he'd nod and smile, and it had been enough to make her believe he agreed with her.

Daniel embraced his own kind of respect for bones. For him, they were game, kind of like the sportsmen around here viewed the deer and elk they tracked every open season. Luckily for him, a defined season for humans didn't exist. No dates to worry about and no license required. All he needed to begin a hunt, he'd received years ago in Tibet.

After dropping his backpack on the floor, he sat in the chair behind her desk and leaned back, his hands behind his head. With his eyes closed, he inhaled and smiled. After a few moments of enjoying the energy surge, he opened his eyes and put his hands down. From his pocket he pulled out his very special prayer beads. Once more he closed his eyes as his lips began to move in silent prayer, the beads sliding through his fingers one by one.

Five minutes later he leaned over and grabbed his pack. Into the center desk drawer, he put the gold and diamond heart necklace he'd pulled from an inside pocket. The moment he'd seen it, he'd known it belonged around Shantel's neck, the diamonds resting against her smooth skin. Twice after he placed it in the drawer, he picked it back up and rearranged it. The third time suited him. Now it looked right, and the message she'd receive would be as he wished. Details were always important.

With a final deep breath, he stood and slipped one strap of the backpack over his shoulder. Not really his style. It was for most of the people on campus, that being the point today. Before he left her office, he reached into his jeans pocket and pulled out a single loose prayer bead. He kissed it and then placed it on the top bookshelf nearest the door. People might consider it weird. Not at all. For him, it became spiritual, just as he believed himself to be a spiritual being. To leave this bead here was a gesture of faith. Of protection. The prayer bead would keep his beloved safe and lead her on the path back to him. She hadn't excised him from her life. She'd only gotten lost on her path. Both his love and spiritual guidance would aid her in the journey back.

As he left her office and the university behind, nothing could dampen his mood. The various setbacks aside, from his view, the world remained on his side, as it always did for winners.

CHAPTER TWENTY-ONE

Johnnie rode with Shantel back to the ME's office after turning down the offer to run her to her own car first. She'd been silent the whole way, and Johnnie didn't push for conversation. She sensed Shantel would appreciate quiet patience, and in her own time, she'd share her thoughts on what happened below that hill.

That she could relate to someone like this made the silence even more comfortable. Usually, she would try to fill it with light chatter. Perhaps because she spent so much time alone, when she found herself with company, constant interaction felt more natural than quiet. That went right out the window with Shantel. Around her, everything flowed easily, whether or not they were conversing.

She wasn't wrong. A few miles away from the crime scene, Shantel glanced over, her lips pressed together, her expression troubled. "Something's really wrong about all this."

"I wasn't even out there, and I have the same feeling."

Shantel returned her eyes to the road. "Whoever did this went to a lot of trouble to give it the same appearance as the older graves."

"Teeth marks on the long bones?"

"Yes."

"But the kill was recent, so I'm guessing the body's essentially intact."

"That's it, for the most part."

It was starting to come together in Johnnie's mind. "Not quite pulling off the same killer thing."

"Not quite."

Alone in the car earlier, she'd run a thousand scenarios through her mind. She kept coming back around to the timing and location of this one. "After the killer took such care to conceal the other graves, why did someone discover this one within hours?"

"Exactly. But that's only one of my concerns."

Johnnie stared at her profile, and a wave of something bad washed over her. "You found something else, didn't you?"

Shantel bit her lip before answering. "Another prayer bead."

The cold chill that raced through Shantel as she told Johnnie about the bead made her want to turn the heater on high. Since the moment the bead had been located, she'd been unable to get warm. The events of the last week started to feel increasingly personal. They shouldn't, but that thought, regardless of how logical, didn't change a thing. She was a college professor, and serial murders having anything to do with her was way out there. Yet she couldn't shake the feeling, and she hated it. Johnnie was the only saving grace. At least she had someone to bounce her thoughts off.

The sight of that bead on the victim's shirt had nearly made her jump back. Fortunately, she'd maintained her composure, thanks to years of experience confronting the unexpected and unusual. It wasn't the first time she'd come across an item out of place when excavating human remains. Those whose lives were stolen often captured something of importance that went with them as they left this world behind. Almost like their last act became an effort to help law enforcement identify their killer.

The bead didn't fit into that category. Not for one minute did she believe it connected back to the victim. In one respect, too random. At the same time, too specific. It had everything to do with the killer, or rather killers, and no one would be able to convince her otherwise.

"It's connected," she murmured as she kept her eyes on the road. She'd share her thoughts with the ME too, but now, she appreciated Johnnie as a trusted sounding board. Without her, this situation might overwhelm.

Johnnie ran a hand through her hair, causing it to stand up on end. She glanced over and thought, cute. A nice diversion from the heavy job she'd just completed. Johnnie stared out at the road too as she said, "Can't argue. Damn if it doesn't sort of blow a giant hole in my werewolf theory though."

She smiled, and a little of the weight lifted. Leave it to Johnnie to keep focused on the werewolves. In a way, she'd like for it to be that simple, if one could call a preternatural serial killer simple. "Don't know that it's any less probable than last night." It would be just as probable to have several werewolves as it would be to have one. Two different killers, two different werewolves. From an odds standpoint, pretty high either way.

"Maybe. Somehow I don't see a werewolf running around with prayer beads." Johnnie steepled her fingers and rested her chin on them. She sounded a little disappointed by her own theorizing.

Shantel reached over with one hand and patted her shoulder. "If the possibility of a killer that stepped right out of folklore exists, then I'd say anything else is as likely."

Johnnie dropped her hands and rewarded her with a smile. "I do like the way you think, doc. Werewolves are back on the table."

"Werewolves notwithstanding, I keep coming back to Daniel."

"I have the distinct impression your ex bugs the shit out of you."

"He does. Very much."

"Is he a violent guy? I mean, you'd said before you didn't think so." Johnnie's question wasn't out of line. "Is it in his makeup to kill people, gnaw on them, and then hide their bodies? That's pretty fucking extreme. Excuse my French."

She shook her head as a thousand memories fast-forwarded through her mind. "Violent? No. Not that I ever saw anyway. I'd characterize him as more intense. The guy can laser-focus on things like you can't believe. It's one reason he's so successful."

"At?"

"Criminal defense."

"Yuck. Don't get that side of the table, if you catch my drift."

Now she laughed out loud. A pattern revealed itself: Johnnie could make any discussion a lot more interesting. "I don't pick sides and didn't even when I was still married to him. I'm a neutral observer. My job is to find the facts and let them speak. I make no judgment calls."

"I appreciate that, and my job is about pointing people like you in the right direction. No judgment from us either. It's just that when you do the kind of work that Cougar and I do, often it's because someone's life has been stolen. Sometimes it's an unfortunate situation or an accident. Many times, unfortunately, it's far more sinister, and in those instances, I want the person brought to justice. Hence, my prosecutorial leanings. It's hard to keep a hold on impartiality in those cases."

Oh, did she understand. Her chosen field brought more than her share of horror, and she longed for justice to rain down on those responsible. Didn't change what she did or her role as a nonaligned party. Daniel? Different story. "His skill is legendary and one of the reasons his father pushed us hard to come back here. A big coup for the family firm. At first Daniel resisted, and then he had some strange change of heart and became excited to return to the homelands. When I got the job at EWU, it all dropped into place. Like destiny at work to drag us here."

"And now the prayer bead brings you full circle back to the former ball and chain."

In some ways, still the ball and chain, though she kept that thought to herself. "That's exactly it. The bead is unusual. Handmade. He takes a trip back to Tibet every year and comes home with a string of them. I could never figure out why he needed so many, and he never explained it other than to say they were important to him. When Daniel didn't want to tell you something, you'd never get it out of him. I stopped asking because, frankly, I didn't care."

"Until now."

She pulled into an empty parking stall at the ME's office. "Until now."

"Let's say I agree the beads tie the murders together. Still a giant leap back to your ex."

"I suppose." Except the idea kept growing in her head, and it bothered her. She shouldn't be thinking about it like this. Thinking about him like this. He'd never done anything to indicate violence toward her or others, except that an air about him, an aura maybe, always hinted that the waters ran deeper than what showed on the surface. The way he obsessed about her now had the same feel. More and more she became convinced that he'd never been a hundred percent open with her.

The longer she pictured that bead in the dirt next to the victim's body, the more her blood ran cold.

❖

The witching hour arrived, and Daniel was more than ready. Older and more experienced, he didn't rely on the moon for the power to change. Shantel never understood the yearly trips he'd take to what he called the motherland. She thought it revolved around his deep faith, and he let her continue to believe the lie. Not exactly a lie, given he considered his visits faithful. Splitting hairs, he supposed.

What the trips were about went far deeper than Shantel, or anyone outside the global pack, could grasp. Perhaps when he brought her in, he'd take her on his next one. If she saw it with her own eyes, she'd internalize the importance of each journey back. Drawing from the master during those weeks gave him something he couldn't secure anywhere else. He returned smarter, faster, and more powerful. It would be the same for her as well.

As he waited in the darkness, he began to wonder if he'd even need to trek to the motherland in the future. He'd learned all the enlightened one could offer, and in the last few years enjoyed the change in scenery rather than build up his already considerable strength. In a way his adventures became little more than a habit he hadn't been able to break even as the student became the master. Surpassed the master.

He caught his victim's scent long before he picked up the footsteps. Just what he'd been waiting for, and as soon as the waft of it hit him, he slipped out of his running shorts, T-shirt, and sneakers. Without ceremony he dropped them into a pile next to the big pine that shadowed him from view. His arms raised over his head, he tilted his head back and silently called the change. Sensations rushed through his body, his bones, muscles, and sinews growing and shifting. Beautiful pain.

"What the fuck, dude?"

The animal in him reacted to the man who'd stepped into the cluster of trees in time to witness the change. Not an accident. He'd timed it to perfection, and the shock caused his invited guest to stop and gape open-mouthed. It happened this way each time he allowed someone to see his true self. The intentional act resulted in the expected outcome. Paralysis.

He pawed the ground, stirring up the dirt. The fun would begin once the fear kicked in and overrode his prey's immobility. It wouldn't take long. First the fingers twitched, and then the eyes widened. The fun commenced a flash of a second later.

Before he'd called the change, he'd been silent for fear of scaring him away. All different now that the game had begun, and he tipped his head back and howled. The man screamed, the sound high enough to have come from a five-year-old, and he began to run. Daniel ran faster, all the while inhaling the heavy scent that wafted through the air. Darkness wrapped around them, and the air filled with the sound of running feet. No rest for the wicked.

He caught up to his intended deep in the woods, where the trails disappeared and the trees thickened, the smell of his sweat and fear heavy in the air. More howls mingled with the screams, and the creatures that typically ran the ground here disappeared. All the better.

Thirty minutes later, he returned to the tree where his clothes remained. He lay down next to them and closed his eyes. The chase filled him with joy and rapture, something he wanted to take time to savor. A brief rest under the stars and he'd be ready to call it a night.

When his eyes opened, the moon had climbed high into the sky. Tendrils of light broke through the thick canopy of tree branches above him to kiss his face. The wolf sighed and resisted ever so slightly as once more the human returned. He stood, stretched, and rolled his shoulders. While he'd love to linger and relish the beauty of the workings of a great plan, time to redress and leave. He picked up his clothes and began to put them on. Under normal circumstances, he'd tidy up to ensure the safety of his treasure. These were not normal circumstances, and he didn't intend to return to where he'd left his prey.

He'd enjoyed the game tonight, but it was a different kind of hunt. He'd done this out of vengeance, not an embrace of his true nature. If someone found this body tonight, tomorrow, or next week, he didn't care. Bastard deserved to be abandoned out here, to be exposed to the elements and the animals. When he'd decided to try to extort Daniel, he'd signed his own death warrant. He'd been a fool when he'd represented him, and even more of a fool tonight. He'd learned that

Daniel wasn't a man to turn on. No one crossed him and lived to tell about it.

Using the sleeve of his shirt, he wiped the blood from his face. It wouldn't do well to run into someone out here with a bloody smile. Not a great probability of that happening at this time of night. Just the same, he cleaned away any trace of the game. Next, he tied his trainers and then jogged back to his car, parked a good three miles away. Even with the hunt tonight he could keep going for hours without getting tired or sore. Nights like this filled him to the brim with good energy. It would hold until the big show on the night of the full moon.

The perfect way to top off a wonderful night like this would be to swing by and spend time with Erin. Two very different kinds of fun made for a great mix. In fact, the more he thought about it, the better the idea sounded to him. He deserved it.

Daniel turned on his brightest smile as he leaned against the door frame and rang the bell. She'd be happy he came by. He knew how to make a woman feel special and valued, another of his superpowers. Hard to list them all, given his many natural gifts. Some drew a better hand than others, and his hand was the best, having Senior as his father aside. He'd been able to rise above his father's questionable role-model status and take his place as a superstar.

When Erin flung open the door, not a trace of a smile showed on her face. "You damn bastard!"

CHAPTER TWENTY-TWO

Johnnie didn't get a whole lot done after she left Shantel at the ME's office. She finished one chapter and took a five-mile run with Cougar. The rest of the time she wandered around the house like she didn't have a thing to do when, in fact, she had plenty. She just didn't want to do any of it and couldn't get her mind into the work.

Besides the fact that she'd become fascinated with Shantel, this whole situation had gotten under her skin. Some of her previous searches resulted in criminal investigation, but this was her first involvement in what looked more and more like the activity of a serial killer.

Regardless, she and Cougar did the same thing every time. Once they finished in the field and Cougar told them where the odor of human composition existed, they walked away. Unless, of course, they ended up in trial, which—knock on wood—hadn't happened to date. Even if they hadn't been called into court yet, all her ducks were in a row, just in case. Their training records were accurate and up to date, their certifications were current, and she completed seminars with the best and the brightest. Every professional handler she knew did the same thing.

Cougar kept coming in to check on her, his intense gaze telegraphing his concern. The tap, tap, tap of his nails on the hardwood floors announced his babysitting arrivals. He'd stand next to her and bump her leg with his nose. Only after she rubbed his head and assured him she was fine would he turn around and leave her. That happened at least a dozen times.

Now, as she stood out on the deck sipping coffee and staring out over the hay fields, Cougar raced in from the yard to do his stop-and-check again. She patted the top of his head. "I'm okay, buddy. I promise." His dark eyes studied her face.

This time reassurance appeared to work. He turned, ran back into the yard, and resumed his patrol duties. When not working, Cougar took security of the homestead as his personal responsibility. That duty included keeping the farm safe from intruders of both the human and animal variety. He didn't tolerate trespassing of any kind, including strangers, coyotes, deer, or moles. Safety in seventy-five pounds of canine, and she appreciated him more than words could express.

She took a sip of her cooling coffee just as her phone rang. When she pulled it out of her pocket, she groaned. "Oh, God. Not again." It was Kay. Seriously, the woman played their lifetime friendship card too often. She didn't divulge information to the press even when the press had been her friend since before puberty.

Her first instinct was strong: ignore the call and put the phone back in her pocket. Might as well answer and get it over with. She'd avoided Kay for days, and if nothing else, she personified persistence. Probably one of the biggest reasons she'd become quite successful in her chosen profession. "Hey."

"About time. You can run, but you can't hide forever." The tone of indignation came across loud and clear. Another consistent thing about Kay: it was always about her.

Johnnie didn't try to hide her own irritation. Long-time history aside, Kay pushed too hard even when she knew the consequences to people she professed to call her friends. "I can't."

"You have no idea what I'm going to ask." A touch of whining for good measure.

"Kay, I always know exactly what you're going to ask."

She switched back to indignation. "That's kind of harsh for your oldest friend."

Johnnie could tick off all the styles of manipulation that Kay could and would employ in an attempt to get her scoop. "And it's precisely why I know the reason you're calling me."

"Come on. Give me something."

"No." Johnnie could be as stubborn as Kay.

"I won't reveal the source." Sweet pleading.

"No."

"It doesn't have to be much. My career hinges on something big. I'm not getting any younger, and this is a young person's business." Guilt based upon their shared ages.

"No." An attempt to justify her pledge to confidentiality wouldn't fly with Kay. Best to keep to one-word answers.

"I have your secrets that I've held close, like a good friend."

Her heart sank, as did Kay's strategy. This was the first time she'd actually threatened Johnnie, and it didn't bode well for the survival of their friendship. "Stop it, Kay. This is beneath even you."

"What do you mean, even me?"

"You've changed over the years. You're now threatening one of your oldest friends. How many others have walked away because you've done this to them? All in the name of advancing your precious career? I've not allowed your dogged determination to get a story at the expense of those you profess to love end our friendship, but I'm finally at the end here."

"Don't be stupid." Ice now entered her voice. Johnnie hit a nerve, and the real Kay surged forward.

"I'm hanging up now. Don't call me again." The end of the line had just arrived. Sometimes it became necessary to walk away from people.

"Wait—"

She hit the bright-red button and shoved the phone into her pocket. It hurt less than she thought. In the back of her mind, a clock ticked as the time approached when she'd have to say those awful words. She'd loved Kay. She still loved her, really. Sometimes that wasn't enough. Some individuals, despite all best efforts of those who loved them, imploded. They couldn't control their toxicity, and it spilled out on those who stayed around. That described Kay. She didn't want that in her life anymore.

When her phone rang again, she hesitated before she pulled it out of her pocket. Kay wouldn't take rejection lightly, and she might have to block her number. When she glanced down at the display, her hesitation vanished. She smiled as she said, "Hello."

"I apologize for calling you yet again." Shantel's voice clearly conveyed her sentiments.

"I don't mind." Far from it. An uplifting follow-up to Kay's disappointing call.

"I went into my office this afternoon."

"Get some work done?" If Shantel was as far behind as Johnnie, they'd both have to kick it into double time soon.

"Not really." Something in her voice made Johnnie's antenna go up. A problem.

"If it's any consolation, I've pretty well bombed today too." Maybe the volume of work Shantel had to catch up on caused the heaviness in her voice. Their shared experience might help her.

"He's been in my office."

"He?" She wasn't following, thanks to Kay, who'd sent her thoughts and emotions reeling. A mix of anger and disappointment could do that to a person. She tried to rally and focus on Shantel alone.

"Daniel."

Okay, now Shantel grabbed her undivided attention. "Your ex." More and more that guy bothered her. Shantel might be confident he wasn't the violent type. She wasn't so sure.

"Only two people have access to my office. Me and my assistant, Erin."

"She let him in?" That would be the logical conclusion.

"She wouldn't do that."

"What are you saying?" Fear pushed her to grab her keys and race to the garage.

Shantel sat at her desk staring into the middle drawer. She'd started to pick it up, and then better sense kicked in, and she put her hands in her lap. After what she'd found on top of her desk, nothing should have surprised her. It pissed her off just the same. Damn him for always finding a way to get to her. He'd done it all the way through their marriage, and afterward, he'd kicked it up into overdrive. She bit her lip and willed herself not to cry.

She'd called Johnnie first. Proper protocol would have been to contact either campus security or Rick before a friend. Johnnie kept a level head and a keen eye, which made her a good person to share her concerns with. Her recommendation echoed what had been in her own mind. If she wanted to be free of Daniel, the time had come to take it to another level. The law-enforcement kind of level.

Call number two went to Rick to report the incident, though she would omit the part about calling Johnnie first. She could have contacted campus security and probably should have. She certainly thought about it in tandem with considering who to get in touch with after Johnnie. They agreed that having a reliable contact in the county sheriff's department carried more weight than campus security, and thus, Rick it had been. He could work with the security folks and be the buffer she could use right about now. Daniel's actions, combined with the intensity of the work, were taking her stress to new levels. She didn't need his bullshit right now. As Johnnie would say, excuse her French.

"How are you doing?" Johnnie sat down in one of the guest chairs, her eyes intent on Shantel's face.

"I'm tired. Between the murders and Daniel, I'm wearing down." To be truthful with Johnnie came naturally. A welcome relief.

"I'm so sorry. I wish I could do something to help."

She met Johnnie's gaze. The warmth in her dark eyes drew her in. "The fact that you dropped everything and drove all the way out here to Cheney helps more than you can imagine."

"Not a big deal."

Wrong on that count. "It's a very big deal to me."

Johnnie's smile banished some of the shadows that hovered at the corners of her vision. "Okay then. Super glad I can help. And, for the record, not a hard drive to Cheney from my place. Anytime you need me, I'm a call away. Deal?"

She smiled back and sat in the chair next to Johnnie, taking her hand. The simple touch banished the rest of the shadows. "Deal."

A knock at the door made them both turn toward the sound. The six-feet-three, fully armed calvary had arrived. "Tell me," Rick said as he walked into the office, his gaze taking in the entirety of her workspace.

At least his prompt arrival meant she needed to tell the story only once. She released Johnnie's hand. She'd have preferred to keep holding it. Like her, Johnnie leaned back in her chair. Better to keep it all professional now that the law had arrived.

It took her a few minutes to walk Rick and Johnnie through what she'd found earlier. All of it, from the card professing his undying love left on top of her desk to the gold necklace in the middle drawer.

Both listened quietly and without interruption until she finished. Only then did Rick walk around to stand next to her chair. "Show me the necklace."

His eyes narrowed, and he leaned closer when she slid open the drawer, Johnnie peering over his shoulder after getting up to stand behind him. The small lamp on her desk shone light onto the small, sparkling diamonds. Like her, he didn't touch it.

For a few seconds he didn't say anything. When he did, the hair on her arms stood up. "I don't fucking like this. I could be wrong…"

"About?" She didn't like either his expression or the tone of his voice.

Rick ignored them both as he put his phone to his ear. A few seconds later, he said, "Jill, text me the picture of Kathy Lourdes. Yes. Right now. I know it's late. I know you're at home. Get me the picture anyway." He punched off the call and held the phone in his hand, waiting. The plink of an incoming text sounded less than a minute later.

Johnnie, who had a full view of Rick's screen, whispered, "Son of a bitch."

"What?" Now he was scaring her. They were both scaring her.

"You need to look at this." He turned the phone around to display the screen and the picture.

It took her a second to make the same connection he had almost immediately after she'd opened her desk drawer. "Oh, dear God."

Fuck, fuck, and fuck. That goddam Shantel had ruined a perfectly good situation, again. He'd had everything under control and going exactly the way he wanted it to, and now this. If she'd kept her big, fat mouth shut until after the full moon, his position as alpha would have been too solid for Erin to ignore. At this stage, she retained too much of her human will, and Shantel's call to Erin and the revelations that resulted came as a major setback to his master plan.

When the car in front of him didn't move quickly enough after the light turned green, he laid on the horn, its scream gratifying. The driver flipped him the bird, the action clear in his headlights. The temptation to ram him, even if it would damage his bumper and hood, was almost too much to ignore. It would serve the fucker right. But he didn't need the added attention and managed to harness enough restraint to resist. The offending vehicle raced away, and he forced himself to drive like a normal, civilized person.

The urge to race back to where he'd left the body rested as strong upon him as the one to ram the car. He needed to run and to feast. It would provide the power to fill him up and banish the fury over the wrinkle in his best-laid plans. He made the same choice about the run as he had about acting on the road rage. He knew better than to make a bad night worse, and that became a very real possibility if he retraced his earlier steps. The risk outweighed the reward.

At the house, he didn't bother to pull into the garage. Instead, he left the car in the driveway, wrenched open the front door, and stomped inside. From a cupboard he grabbed a nearly full bottle of fine whiskey. He rarely imbibed in the hard stuff because he had no need of an artificial buzz, given the natural high he got from the simple beauty of his special life. Tonight, he called on reinforcements and poured a healthy amount of the deep amber, rich, and well-aged liquid into a glass, nice and neat. It burned all the way down his throat in a most delicious way. Less of an artificial buzz and more like a perfect fire for the beast. Not quite the same as the glorious sensations achieved by a hunt, but it would have to do.

After the second glass, he managed to steady himself and regroup. The whiskey did its job, and Plan B began to form in delicious detail. Being the best criminal-defense attorney ever gave him the tools to revise, adapt, and overcome. Those he defended often had a way of bringing up surprises when least expected. Kind of like right now. Part of his brilliance came in understanding how to deal with each and every one of those surprises in order to prevail.

His phone rang, and he groaned when Senior's number appeared on the screen. Not in the mood for his particular brand of bullshit, he picked it up just the same. The old man would call over and over until he did. Might as well get it over with. "Hello, Father."

"Why aren't you here?"

"Why would I be?"

"It's your brother's birthday." As usual, he didn't try to disguise his disgust. The brilliant yet disrespectful black sheep disappointed his ever-supportive family yet again. Little did he realize, Daniel was something far better than a black sheep.

"Bad me, and I didn't get him a gift." He'd already called and apologized to his mother for the last missed soiree, but he could frankly give a rat's ass about his perfect younger brother, the surgeon they were all so proud of. Fuck him and his pretty little trophy wife with the long blond hair and perfect body.

"Get your ass over here now." He used his Daddy's-the-boss voice. Didn't work when he'd been a kid. Didn't work now.

"Tell Mother I'm on my way." He could give a shit about the old man or his brother, though he did retain a modicum of respect for his mother, her morning, noon, and night reliance on expensive vodka aside. She tried even if the task was Herculean. Hence, the vodka. On the way up the hill, he'd stop at a convenience store and buy baby brother or, should he say, the golden boy, a birthday card.

CHAPTER TWENTY-THREE

How can that be?" Shantel's question echoed Johnnie's unspoken one. Between the picture on Rick's phone and the necklace in Shantel's desk, the term shock didn't cover it. Impossible a far better word. The proof in front of them couldn't be denied.

"That's what I'm wondering." Rick's face reflected his concern.

"You said he's never shown any signs of violence, right?" Johnnie flashed back to their earlier conversations. If Shantel hid a dirty secret, it didn't show. Most victims of domestic violence went to great lengths to conceal the undeserved shame. None of that characterized Shantel. Open and honest best described her.

Shaking her head, Shantel confirmed Johnnie's assessment. "None at all. In the time we were together, I never saw one thing that raised an alarm in that respect. Controlling and obsessive, without a doubt. Not one hint of violence directed at me. Trust me. I'd have left him a lot earlier if he'd been inclined toward brutality."

"Nothing toward you. What about someone else?" Rick's investigator's hat was firmly on now. Even his voice changed from the search manager she'd worked with time and time again to something much different.

Shantel shook her head again. "Nothing that I ever saw, and that's what confuses me. How could he have a missing woman's necklace? He's not the kind of man who'd buy from a pawn shop. He's a high-end, brand-new kind of guy."

"We're going to find out exactly how and why he got this." Rick put his phone to his ear and spoke quickly. After he finished, he motioned for them both to leave. "I've called in the techs and plan to have them go over everything in here. You need to step outside and not touch anything else."

"You believe this is really her necklace?" Shantel's voice shook. Johnnie took her hand and held on tight, hoping her reassurance would ease the trembling.

"Maybe and maybe not. This isn't the time to make assumptions. We'll check it all to make sure."

Johnnie approved of the path Rick was heading down. As soon as he showed them that picture, her stomach sank, and a boulder had settled there. Something wasn't right about all of this. A persistent ex-spouse wasn't that unusual. Shantel's might be taking it to the extreme, but could he be murderous? Or, even worse, twisted enough to leave a presumably dead woman's jewelry as a gift? That felt like a gigantic leap and, at the same, absolutely true. She wanted to believe it nothing beyond a sick coincidence. The problem was, she didn't.

Once out in the hallway, Rick turned to Shantel. "Explain to me again how he got into your locked office."

She ran her hands through her hair and sighed. "Erin."

"Who?"

"My graduate assistant, Erin."

It didn't sit right with Johnnie that Shantel's trusted assistant would let her ex-husband in. She needed to make some kind of sense out of it, and unless Rick had made a leap she'd missed, he'd want more as well. "Why would she do that?" If Shantel had been trying to keep her ex away, her assistant surely wouldn't allow him free access to her personal space.

Shantel looked from Johnnie to Rick. "After I talked to both of you, I called her. I wanted to be angry with her for allowing him into my office because that's the only thing that made sense. I was furious until she explained what she'd been doing over the last week. Or, rather, whom she'd been doing over the last week. The story wasn't pretty and not her fault at all. That shit used her, plain and simple."

Johnnie still wasn't following. "Are you saying she didn't recognize your ex?"

"That's exactly what I'm saying."

Now Johnnie was confused. "How did she not know?"

Shantel shrugged. "For starters, we have different names. I never took his, though he threw that decision in my face over and over again. Daniel is a little old-school in that regard and believed I should embrace the Mrs. moniker. I preferred the name I was born with, particularly with Dr. in front of it. I worked hard for that privilege. When it came time to sucker my assistant, that difference became an advantage."

"And you're also saying she'd never seen him before?" Rick asked the follow-up question rolling around in her mind.

"No," Shantel said. "Not in person or in a picture. By the time Erin came on board as my graduate assistant, the divorce was long final, and I'd made it crystal clear to Daniel that he was to stay away from campus. All Erin knew was that I had an ex-husband and the split was not amicable. I didn't ever talk about him and had no pictures laying around."

"The flowers?" Johnnie thought about the first time she'd heard about Daniel's obsession with Shantel. Someone allowed him in the office to leave flowers.

"Technically, he's sticking to our agreement. He doesn't personally bring me flowers. He has them delivered. Yes, Erin took custody of the flowers, but not from Daniel directly."

"Maybe he did that this time too."

"I'd think that too if not for two things. First, Erin wouldn't have put a necklace in my desk drawer."

"I guess that makes sense."

"And second, that." She pointed back toward her office and the single bead sitting on the bookshelf. "That wasn't there when Erin left on Friday. My office was clean and tidy when she took off. No bead. No necklace."

A chill ran through her again. The deviation from normal couldn't be a good thing. "I don't get why he did this himself then? Stick to the tried and true, and have it delivered."

"That's what's so disturbing. He's always been a bulldog when he wants something. He's the kind that goes around saying 'failure isn't an option.' This goes way beyond what I thought he'd ever do. The creepy level is off the charts."

Johnnie considered her words. In her mind, the creepy level had been breached before today. "The wine…"

Rick stopped and turned to stare at Shantel, his eyes narrowing. "What does she mean, the wine?"

❖

The uneasiness that had been with her since she unlocked her office door and walked in ratcheted up about a hundred notches when Johnnie mentioned the wine. In light of everything else, Shantel pushed the breach in her house to the back of her mind—something to take care of in the near future once the immediate mess got handled. Now that Daniel had also breached her office, she couldn't ignore the facts about his obsession. He couldn't be trusted to maintain boundaries or, from the look of things, to stay rational.

"Well…" A guy that big, with a gun at his hip and staring down at her with eyes blazing, made her want to step back. She got it though. Rick needed all the facts to help protect her. In his view, he probably thought she'd been withholding information. She had, in a way, just not intentionally.

She took a breath. "Daniel broke into my house and left a bottle of wine on my kitchen counter."

He raised a single eyebrow. She guessed he expected something a little more at the bombshell level. "How can you be so certain it was him?"

"Easy enough to whittle down the suspects to one. Only Daniel would know about my love of that particular wine, and trust me. It's not something you can go to the grocery store and pick up. He went to a great deal of effort to get that bottle."

"We need to talk." Rick's tone of voice was the same one she'd heard other detectives use in the midst of a critical case. All business and no bullshit.

Shantel glanced back into her office, which until now had been a peaceful sanctuary where she worked and helped guide eager students. The office itself was standard, nothing special in terms of architecture. What happened in the room is what made it special. Now, Daniel had managed to tarnish a once bright and shiny place. She ran a hand over her eyes and sighed. "This is unreal."

Johnnie put a hand on her shoulder, and the simple touch pushed away some of the tension making her shoulders scream. The touch of her hand, her mere presence had a steadying effect. She'd like to bottle what Johnnie possessed so she could take it with her everywhere.

"We'll get to the bottom of this," Rick reassured her, also putting a hand briefly on her shoulder. "After all, it's what I do."

Shantel trusted him and had since the moment they'd met. He'd have her back. Yet overload hit her hard despite her faith in him. "Can we talk later? I would *really* like to decompress for a bit. I thought I was used to his tricks and that he couldn't get to me anymore. This," she waved a hand in the direction of her office, "has thrown me way off. It's like he physically kicked me in the stomach."

Rick nodded. "I understand," he said. "I'll either call you later or swing by your house."

Johnnie stepped in, her hand still on Shantel's shoulder. "She'll be at my house."

Rick looked first at Shantel and then at Johnnie. "Your house?"

"She hasn't had a chance to change her locks after the wine incident," Johnnie hurried to explain.

"She's right. I'll get to it. I swear. As soon as my life gets back to normal."

Johnnie's clear thinking and even clearer plan for the evening rocked. Shantel might take offense at the way she'd stepped in and told Rick she wouldn't be going home. Under different circumstances, maybe she would have. She didn't now because, after this most recent turn of events, her logic and clear-headed analysis made perfect sense. If she were being smart and safety conscious, she shouldn't go back to her house until her security had been brought up to Daniel-proof status. Whatever was going on with him, she would prefer Rick get to the bottom of it rather than find herself in an uncomfortable confrontation with him. So, Johnnie's house it would be.

This time Rick nodded. "I like the way you're thinking, Johnnie. You two go to her place, and I'll buzz over once we finish here. We can walk through this all again with clear heads."

"There's one more thing." Rick would eventually find it in the search of her office, but she wanted to bring it up now. It couldn't be a coincidence, and whatever sick game Daniel might be playing, they all needed to be on the offensive. She pointed to her bookcase. "The bead."

He nodded. "I saw it."

"Your techs are going to find that it's the same bead as the one found near the clandestine graves and on the shirt of the latest victim. It's identical to the prayer beads Daniel has been using for decades."

"Lots of people use beads. We'll have to keep an open mind." The words of a good investigator who didn't jump to conclusions.

"I appreciate that. Just want you to be aware that it's got to be his."

"What makes it special? I mean, I agree. He probably left it here, in light of everything else. Ruling out any other possibility wouldn't be a good idea."

Shantel knew it belonged to Daniel. No one would be able to convince her any different. "The bead is not a generic type you can pick up at any souvenir store. It's unique and can be purchased only in Tibet."

Rick's eyes did the narrow thing again. "This isn't looking good for your ex."

"No," she whispered. "It's not."

Daniel suffered through the cake-and-champagne event that his father insisted on every year for his brother's birthday. It grated on him, as it always did. If his father had been the kind of man who meant the gesture, it might be different. As it were, everything the old man did lacked sincerity, even when it came to his precious baby brother. All about the show.

It might be hypocritical to hold his father in low esteem because of that trait, since he employed a similar strategy. No one except his maker knew of his true nature. He, too, put forth a public persona that didn't have much to do with the real him. Still, for Daniel, it had less to do with being an asshole and more to do with self-protection. Most wouldn't fully appreciate his secret and would react on gut instinct if they were to encounter him after a change. They'd want to stop him, in a fatal way. For his father, the opposite held true. Asshole should be his middle name. His father simply wasn't a good person, despite what he liked to proclaim and portray.

Tonight, with everything in his world upside down, a mere filament kept him from losing his patience with Senior. For years he'd played the dutiful son, for the most part anyway. He even came back into the family business, knowing full well it had little to do with him being the son of the senior partner and grandson of the partner emeritus. The old man wanted him to come home and join the family business because of his renown as an unbeaten criminal-defense lawyer. Dear old Dad knew that sonny-boy could make the firm a shitload of money. That's what it all revolved around for Senior.

It pissed him off. Unlike little bro, he'd never gotten full credit for his intelligence and skill. Since he'd come home, more than once he'd witnessed his father explain to clients how his son learned at his knee and thus Daniel's success was a direct result of those lessons. Not true on any front. He could count on one hand the number of times his father brought him to the office to learn at that so-called knee. If he'd learned from a parent, it would be his mother. What had he learned from her? Tell the old man what he wanted to hear and avoid his rage.

Now, his brother? That story had a different spin. By going into medicine rather than the family business, Spencer, named after their grandfather, got to brag on his achievements all by his lonesome. Did he learn at Daddy's knee? Oh, no. Spencer-the-brilliant had been the sole architect of his success. Behind the closed doors of the family home, double standards were the standard.

"When are you getting back together with Shantel? This divorce thing doesn't look good for the family." Senior puffed a big cigar, the smoke rising in front of his face and blurring his features. Daniel preferred it that way.

Daniel took a sip of his water before answering. "My relationship with Shantel is my business." He refused to discuss this with him. Not now. Not ever.

"That's where you're wrong, son. Everything you do is family business." He blew smoke in Daniel's face.

He waved a hand, dispersing the offensive smoke while refusing to rise to the bait. "So, your little legal-assistant girlfriend is family business too?"

True to form, the old man didn't even blink. "Do not disrespect your mother."

He could play the game too. He calmly answered. "Don't think it's me who's disrespecting my mother."

"My business is my business."

"Right back at ya, *Dad*."

"Enough."

"Couldn't agree more. You stay out of my business, and I'll stay out of yours."

"I believe it's time to call it a night." His father ended every conversation he didn't like that way. Daniel didn't have a problem with the suggestion. He'd been ready to go before he ever stepped into the house.

He got up and walked around the table to give his mother a kiss. He whispered in her ear, "Sorry, Mom. I didn't mean to stir it up."

She patted his cheek and smiled. "Thank you for coming."

He waved at Spencer, who, accustomed to the ugly banter between Daniel and their father, sat drinking wine as though they were another normal family enjoying a pleasant birthday dinner. His expression never changed, his arm casually draped around his wife's shoulders. It all rolled off the good doctor without ever sticking.

Outside in his car, Daniel tapped his fingers on the steering wheel. While Senior might have ended the little birthday celebration, if Daniel knew him as well as he believed he did, the night still had legs to it. The filament holding the remains of his patience snapped. Instead of going home, he backed out of the driveway and drove half a block down to idle in the shadows of a large blue spruce. Dark car, dark night, dark shadows. Invisible.

As he suspected, Senior drove out of the driveway less than ten minutes after Daniel made his ungraceful exit. He pulled in behind his dad a few seconds later, betting that his father would pay little attention to the traffic around him. Arrogance had its advantages, like believing in invincibility, self-importance, and no accountability. Twenty-five minutes later, his father parked in front of a small, tidy home on the city's north side. Nice enough, though not high-end by any stretch of the imagination. The sort of home a fairly well-paid legal assistant might be able to afford.

He caught up with him just as he stepped onto the sidewalk leading to the bright-red front door. "Hey, *Dad.*"

Gratifying jump and spin. "What are *you* doing here?" Even being caught in the act of cheating, he still maintained an abundance of righteous arrogance.

His father didn't even see the punch coming.

CHAPTER TWENTY-FOUR

All right. Let's get to it." Johnnie had been thinking through the strange turn of events all the way home. Her childhood encounter gained more and more significance over the last few days. Though impossible on the face of it and easily rejected as the fantasies of a young girl, she couldn't dismiss what she'd seen out there. Not just what she'd seen. What she'd been feeling. A germ of an idea had begun to form, and it took solid root.

"Get to what?" Shantel sank to a chair in the living room, the stress of the day clear on her face. As she settled back into the softness of the cushions, Johnnie thought about how natural she looked in that chair. Not just the chair, but how natural it felt to have her here in the house.

Holding up a hand, she said, "Hear me out." A quick thought before she launched into making her case. "You want a glass of wine before I dazzle you with my proposal?"

Shantel cocked her head and studied Johnnie. A little light came back into her face. "Am I going to need it?"

Valid question. Honest answer. "You might."

"Then hit me with whatever you have that's got a good punch. No wimpy rosé, please."

As a matter of fact, she did have a nice dark-red, courtesy of a friend who owned one of the local wineries. A few minutes later, she handed Shantel a glass with an ample pour and then sat on the low table facing her. "Let's revisit the werewolf scenario."

Shantel took a sip of the wine, her eyes closed. "Given Daniel's link to all this, maybe it would be a good idea to focus on the flesh-and-blood man rather than a folktale. Besides, it's hard to wrap my head around…"

"I hear a 'but' in there."

She opened her eyes and stared at Johnnie, her expression hard to read. "But, the beads and that damned necklace have me thinking twice. I want to focus on Daniel, yet something's pulling at me I can't really explain."

"There's more, isn't there?" Johnnie could almost see the wheels turning in her head, visions of something flashing behind her beautiful eyes. She took Shantel's hands, the sensation of her skin against Johnnie's both exciting and comforting.

Staring down at their joined hands, Shantel sighed. "All the way over here, I thought through the years Daniel and I were together. He's unique, and when I met him, that's one of the things that drew me in. The excitement of a man not like others I'd met. Or, God forbid, the men from my mother's church she loved to try to set me up with."

"What do you think now?"

"I'm starting to put some pieces together, and the picture they're painting isn't pretty."

"Like?"

"Like random trips to out-of-the-way places." She thought back over all the times he'd gone away with no explanation either before or after. Of the silent treatment he employed whenever she questioned him.

"Did something weird happen?"

"Not exactly sure, and to be honest, I'd like to find out."

"Now you're talking, and as it happens, I'm a pro at research." Johnnie smiled.

"As a matter of fact, I have already figured that out about you. What do you say we do a bit of sleuthing together? I'm not so bad at research myself."

Johnnie squeezed Shantel's hands gently, and her smile grew. "Absolutely, and afterward, I have another proposal for you."

❖

Shantel tapped on the tabletop. "You're catching the pattern, right?"

Johnnie's eyes were on the laptop screen. "You'd have to really suck at this to miss it."

"Impossible not to now. And, neither one of us sucks at this." Once more chills hit her all over. Damn that man.

Johnnie leaned back in her chair. "He's been up to something all right. No wonder he didn't want to talk about his mystery trips."

"I may be sick." She wasn't kidding. The more they dug into things, the more a picture started to emerge. A very ugly picture. She dug her fingers into her palms, and the pain helped her focus. Might keep her from throwing up too. She didn't want to do something like that in front of Johnnie.

"I have an idea." Now Johnnie tapped on the table.

"I'm open to anything at this point." Her head reeled. In the last hour, memories had become suspect, and her ability to tell good from bad, equally suspect. More and more she believed Daniel had played her. Most likely from day one.

Johnnie nodded. "Good, because I bet you're going to think I'm a little out there. Well, you probably already do, and now I'll simply prove you right."

Shantel laughed, and it felt good, for just a moment, to let some of the darkness go. "Tell me."

"Let's use Cougar."

What? That comment came right out of left field. "Go out and look for more bodies? Is that what you're saying? How will that help find more to the pattern?"

"Stay with me here. It's a little more complicated than finding bodies. Cougar is certified in human-remains detection, and that's his main job. The thing is, we've also trained quite a bit in trailing. You might say he's a multitalented kind of guy."

"I don't understand the distinction. You're going to have to explain in more detail."

"It's about scent discrimination. He's an expert at finding the odor of human decomposition, which is why we do what we do. Here's the thing with also learning to trail. It taught him how to follow a specific scent. He's not certified in it so I'd never deploy him on a mission, but he can sure do it."

Johnnie's point finally started to click for her. "You mean like what you see bloodhounds do on all the television shows?"

"Just like the TV shows, only better. If you can get something with Daniel's scent on it, like a shirt or a jacket, we can have Cougar track him. It might give us a clue where he's been going and what he's been doing. A little canine stalking, if you will. Turn the tables, so to speak."

Shantel had to think about that. The idea didn't repel her. In fact, she rather liked the plan. The problem? How could she get her hands on something of Daniel's? She hadn't taken anything of his when she left. A house Daniel-free in all respects was a big priority. The whole point had been to move on from the life that crushed her soul.

Then she thought about a key ring back home. A possibility clicked in her mind. "I'm pretty sure I still have a key to his house."

Johnnie clapped her hands. "A little larceny. I'm liking you more and more all the time."

Her eyes met Johnnie's, and despite her light tone, what she saw there wasn't light in the least. "I like you too." For at least a couple of seconds, thoughts of Daniel and obsession and murder disappeared.

A slow smile pulled up the corners of Johnnie's mouth. "Good."

For years and years and years, he'd dreamed of this moment. In his mind he'd built it up to levels no rational person could possibly achieve. Wrong on all counts. The reality of it surpassed every scenario he'd run through in his vivid imagination, every single one.

Freedom came as the most surprising result. He hadn't anticipated how untethered he'd feel, and a trickle of annoyance almost spoiled the moment when he decided he should have done it eons ago. Nothing now remained to hold him back, and the new world order, as he saw it, spread out before him full of possibilities.

First, he needed to tidy up. Earlier he'd left the asshole client's remains out in the open. That one didn't matter. Not a hunt and not a kill of any significance. Simply a means to an end for one who'd made a miscalculation of gigantic proportions. That it had been fun for Daniel came only as icing on the cake. As far as he was concerned, the sooner his remains were found, the better. He didn't want his treasured wilderness to be cluttered with trash like that.

This one was totally different—a kill of supreme importance more righteous than fun. It wasn't the sport he typically engaged in. Those had a different flavor to them and were special each in its own right. This one brought an almost orgasmic high, and he needed to clean it up carefully. He liked his secrets. Keeping them well hidden meant he could revisit them, which also let him relive the high over and over. A priceless benefit.

He'd most assuredly want to revisit this grave many times and suspected he'd enjoy the same high each and every time he returned to stand on the ground hiding his secret. It didn't take him long to tuck dear old dad away. Experience made him both tactical and skilled. He could find the right place in a matter of minutes and use the surrounding landscape to hide the disturbance until the natural world took control once more. His eidetic memory made it easy for him to find each and every special place. His frequent runs were, in many ways, reconnaissance missions.

He did have to go back to the car to get dressed and grab the foldable shovel he kept in the trunk. In human form he didn't possess the same speed, which was okay. No one else would be about this time of night. He'd run these woods enough to know exactly where to be in order to avoid detection. Easy for someone with his level of intelligence.

On the way back, he hummed the same little tune his mother used to sing to him when he was a child and couldn't sleep. Tonight, insomnia wouldn't be a problem for him. Instead, he'd sleep like a baby or a well-fed puppy.

CHAPTER TWENTY-FIVE

Johnnie couldn't recall a time when she'd ever experienced this level of excitement—or stress. She wasn't sure right now if she could distinguish between the two. She sat at the curb in front of the lovely two-story brick home on the upper South Hill. Considering everything Shantel shared about her ex, this neighborhood suited the man she'd described. It represented historic Spokane families and old money. From what Shantel explained, he possessed both and liked everyone to know.

All the windows were dark, and the driveway empty, although that didn't mean much since the house boasted a three-car garage. They watched for a few minutes to be sure he wasn't home. Then Shantel ran around to the back because she didn't want to risk someone witnessing her open the front door. Good plan. The only glitch would be the surveillance cameras attached to the garage and house. Shantel assured her they wouldn't be a problem.

Earlier they'd taken a quick trip to Shantel's house, and after digging through a drawer, she'd come up with a key ring complete with a set of house keys. She'd explained that Daniel had insisted she keep them because he'd expected her to move back in at some point. The picture of an arrogant, entitled man solidified in Johnnie's mind. That quirk on his part, however, made it easier for them to put Johnnie's plan into motion now, even if it took Shantel a while to remember where she'd tossed the keys.

Now, as she waited, Johnnie kept repeating, "Hurry, hurry, hurry." If they were even close to being right about this guy, getting caught in his house was the last thing they wanted to happen. The sooner Shantel got out of there, the better. Her gaze kept going to the visible camera on the corner of the garage.

While she waited, Johnnie also peered intently at the driver of every car that passed her. She made a point of remembering each vehicle, which, fortunately, were not many. Shantel finally trotted back down the driveway after what felt like an hour. According to the dash clock it had been seven minutes.

The overhead light came on when Shantel opened the passenger-side door, and Johnnie almost gasped at the sight of her pale face. "What happened?"

Shantel slid in, dropped the plastic bag she'd carried out of the house, and then clicked her seat belt into place. "Let's get out of here now."

Johnnie didn't wait to find out why. The tone in Shantel's voice told her everything. Once they were a good mile away, she finally spoke. "What happened in there?"

"I got one of his socks out of the laundry basket. Should be heavy with scent."

"Okay, that's great. Cougar can work with that. That's not what upset you, is it?"

"No."

"Tell me."

Shantel turned and gazed out the window. "I saw a bloody shirt on the bathroom floor."

Johnnie forgot all about the cameras. "Oh, fuck."

A shudder ran through Shantel as she closed her eyes and recalled the condition of the downstairs bathroom. Daniel hadn't changed much. He'd always favored that bathroom to clean up in when he'd come home particularly sweaty after a run. It had been his very vocal preference that the master bath be kept pristine. No dirty clothes on the floor. No untidy towels. No water spots on the glass shower doors. That's why she'd beelined for the downstairs bathroom. She'd be able to grab something quick and get out. Her plan had been spot-on.

She'd side-stepped the cameras, unlocked the door, and made it to the bathroom. All perfect until she'd seen that shirt on the floor.

Her theoretical discussions with Johnnie thus far intrigued her. Abstract and interesting, they kept her mind rolling without leaving room to get scared about how intense Daniel had become of late. The blood-smeared shirt took it all out of the remote realm and plopped it right into the here and now. Never would she have thought Daniel capable of violence, yet that shirt suggested the opposite. No bloody nose there or accidentally cut finger. The rational part of her said that evidence of a serial killer could make anyone jump at the slightest irregularity, like a bloody shirt on the bathroom floor. And, while she might be jumping to conclusions given everything they'd been involved with lately, she didn't think so. The chill she'd felt the moment she'd laid eyes on that shirt came from nothing short of evil.

"Well, now isn't that interesting."

"Frightening is more accurate." Her hands still shook.

Johnnie reached over and squeezed her shoulder. "It sure as shit is. What, inquiring minds would like to know, has he been up to?"

She turned in her seat and looked at Cougar, who rode in the back. "I'm hoping he can give a little more insight into that subject."

"I'm about half afraid to find out more now. I mean, here I've been all hot on proving werewolves really do exist, and all of a sudden, I'm a little freaked out."

"I'm more than a little freaked out. I lived with that man for a long time. What don't I know about him? What has he been doing? Who is he?"

Johnnie pulled over to the curb and turned in her seat. "Let's not jump to anything until we get more info. You're a scientist, so let's use your science to understand it. Don't let him freak you out."

"You and Cougar have your own science."

"We do, and we're going to start with our skill set. We'll just do what we do best and go from there. Okay?"

"The blood," she murmured and shivered.

Johnnie put her palm against her cheek. "One step at a time. Don't jump ahead, and don't let your ex get into your head."

Outside the window, deep darkness settled over the city. "We can't do it tonight."

Johnnie shook her head. "Definitely not tonight. We're going to need daylight. As soon as it gets light in the morning, we'll go. We can give some serious thought to where we want to start."

"Let's go back to your house and make our plans."

Johnnie smiled. "Now you're talking."

❖

Daniel's thoughts turned to Erin on the way home. She'd made it clear she didn't want him to come by, and in a way he understood. In another way, he didn't. He was her alpha, and that bond should be strong enough to override anything else, even Shantel's meddling. All his plans derailed just because Erin now knew that her Danny happened to also be Shantel's Daniel.

If only she'd waited a few more days, the full moon would happen, and nothing would be able to come between them at that point. With Erin at his back, he'd have righted what Shantel turned upside down. Unfortunate, though Erin's betrayal didn't alter his overall plans. He simply needed to revise them. His thoughts kept him occupied all the way into the house.

He stopped two feet in and lifted his head. "Well, well, well." He'd considered the Erin situation a surprise. This intrusion trumped that by a long shot.

"What have you been doing, my little darling?" Could be a quid-pro-quo situation. He'd let himself into her house, and now she'd come into his. No need to check the security cameras. Her scent lingered, and though faint, enough for one of his abilities to easily capture it. He smiled and clapped his hands.

Now he just needed to figure out why she'd come here. It wasn't like her. She hadn't stepped foot in this house since she moved out six months before the stupid divorce had been finalized. If she'd looked around, she'd have noticed he'd kept everything just as she left it. Her skill at decorating far surpassed his, and he liked what she'd done. The house felt like a home when she'd finished, and he wanted her to experience that comfort once she moved back in. He never would have guessed that she would venture here while he'd been out.

"Why were you here, my love?" He continued to follow her scent from the back door, through the kitchen, and into the first-floor bathroom. His shirt still lay on the floor where he'd dropped it. Typically, he didn't leave a mess like this. The call from his father had interrupted him.

That she'd come in here wasn't a question. Her scent lingered within the walls of the small room. He inhaled deeply and closed his eyes, letting sensation wash over him. He missed the smell of her.

He opened his eyes and dropped his gaze to the crumpled shirt. He picked it up, and stared at it. No way to overlook the blood he'd wiped on the sleeve. A smart woman like Shantel wouldn't miss that detail. What would she think of it? Without any context, she'd have to assume it came from something as simple as a bloody nose. A good assumption except she would be aware he didn't suffer from bloody noses.

Best not to take chances. He went to the kitchen, pulled a trash bag from the pantry, and returned to the bathroom, where he picked up the bloody shirt and stuffed it into the bag. He'd kill two birds with one stone, so to speak.

Back out in the car, he tossed the bag into the driver's seat as he backed out of the driveway. Halfway to Shantel's house, he stopped at a coffee shop. Closed for the night, the windows were dark and, more important, the parking lot empty. He pulled next to the dumpster, got out, and tossed the garbage bag into the big yellow container. The black plastic lid banged as he dropped it, and he glanced around. Satisfied that no one heard or saw him, he got behind the wheel and drove away, the dirty deed completed.

At Shantel's house, disappointment made him frown. Dark and quiet again. She still wasn't home, her behavior totally unacceptable. He tried her cell without success. In consistent style, she ignored him. He'd have been more surprised if she'd taken the call. A guy could still hope.

The night was growing deep and dark as he waited. Normally she'd be home by now, either working in her home office or relaxing in front of the television. She wasn't in her office or watching a mindless comedy.

He whispered into the darkness. "What are you up to, my princess? Not like you to change things up like this."

By eleven, he gave up. As much as he wanted to stomp on the accelerator and race away from her house, he didn't. It wouldn't be good strategy to let temper draw attention to a car sitting outside her house. Not all the windows in the neighborhood were dark, and people were quick to take pictures and videos these days and post them all over social media. Best to be a normal guy driving down the street minding his own business.

He studied everything on his way home. He hated the world as it stood because it denied him his true nature and made it out to be something unbelievable or mocked. It wasn't right and never had been. He owed nothing and deserved everything. Time for the world to change to suit him.

CHAPTER TWENTY-SIX

Johnnie tossed and turned for hours, her mind not wanting to turn off. They'd developed what she considered a solid plan by the time they headed to their respective bedrooms a little before midnight. Funny how she already thought of the guest room as Shantel's.

Every time she woke up, she thought about their discussions. She hadn't met this Daniel, yet every instinct screamed bad man. Shantel insisted he'd never given her any reason to think him violent, and she got the validity of that belief, but her gut said otherwise. The proof might be hidden, but she felt certain it existed. All they needed to do was find it.

Breaking into Shantel's house went beyond what a reluctant ex-husband would do. Lots of people got divorced, with one of the duo having trouble letting go. Far fewer continued to show up, send gifts, and go to the trouble to break into the house of an ex-spouse. The ones that did? They often made the six o'clock news.

In Daniel's case, everything Shantel shared with her painted the picture of a rich, entitled man who also happened to be borderline brilliant. That scared her too. Money always upped the ante. Throw in brains and it got doubly frightening. She also thought about how many of the truly brilliant stepped over the line to mental illness. She couldn't help wondering if that were the case with Daniel.

At five, she finally gave up and rolled out of bed. She'd gotten maybe two or three hours of sleep total. It would have to do. It wouldn't be the first time she went out to work in the field with Cougar with only a few hours of rest. Part of the gig. Search-and-rescue meant being on call 24/7.

She had just finished her first cup of coffee when she noticed Shantel standing in the kitchen doorway. Interesting that she hadn't heard her. Cougar, who was outside, normally would have made a fuss over a morning guest. Not that she had many overnight guests who weren't family. Maybe he was growing accustomed to Shantel's presence in their house.

"Good morning." She smiled. "Coffee?"

Shantel nodded and moved to the table. "I'd love it."

"How'd you sleep?"

"Like crap." She leaned her elbows on the table and rested her head in her hands.

Johnnie snorted and was instantly mortified. Way to impress. "I can relate to that." Yeah, she sounded cool.

"I kept thinking about that bloody shirt."

"Me too." She walked over and handed her a mug of coffee.

Shantel took the mug and set it down without taking a sip. "I have a doctorate, for Christ's sake, yet all of a sudden I feel like a complete idiot. How could I be so oblivious when it came to him?"

Johnnie acted on instinct and put her arms around Shantel. "You're not an idiot, and we don't want to jump to any conclusions yet. Even if he turns out to be what we think he might be, that still doesn't reflect back on you."

"How can it not?"

"Because that makes him a psychopath, and you know as well as I do that those kinds of people are masters at manipulation and cover-up. It's not on you."

"I lived with him."

"So did other women who had no idea their husbands and lovers were serial killers."

She stiffened in her arms, and Johnnie held her tighter. "I still feel sick."

Without giving herself time to resist, she kissed the top of Shantel's head. "You're entitled, but we're in this together. You're not crazy, and you're not alone."

Shantel turned in the chair and wrapped her arms around Johnnie's waist. Through tears, she said, "Thank you."

❖

Having Johnnie close to her was all it took for Shantel to unravel. Sobs shook her shoulders, and without thinking, she stood and wrapped her arms around Johnnie's neck. The scent of lavender soap filled her senses, and she tightened her grasp. She wanted to stay right here and forget the insanity growing with each passing hour.

Johnnie brushed the hair away from her face as she sprinkled kisses on the top of her head. "It's okay," she said softly. "I'm here for you. You're safe."

"I'm sorry." She stepped back a little, though she didn't fully break contact. The nearness of Johnnie steadied her, and a sense of being home didn't hurt either. "I don't typically fall apart."

Johnnie's small smile lit up her face. "Gee. Getting pulled into a serial-killer investigation, your ex-husband stalking you, and now finding a missing woman's necklace in your desk drawer, presumably placed there by said ex, and you're apologizing? Beautiful woman, you have exactly zero to apologize for."

She returned the smile. "How can you always be so upbeat? I've never met anyone like you."

Johnnie shrugged. "Upbeat is just one of my natural gifts."

Without stopping to think, Shantel kissed her, right on the lips. Warmth exploded in her, and the despair of seconds ago vanished. Then she jumped back. "Oh, my God. I'm so sorry."

Johnnie caressed her cheek. "I'm so not."

Those three words changed everything. She stepped back into Johnnie's arms and leaned into the kiss. This time, it was slow and full of heat like she'd never experienced before. Yes, she'd dated after leaving Daniel, and, yes, she'd kissed other women. This was different, like the universe opened up and welcomed her into a new world.

She moved her hands across Johnnie's back. Nothing on beneath the T-shirt. She didn't think she could get any hotter, but she was wrong. Her pulse started to race, and the fire inside her raged.

"I need more," she whispered against Johnnie's lips. "I want more."

Johnnie whispered back, "Ask and thou shall receive."

An hour later, Shantel opened her eyes and smiled.

"Feel better?" Johnnie asked.

She rolled over and met Johnnie's eyes. "I do."

"Funny thing. I do too. You got a little sleep."

"How long?"

"About twenty minutes. Ugh…" Cougar jumped right into the middle of Johnnie.

Shantel laughed and rubbed Cougar's head. "You're a beautiful boy."

"And heavy."

"I'm ready to face today now."

"I'm ready to face a lot of todays now." Johnnie kissed her.

Shantel laughed, rolled out of the bed, and headed toward the bathroom. "This girl has to clean up first."

Johnnie followed. "I'll wash your back."

Daniel went back to Shantel's house first thing in the morning. His phone rang while he sat studying the house from down the block. The expected call came a little later than he would have imagined. Mother must have slept in. A bottle of vodka polished off could do that to even the most seasoned.

"Have you talked to your father?"

"Not since last night." Not a lie. His last conversation with the old man had, in fact, been late last night. The only detail he left out was the part about it being after he left the family home. Mother would assume their last conversation had been at the front door while he'd been leaving—the usual berating him about being a poor son. He'd let her believe that. She'd make a very good witness that way.

"He appears to have left last night and hasn't returned."

"Did you check with his *assistant?*" Honestly, he couldn't resist that one, even as much as he loved his mother. Sometimes her refusal to see Senior for the complete and total asshole that he is—was—pissed him off. A tiny twinge of regret assailed him after the words left his mouth. But only a tiny twinge.

"I didn't call you because of your complaints about your father. I've heard them too many times. Get over it, Daniel. Haven't you figured out by now I don't give a tinker's damn about his whores?"

Whoa. Mommy was on a roll this morning. He kind of admired her spunk. Not something that happened often or when relatively sober. "My apologies."

"Insincere as they might be, I accept. Now, do you have any helpful thoughts on where your father might be?"

"Did you try the office? He will crash on his office sofa when it gets late." He didn't add, with his legal assistant and pants down. No sense really pushing her buttons. She'd pretty much made her position clear.

"Of course I tried the office. I'm not stupid."

The bit of snap in her voice made him wonder if she had a bit of intuition going. Fueled by morning coffee fortified by her favorite vodka, perhaps she sensed Senior wouldn't be coming home at all. Technically not incorrect. At some point in time, he'd return. In a box. If he got a say, it would be a beat-to-shit cardboard box, because that's all the old bastard deserved. Mother wouldn't see it that way. She'd make certain all was supremely proper, with an expensive coffin befitting a man of his standing in the community. Made him want to throw up. Or, better yet, shit on said coffin.

"Mother, I'm not sure where else he got off to." Now he did lie, but damn if he didn't do it well. "You'll just have to wait him out. You know how he can be. He loves to make a grand entrance. Adds to his self-importance."

Her sigh was audible. "That he does. Please don't be like him in that respect."

"I do my best, Mother." He wasn't like his father in any respect because he actually possessed the supremacy his father only dreamed of.

"See that you do. Call me if you see or hear from him."

"Of course." Wouldn't be a problem, given he'd never hear or see from Senior again. Perfection on a nice sunny morning.

He ended the conversation and glanced back at Shantel's house. Just as quiet as last night. Not acceptable. High time for her to get back to normal. Though he'd been waiting for the power of the full moon to make everything turn, it might be wise to speed things up, as in no more waiting at all. Yes, it all solidified in his mind.

When the moon rose tonight, things were going to change.

CHAPTER TWENTY-SEVEN

Johnnie wondered if she'd ever felt as alive as she did right now. With Shantel in the passenger seat and Cougar in the back, they were off on their rather bizarre fact-finding mission. She wished they'd been able to glean more information. Rick said he'd come by last night and then called to say he'd talk with them today. He'd gotten another call-out right after leaving Shantel's office, and from the sound of his voice, wasn't exactly happy about it. She felt for him. Poor guy was getting hammered right and left.

Johnnie and Shantel carried their fully charged phones. When Rick called, they would be readily available. In the meantime, they put their own plan into motion. Cougar could do the job, even if tracking wasn't his primary skill set. He'd rocked it every time they'd worked in the discipline and could do it again today. The plastic bag at Shantel's feet held a sock full of Daniel's scent—all they needed to give it a credible shot.

They decided to go with trailhead starts in the areas Shantel indicated he preferred. Or at least he had during the time they'd been together. They couldn't dismiss the possibility he could have changed his habits after she left him, but they had to go with what they had.

They started at the Seven Mile trailhead. As Shantel explained, always one of his favorite places to run and cycle. It would be a good test for Cougar, given its immense popularity with the outdoor-loving community. He'd have to try to find a direction of travel in a highly contaminated area, if one existed.

At the trailhead, she skipped putting Cougar in his vest. This wasn't official, and she didn't want anyone to think they were working for the sheriff's department. Cougar never cared because work was work, vest or not. For the dogs, it became very simple. While no vest, she did put on his trailing harness. Given they were in Riverside State Park, she would obey the rules and put him on a long line. The last thing they wanted was for someone to report an off-lead dog. Rick would not be pleased, and personally, she didn't want a $250 ticket.

"So," she said as she clipped the long line to the harness. "He may or may not pick up something. If Daniel has been here recently, he can grab it. If not, we'll have to try somewhere else. It's a crap shoot. Cold trails are incredibly difficult, despite some handlers telling you their dogs are capable of following ice-cold ones. They're either full of it or delusional. Some people want to believe it so much, they convince themselves it's true. I fall on the it's-not side of the argument."

Shantel nodded. "I understand."

She wasn't sure she really did. Most people saw television shows where the dogs appear to do the impossible. Too many handlers reaching for glory claimed credit where it wasn't due, which made it difficult for the many wonderfully skilled teams in the field for all the right reasons and with all the requisite skills. They didn't claim the impossible. They worked instead with professional dedication.

"Ready?" When Shantel nodded, she opened the plastic bag and held it to Cougar's nose. He inhaled deeply, and she closed the bag and handed it to Shantel. To Cougar, she said, "Search."

Ten minutes in the large area and then she called it. "Nothing here." Shantel's expression darkened, and Johnnie put a hand on her shoulder. "Remember, if it's been a while since he was here, Cougar won't pick up his scent. It just doesn't stay here that long, even if TV makes it look that way. Don't get discouraged. We're just getting started."

"But he found bodies buried years ago."

"That's different. Here, he's searching for the specific scent of a specific individual. Human-remains detection means that he's trained to detect the odor of human decomposition. It's scent specific, just not individual specific. Does that make sense?"

"It does, of course." Her face still held shadows. "I was hoping…"

Johnnie gave her a hug. "Cougar and I are always hoping. Don't let it get you down. The first rule of searching is you'll probably find nothing."

"Really?"

"Really. In more searches than not, we don't find a thing. The last few days have been unique, to say the least. Cougar has done far more negative searches than positive ones. The nature of the beast."

"Oh." Her shoulders slumped.

She squeezed her again. "No giving up. Again, we're just getting started."

Two hours and two more trailheads. Nothing. "Okay, one more and we call it a day." Her own hopes were beginning to dim despite the constant encouragement she'd been giving Shantel. It sounded like such a good idea when she first lobbed it at Shantel. And after the beautiful start to the morning, she'd really believed they'd have some measure of success.

This time they traveled to the opposite side of the city. Far up on the South Hill, they parked in the newly completed parking area for a county-owned natural area. Three other cars were in the lot. Normal for a nice day.

They repeated their preparations for the fourth time. Despite the lack of success in the other three locations, Cougar's high level of enthusiasm didn't wane. She loved his work ethic. He could go for hours without giving up on the hunt or losing his focus. He truly was a one-of-a-kind dog who loved his job.

Ready to go, she leaned down, let him sniff the sock inside the bag, and one more time said, "Search."

His head went down to the ground, and he began to move with intention. "That's different," Shantel said.

"Nice read," Johnnie told her as her own hopes rose. The difference in his body language the second his head went down was what she'd been hoping for. Cougar had scent.

While Shantel might not be an expert on canine search teams, she could tell that everything just changed. The body language for both dog and handler was completely different from their last stops. A thrill raced through her, and the discouragement that followed her here disappeared in an instant.

Several trails led into the wilderness from the parking lot, and Cougar started toward the lower path. Johnnie moved easily behind him as she handled with practiced skill the bright orange line she guessed to be at least fifteen feet long. She managed to keep hold of it no matter what direction, how fast, or how slow Cougar moved. Impressive.

He stayed on the path for only about a hundred meters and then veered right and into the thick pine trees that covered the hillside. He moved quickly up and up, and her breathing became labored as she tried to keep them in sight. Daniel loved hill running and always told her it filled him with power. He'd been big on power, in all its forms and if he could show up anyone, but especially other men, all the better. Early on in their relationship, she'd rolled with it. Later, it made her want to scream and run in the opposite direction. She supposed, in a way, that's what she'd done, sans the screaming, that is.

Near the top of the hill, Cougar slowed, and to Shantel it appeared that something in his behavior changed. He'd been charging with intensity through the woods and up the hillside with his nose near the ground. Now, his head came up, and he smelled the air, or that's how it appeared to her.

"Is something wrong?" She came up behind Johnnie, who'd stopped and was watching Cougar intently.

Johnnie shook her head. "No, but this is pretty fucking weird."

"What is?"

"He's in scent."

"I get that. It was pretty clear to see he was following Daniel's trail."

She slowly shook her head. "No. That's not what I mean. He's in scent for human remains. What you're seeing is his change in behavior when he's caught a scent cone. Something's here, and it's not a good something."

Dread dropped to the pit of her stomach. "Oh, no."

"Oh, yes."

Johnnie unhooked the long line from Cougar's harness, winding it up and slipping it over her shoulder. Cougar didn't notice as he began to move with intention through the trees. She understood what Johnnie told her. His movements were not the same as when he'd been following a trail from the parking lot. He searched in a completely different way, his focus intense.

He continued up the hill, working the air and covering a lot more area than either Johnnie or Shantel could do as mere humans. Near the top of the hill and beneath a massive ponderosa pine, he slowed and then went down. His big head turned, and he stared at Johnnie, his eyes intense.

"Son of a bitch." Johnnie ran up to where Cougar waited for her. She was pulling her phone out of her pocket as Shantel reached them.

What she saw chilled her. "You better call Rick."

Johnnie had her phone to her ear. "Already on it."

Daniel's stakeout at Shantel's yielded nothing. She simply didn't come home. Earlier he'd picked up a burner phone and tried her office, rationalizing that she'd take the call if it wasn't his number. He had no idea where to go next. Except, perhaps, he did have another avenue for gleaning information about his beloved. Erin might be pissed off at him, but he could sway her. She'd come back to his side. No one could resist him forever.

Like Shantel's, Erin's house was quiet. He knocked loudly and waited, tapping his foot. He didn't turn around and leave because when he peeked through her garage window, her car was parked in the same place as when he'd last been here. That she didn't answer the door could mean a couple of things. First, she could still be mad at him for his supposed deception, or second, someone picked her up and she was simply gone for the day. That no sound at all came from inside made him wonder more than become concerned.

He went to the back door and tried the knob. Open. He took that as a sign signaling for permission to enter and walked into the kitchen. Tidy and clean. No half-full coffee cup. No breakfast plate. It didn't look like anything had happened in here for hours.

At the stairs, he paused. Her scent wafted down strong enough that he felt certain she was here. The odd part, not so much as a creak indicated she might be up there. Things were a little strange, so he might as well check it out. He didn't bother to try to sneak up the stairs. Even if he scared her, she'd relax the moment she saw him. Her anger surely had cooled by now. No one could stay mad at him. Even before he'd been turned, he'd been skilled at turning on the charm.

The empty bathroom gave away nothing except to highlight that it hadn't been used for a while. He passed by the two bedrooms, heading for the master. Then he stopped at the door and sighed. "Damn."

He'd seen it happen once before, and the old ones warned against cutting the young ones loose too soon. He'd been a mere bystander last time. If he was being honest, it didn't feel a whole lot different. A little bit of a letdown, given he'd wanted to release some of the tension caused by not being able to find Shantel. Now she'd gone and ruined that plan.

The risk of madness existed in every population, and his was no different. The majority of those turned took to it well. Some, like him, exceptionally well. Others, like Erin, went in a different direction, the final result permanent. Unlike the legends and stories told around the campfires, it didn't take a silver bullet to end it all. Good, old-fashioned methods worked as well as a shiny bullet or a polished sword.

Nothing he could do for her and nothing he could get from her. Besides, he didn't care for messes. He turned around and walked back down the hallway. Weariness made him consider taking a nap in one of the guest rooms. It wasn't like she'd object. He continued past the two rooms and down the stairs. He opted not to stay here, where disappointment added to the weariness. Someone would find her eventually, and they'd all wonder why the bright doctoral student had taken her own life. They'd never get their answer because he would be the only one who really knew what drove her to the bottle of pills and glass of liquor.

That reminded him why he'd resisted bringing Shantel into his world. His love for her eclipsed everything, and to run the risk that she might take the same path as Erin? Unthinkable. She had to be protected at all costs.

Still…

CHAPTER TWENTY-EIGHT

Rick allowed them to stay and view the excavation, and given the gravity of the situation, it was a big favor on his part. Like all the others, grids were laid out and white suits donned. This time Shantel stood with Johnnie as they watched the techs do their work. The county had an exceptional forensics unit, and no one doubted their skill at retrieving the body and all the relevant evidence. It was more than the fact the county could do the job that excluded her from this one. Part of the discovery, it would be inappropriate for Shantel to work it, even as much as she wanted to.

They watched in silence, everyone somber in the face of yet another victim of the mystery killer. What no one expected came at the end. Beth, running point for the unit again, gasped as she used a brush to move dirt from the victim's face. She stood up and stepped away from the clandestine gravesite. Only when she had moved outside the tape did she speak. "Rick..."

"What's wrong?"

Beth pointed. "I know who that is."

"Say what?"

"I recognize him is more accurate. I went to school with one of his kids."

"And?"

"Daniel Rodger."

Shantel grabbed Johnnie's arm in a vise grip. "What?"

The expression on Rick's face grew dark, and he held up a hand to cut off anything else Shantel might have been ready to say. Johnnie thought she understood. "Age?"

Beth clarified. "It's Rodger senior. Not the hotshot oldest kid who likes to dispute our solid evidence."

Shantel's grip on her arm relaxed, though not by a lot. "Senior?"

Rick turned to Shantel. "You go to school with his kid too?"

Beth tilted her head and studied Shantel. "No. You didn't go to our school."

She shook her head. "I'm not from around here. But, Daniel Rodger Sr. is my ex-father-in-law."

Rick's expression cleared. "Father of the same guy who messed with your office."

"Yes."

"Holy crap," Beth muttered.

"Back to my question." Rick said as he turned to Beth. "What do *you* know about him?"

"A difficult man, but I can't believe anyone would want to kill him like this."

The name rang familiar to Johnnie, though she knew nothing about Daniel Sr. beyond his connection to Shantel. As she thought about it, she put two and two together. An old, wealthy Spokane family whose name immediately brought up images of the massive homes on Rockwood Boulevard. As a teenager, they'd drive by the homes on the tree-lined street and make up stories about those who lived there. None of the people who resided in the fancy houses were in the circles her family rolled with. It made her wonder about Shantel. Despite their amazing morning and their strong connection, did they come from two different worlds? Shantel ran in high circles. Hers were most definitely on the middle-class side.

Shantel took her hand, and all of a sudden, she didn't care where either of them hailed from. All that mattered was the here and now. Right here, right now, they were together. "I don't like the feel of this."

Shantel shook her head slightly. "Neither do I. We need to find Daniel." Her eyes met Rick's.

"We're already checking him out," Rick said.

Johnnie didn't like the sound of that. "You need to do more than check him out. There's a lot you don't know about him."

Shantel squeezed her hand. "He's working on it."

Rick's narrowed eyes now met hers. "What precisely do you mean by that, Johnnie? What don't I know about him?"

Again, Shantel squeezed her hand. Message received. "He's just an asshole. That's all I meant."

"Right…"

"Probably time for us to leave."

"Keep your phones on."

Johnnie knew when it was time to exit stage left.

Back in the car, Shantel turned to Johnnie. "This is wrong."

"You think?"

"I hate to say it, but I believe Daniel did this." Her hands curled in her lap. She didn't like Daniel's father. She also didn't wish him dead.

"I agree. It's my first assumption too. I also don't want to jump to conclusions. I don't work that way. Kind of like the history books I write. Don't take anything at face value. Dig deeper."

"No. I don't want to jump to any conclusions either, and I'd be disappointed if you did."

"Nice that you're not disappointed. For the record, I really like that scientific mind of yours. Still, your ex is looking pretty good for all this."

"You think he's a werewolf?"

"I'm convinced he's a killer, and I'm beginning to lean really hard in the direction of werewolf."

"You want to believe it." At this point Shantel didn't disbelieve. She also didn't quite believe either.

Johnnie paused. "I suppose I do. The kid in me who was sure she'd seen one really wants to be validated. The adult in me has a bad feeling about a guy who's showing all the signs of being someone capable of murder. Does that make him the werewolf I've been searching for most of my life? I don't know."

As much as Shantel wanted to disagree, she didn't have it in her. She'd been uneasy for a while now. Daniel's obsession had been ramping up. Too intense to pass off as merely a heartbroken man who didn't want to let go of a relationship. People often struggled in those situations, and this thing with him went deeper and darker. Because she didn't want to deal with the reality of it, she found ways to rationalize his behavior and her lack of action. For a smart woman, sometimes she could embrace dumb quite well.

Outside the car window, scores of law enforcement went about their work. The press trickled in, and soon the cameras would be rolling. Out of the corner of her eye she saw a reporter heading their way.

"We need to get out of here."

Johnnie glanced in the rearview mirror and started the car. "We don't need that, on top of everything else."

"No, we don't."

The reporter's disappointment was easy to see as they pulled away before he could reach them. Even if he had made it to her window, she embraced a simple rule in situations like this: no comment.

Johnnie drove toward town. "What now?"

She'd been thinking about that same question since she'd glimpsed Daniel Sr.'s lifeless face, dirt marring the features that even in death were stern and humorless. "We have to find him."

Daylight was boring. He had to pretend to like people he didn't. Had to work behind a desk when all he wanted to do was run through the great outdoors. Had to keep up appearances so as not to sully the good family name. The only fun time was during a criminal trial. When he got to play the chess game that criminal defense entailed, that's when he felt almost as alive as when he ran through the woods under the full moon. Almost, because nothing rivaled the sheer joy of that.

Now he allowed the weariness to wash over him. Thwarted in all his good intentions this morning, he would recharge and let the day wane. Later, he would enjoy the night and all the benefits of being himself. He'd build his world the way he'd desired for so long. He'd take the step he'd been hesitant to before now. No guts, no glory. The old man used that phrase a million times or more. Wouldn't hear it again, now would he? He tipped his head back and laughed.

An idea struck him, and he rolled with it. Lately, despite the interference of the police, he'd had some of his most brilliant ideas. He turned his car around and drove back to Shantel's, resisting the urge to park right in her driveway. Hiding didn't appeal to him any longer. Too much water under the bridge at this point.

He nonetheless parked a good block away and walked casually to the house. As empty as his last few trips here. The unusual extended absence told quite a story. What exactly was she up to? He intended to get the answer. The secrets that put a wall between them before had to come down. That would be the only way they'd be in a position to share their eternity. The truth would set them free. Again, he laughed at his own turn of phrase. No wonder juries loved him.

With the stolen key he carried in his pocket at all times, he let himself in. After the wine gift, he was a little surprised she hadn't changed the locks. Not a good sign for someone as smart and well-educated as Shantel. Perhaps of little significance when thinking of everything overall. She'd be moving out of here soon enough, and thus a change of locks would be an unnecessary expense, especially since she survived on a university salary. Not exactly up to the kind of money he brought down. She deserved a better standard of living than her income provided, and he would give her that and more.

He did give her props for a comfortable bed. He closed his eyes and relaxed seconds after stretching out on it. Her scent flowed over him, both soothing and exciting. He leaned toward soothing at the moment. Exciting would come later.

The trill of his cell phone brought him upright. The light had receded since he'd drifted off into slumber earlier, the room now dark and full of shadows. He shook off the remains of sleep and pulled the phone from his pocket. "Yes."

His mother's voice had a raw edge to it. "They found him."

All traces of sleep vanished. Good thing she hadn't video-called him. The smile on his face would most certainly offend her sense of propriety. "I presume you mean Father, but who is they?" No mystery about the who. Just had to play the game.

"I do mean your father." Her voice rose. Mother never did handle stress well unless she had plenty of vodka on board. She liked to hide and pretend all things in her world were perfect and pretty. She turned a blind eye to anything that conflicted with that view.

"All right," he replied with exaggerated calmness. "Father has been found."

"He's been found dead."

He continued the game. "Probably cardiac arrest in the middle of an orgasm."

She ignored the dig. "Murder."

"No way. He was an asshole, but that's a little extreme even for his enemies."

"Be respectful. He was your father."

"Sorry." Not sorry. His father earned the moniker of asshole, and his mother's denial, or her gallons of vodka, could never change that fact.

"They won't let me see him."

His smile enlarged. "I'll talk with them. I have some friends on the force."

"I deserve more respect."

"I'll talk to them."

"You do that, and then you call me. I want this handled today."

"Mother, if it's murder…"

"Today."

"I'll do what I can." He ended the call. She could go on like this for hours, and he'd learned a long time ago to cut her off. A nice dirty martini or twelve, and her world would once again be orderly.

He swung his feet to the floor and stretched his arms over his head. God, he felt good. Napping on Shantel's bed for several hours made all the difference. His promise to call law enforcement about his father had been empty. He didn't intend to call anyone. Besides, no need to ask what happened. His intimate knowledge could fill in all the holes for them while they wouldn't be able to tell him one damn thing.

CHAPTER TWENTY-NINE

Johnnie bit her lip. How she wished she and Cougar could do more. She said as much to Shantel as they sat not far from her ex-husband's home. They'd been here once already without success. They tried his office. Again, nothing. No sign of Daniel or his car. They'd come back hoping that maybe he'd returned in the interim.

"Are you kidding me? Do more?"

She drummed her fingers on the steering wheel. "It hasn't been enough. We haven't been able to find him." Frustrating. The haunting thought at the back of her mind that warned until they found him Shantel remained in danger refused to leave her.

"Dear God, woman. This has all happened because of you. You and that incredible dog of yours have brought this all to light. We will find him."

"Rick wants us to stand down." A marked cruiser pulled into Daniel's driveway. Were they being tracked? Rick would be less than happy to find them here.

Shantel sighed. "I think that's our cue to leave."

"Definitely. No big deal, given we know he's not here." They'd parked down the street, just in case. Shantel used her key to get them into the house, and this time they didn't even bother to worry about the cameras. Screw him. After she recovered from her first reaction to the house, which was *damn*, they got down to business. When Shantel said he was loaded, she hadn't been kidding. They searched, top to bottom. The disappointing part: nothing, nada, nyet.

The downstairs bathroom where Shantel found the bloody shirt was now so clean it sparkled. Johnnie's singular thought: obsessive-compulsive. No shirt, no nothing. Even the hamper where she'd grabbed the sock had been emptied, almost as if he'd intuited someone had been there and seen what could be damning evidence.

She'd so wanted to find any clue that might validate her belief that Daniel, the high-powered criminal-defense attorney, led a double life. Instead, they found only expensive suits, expensive furniture, and paintings purchased to impress. Didn't take a licensed professional to make that call. The guy wanted everyone to believe him to be all that. It made her wonder all the more how Shantel stuck it out in the marriage as long as she had.

"It's too…" She started thinking out loud.

"Too what?" Shantel sounded defeated.

She walked around the living room, waving her arms towards the paintings and the high-end leather furniture. She pointed to the oriental rug that no one had to tell her didn't come from a department store.

"Too contrived. Like he's painting a picture for everyone to see and believe, and it has nothing to do with the real guy underneath. There's no authentic representation here. It's all an image contrived to lead the viewer to a place of his choosing. To the person he wants everyone to believe he is."

Shantel leaned her head back and closed her eyes. "You're right. I just never thought about it like that before. I kept my eyes closed to reality because it was the easy route. When I think back on everything now, it fits. He always had to have things so particular, like if they weren't, the world would end."

"Or you'd see him for what he really is."

She opened her eyes. "Yes."

"Like a werewolf."

She didn't blink. "Yes."

❖

The last few hours made Shantel think about things in a completely different way. After learning about Daniel's father, she'd been unable to shake the uncomfortable feeling that everything about her ex-husband had been a lie.

With a deep sigh, Johnnie said, "I wish Cougar could track him now. I can't tell you how much I want to find him."

Johnnie squeezed her arm in a gesture that was becoming familiar and powerful in the amount of comfort it provided. Shantel patted her hand in return. "Cougar has done so much. I just don't think he can help us now. It's like Daniel has figured out we're on his trail." She thought about the call earlier from Rick and the admonishment about trying to find Daniel. They were actively searching for him, and yet here they were outside his house. "We'll figure this out."

"We will." Determination made Johnnie's words come out hard, and she understood the emotion behind them.

"We don't want to trip over Rick." She watched the officers get out of the car and head to Daniel's front porch. "We better go before someone spots us."

"What's your next thought? You know him as well as anyone."

A month ago, even a week ago, she'd have said that statement was true. Now she wondered if anyone knew him. Think. She had to think. Where would Daniel go? "Give me a second."

"I'm going to start driving. I don't want to risk Rick seeing us here. He'll be pissed, and we do not want to go there."

Nothing came to her. She closed her eyes and leaned her head back. When she'd been in grad school and exams loomed, she developed a ritual to help her relax before each one. It helped her then, and she hoped it would help her now. She concentrated on her breath. In through the nose. Out through the lips. By the fifth repetition, an idea struck.

"Go back to the beginning."

"What do you mean?" Johnnie drummed her fingers on the steering wheel, and Shantel decoded the movement as concentration rather than stress. In their brief time together, she'd already begun to identify how Johnnie reacted in certain situations. Like a couple who communicated easily without ever saying a word.

"Back to the Fish Lake area."

Johnnie glanced sideways at her. "With all the police activity, who in their right mind would go back there?"

"That's what makes rational sense."

"We're not dealing with rational here."

"Exactly. You can't rationalize with the irrational."

"That's brilliant, Doc! Let's do it."

Cougar whined in the backseat as if he wanted to add his voice. Shantel reached back and rubbed his head. "It's starting to get pretty dark." Perhaps tomorrow would be a better day to continue the search. If she didn't have such a bad feeling, that's what she'd suggest. Yet something in the back of her mind said they needed to find him now. No waiting until the sun rose again. It would be too late.

"All right. We'll give it another go and let Cougar run, do his thing. At this point we have nothing to lose."

She was about to disagree and argue that they had a lot to lose when her cell phone rang. A glance at the display made her stomach drop. "No way."

"What?"

As she put the phone to her ear, she said, "Hello, Daniel."

Her voice made him smile. It reminded him of bells. Not the clanging-church-tower-bells variety but more the melodious, gentle sounds of the bell ringers in a church choir. Beautiful and soothing. "It's time."

Her pause was barely discernable. It couldn't go on forever like it had been. They would have to come face-to-face at some point. That point was now.

"Where?"

A hard edge to that single word. Not at all like his loving wife. They'd have to work on that. Her preferred gentle subservience.

He'd already given great thought to the inevitable question. "Our place."

"At this time of night?"

He'd expected her question, if not outright resistance. "It's important."

"What have you done, Daniel?"

"Everything I've done has been for you."

"Did you kill your father?"

He almost laughed and caught himself. She wouldn't get it, no matter how detailed an explanation he gave, so better to leave it be. "We can talk about that later."

"I don't want to drive up there tonight. It's dark, and that road is narrow and dangerous."

"If you want to see me, that's where I'll be."

"Fine," she snapped.

"Come alone. This is between you and me."

"How can I be sure I won't end up like your father?"

Good point. Smart woman, that Shantel of his. "I would never hurt you, and you can take that to the bank."

"I don't trust you."

"Have I ever lied to you?"

This time her pause was longer and more noticeable. "I don't know."

"Come on, Shantel. Don't be stupid. If I wanted to hurt you, I could have done it a thousand times over."

"There you are."

Damn it, she'd baited him, and he fell for it. "Sweetheart, I swear, you'll be safe. Just meet me, let's talk, and then you can do whatever you feel is necessary."

All he had to do was get her there, and then it would be a simple matter to bring her into his world. Once there, she'd never want to leave him. It would be brilliant, and she wouldn't take the same path as Erin. He had to believe that.

"Fine. Give me an hour."

"I'll be waiting."

He ended the call, walked out the door of the Vista House, and stood gazing out over the mountain where, soon, he'd reunite with Shantel, and the life they deserved would begin.

CHAPTER THIRTY

Y ou're where?" Rick's anger wasn't unpredicted.
"Heading to the Vista House on Mt. Spokane."
"What in the actual fuck, Johnnie!"

She'd expected him to be pissed. She didn't anticipate almost experiencing a slap on her head through the phone. "He called Shantel and wanted to meet her in their special place."

"Damn it, Johnnie. You should have called me immediately."

"I'm calling you now."

"Big fucking deal. You both could be dead by the time we get there. Where are you exactly?"

She scrutinized the area. Though it was dark and a bit cloudy, she maintained her bearings. Each year the county did a mock exercise on the mountain, and she'd been here enough times to have a better than fair idea of her location. It would be nice if she'd grabbed her GPS, and then she'd have been able to give Rick her exact coordinates. Since that wasn't possible, she described her location as best she could. He'd be able to figure it out. He knew this mountain better than she did.

"Where's Shantel?" His voice had gone low, not a good sign.

This question she didn't want to answer. "She's gone on up to the Vista House."

"Alone?" Even lower this time.

"He told her she had to come alone."

"And you let her?" She liked it better when he screamed at her.

"She didn't give me a choice."

"For Christ's sake, Johnnie. Please tell me you at least have Cougar with you. That dog is smarter than the two of you put together."

"Yes. Cougar's with me."

"Why the fuck did he want to meet her up there at this time of night?"

"Apparently, it's the first place he brought her to when he convinced her to move here. Roses and champagne. Moonlight and magic, and all that romantic stuff. That's why he kept calling it their special place."

"Great, a potential serial killer who's a romantic. What is this world coming to? I'm sending the closest deputy your way now. In the meantime, keep your ass right there and try not to get killed."

As soon as she put her phone back in her pocket, she and Cougar started running, all uphill. Technically, she kept her ass right on the mountain, so she was following Rick's instructions. She couldn't leave Shantel at the Vista House alone with that monster. Rick would get over it.

Honestly, she thought Shantel's plan sucked just as much as Rick did. Shantel hadn't given her any choice in the matter. At one of the turnouts on the way up, she'd had Johnnie pull over and presented her counterattack to Daniel's directions. She'd drive up alone, as Daniel demanded, and Johnnie and Cougar would bushwhack their way up to the Vista House. Daniel would believe she'd come alone, when in reality, they'd be there for backup.

Johnnie had neglected to tell Shantel she intended to call Rick because she'd made it clear she wanted to do this alone. That idea hadn't seemed very smart to Johnnie. Apparently, Shantel still didn't think Daniel was quite as dangerous as she believed him to be. Throw in her belief that he could shift into a werewolf, and the danger factor went up tenfold.

All the way up the mountain, she thanked the gods for all the training she and Cougar did, because without it, the trek up would have been excruciating. As it turned out, they made it to the stone house that sat atop the mountain in good time. No trips. No falls. No injuries. She'd been here enough times to be familiar with the layout and the paths that had brought hikers and skiers to its door for nearly a century. At least no snowfall yet.

On her command, Cougar stopped and went into a down. She wanted to take a moment. Shantel had parked the car in the small parking area below the rise where the Vista House stood. From her vantage point behind a big pine, she heard voices coming from the stone patio. Outside rather than in the house. She liked that better. More options for escape.

Cougar watched her intently. With a hand command, he rose and moved with her as she left the cover of the tree and inched toward the house. At the corner, they stopped, where they remained out of view. She could make out Shantel and Daniel as they talked. A thought occurred to her as she crouched in the shadows and Cougar went into a down. She pulled her phone from her pocket and set it to record before putting it back in her pocket.

Daniel's laugh gave her chills, though not as much as his words did. "Ah, my darling Shantel. Now why was I certain you'd defy me still?"

"I don't know what you're talking about." Shantel's voice stayed strong. God, how she liked this woman.

"Come out, come out, wherever you are. No sense pretending you're not there. I can smell you."

Shit.

❖

Shantel's hands had started to shake the moment she'd laid eyes on Daniel. How she'd wished her life could be free of him forever and that he could no longer affect her like this. Given that wasn't happening and the tragedies that brought her and Johnnie together had shaken an entire city, the time had come to face him down one last time. She'd managed to keep her voice steady, even if her hands weren't.

She'd asked Johnnie to come up but to stay out of sight and keep an eye on things to make sure Daniel didn't try to hurt her. Although nothing had been said, she'd been convinced Johnnie would call in reinforcements the moment she'd driven off. Johnnie was smart and caring, and regardless of what Daniel might or might not be, they would need help with him. In fact, she'd banked on her making that call. All she'd wanted before the cavalry arrived was a little time to get the why. She had to make sense of this one way or the other.

Unfortunately, things weren't going quite as she'd hoped. The Daniel standing here now, hands in his pockets, smile on his face, was a complete stranger. Everything about him screamed different. Screamed frightening. Had he been this way all along and kept it hidden? Her stomach rolled, and she shoved her hands into the pockets of her jacket. The warmth helped.

Johnnie came around the corner of the house and stepped up onto the stone patio. Shantel silently said a thanks that Cougar wasn't with her. That the powerful dog stayed out of sight gave her a sliver of hope. She didn't know what he could do to help their situation, and it didn't matter. That he waited in the shadows was enough for the moment.

"I'm here." Johnnie stood tall and defiant. To Shantel, she looked powerful and ready for anything Daniel might come at her with. Her breath quickened.

"My, my, if it's not the trouble-making search-and-recovery bitch. You and your dog have caused me to lose quite a bit. You will have to pay a price for that."

Shantel couldn't quite stop her quick intake of breath. She'd suspected something over the last few days. He confirmed it. "You killed them all?"

Daniel shrugged as he threw out his hands. "I don't think of it as killing anyone. More the end result of a truly fabulous game." His laugh was ugly.

"What are you?" She no longer saw a man. The mask had dropped, and what she'd never seen before—or what she'd refused to acknowledge—met her eyes. She would never be able to unsee it now.

He put his arms in the air and turned full circle, his laugh carrying on the wind. "I am everything."

"You are nothing." The coldness that swept over her brought a clarity she had never experienced before. More than even the day she embraced her new life and walked away from the one she could no longer tolerate.

His arms dropped, and darkness crossed his face. "We shall see, my darling. Little friend, come over and sit."

Shantel didn't like the tone in his voice. It didn't even sound like the Daniel she spent years around. The air changed as Johnnie did as he asked. She sat in the corner, her eyes never leaving Daniel's face.

What he missed had been the motion of Johnnie's hand before she sat down. She'd noticed her do it before. Unspoken communication with Cougar: wait.

❖

Delicious was the only word for what would happen next. Daniel had counted on his belief that Shantel wouldn't follow his instructions. When had she ever done as he asked or expected? She did march to the beat of her own drummer. In the early days, that trait amused him. In the end, it irritated him right to his core. Tonight, it would be just plain fun. The more the merrier in this party.

"Where's the amazing doggy?"

"In the car." Shantel's friend stared him in the eyes. Props for being a bold bitch. A shame she cut her hair all short like a man or that she wore clothes that looked like one too. She'd be a pretty woman if she groomed herself like one. Made him sick to think this is what Shantel thought she wanted. Soon enough he'd have her back on the right path. The only path.

"Really." He didn't trust her. Hard to believe she'd walk out here without her sidekick. She had to pick up on how dangerous he was, so perhaps she'd decided to protect her canine companion.

"Really." Her bravado didn't waver. Wanted to act like a man too. What a waste of a woman.

"All right then. It's just between the three of us."

Because he'd known how Shantel would react, he'd come prepared. He had big plans for tonight and didn't intend to have them thwarted. From his pocket he pulled several zip ties big enough to secure a person. He tossed them to Shantel.

"Here, darling. I want you to secure your little friend. Nice and tight."

She didn't catch them, and instead let them fall to the stone floor. "No."

He'd anticipated this reaction as well. From his pocket, he pulled a gun that he pointed, not at Shantel, but at her buddy. He would never risk harming his beloved. Her friend...he really didn't give a good god damn what happened to her.

"Don't be difficult. This can go down easy or hard. It's up to you. What's your pick, my beautiful mate?"

He rolled his head, the draw of the moon starting to warm him. The sensation, like everything about the night, so far—wonderful. Energy made his fingers flex and his eyesight sharpen. The sounds and scents of the mountaintop wrapped around him like the hug of an old friend.

"Come on, darling. Truss her up so we can get on with this. Let me be clear. I don't care about your friend. She can live or she can die. It's all up to you. All I really care about is you and me. This is the moment I've waited for since the night I was turned. This is the nirvana the monk who opened my world to all that is possible promised me." He waved the small gun in the direction of her friend's face. Until he made his shift, mortal weapons had their purpose. Once he shifted, he needed nothing beyond his own sheer power.

"This is all about nirvana? You're insane."

"Quite the opposite. I'm fulfilling my destiny, and you are part of it. You were promised to me, and it's time for that promise to be fulfilled. In my universe once a mate is selected, it's for life."

"We are divorced. Get over it."

"Man's laws have no effect on our relationship. We are forever, period. Now do as I ask if you want your little friend to see the sun rise tomorrow morning."

Shantel's jaw tightened. His beautiful mate was angry, yet she'd do what he asked. The good doctor knew when she'd been backed into a corner. She went over to her friend and took her hands. Now the games could truly begin.

CHAPTER THIRTY-ONE

Johnnie's mind raced, and silently she prayed that Rick's troops would arrive soon. The ill-advised route they'd taken became super clear to her now. The risks they'd discussed on the way up here all came crashing down. They'd both been in serious denial about how quickly it could—and did—go wrong. Talk about over-estimating abilities.

Now she had to figure out how to get out of the restraints. Rolling her hands into fists as Shantel fitted the zip ties around her wrists gave her space once she relaxed them. Wasn't as easy with her feet. No way to enlarge her ankles. The tiny multi-tool she always carried in her pocket would help, if she could get her hands free. All she had to do was wait for his attention to turn away from her, and then she could make her move.

At the same time, she needed to stay calm. Cougar waited, as he'd been trained to do, and she didn't want to give him reason to break. She didn't trust the crazy man in front of Shantel, who pulled out the weapon he pointed at the middle of her forehead. His obsessive behavior toward her already painted a frightening picture. The deaths she felt certain he perpetrated made the picture even more bleak. Here, in the moonlight, on top of the mountain, beauty spreading out in every direction, sheer terror filled her.

Daniel clapped his hands slowly. "Bravo, darling, bravo. I knew you'd come around. Just think, tonight is the first night of the rest of our lives."

"No, it's not the start of anything. It's the end."

He raised an eyebrow. "I respectfully disagree, my beautiful wife. It's only the beginning. You'll see soon enough. I will open the world to you, and you will find it magnificent."

"And have me become a monster like you?" The truth in Shantel's words rang clear and loud. She believed. "Never."

"A monster?" His laughter carried large on the night air and raised goose bumps on Johnnie's arms. "Not even close. I am a god."

The chills went glacial. Despite her years-long search to validate her younger self and the belief in the existence of werewolves, the reality of the truth filled her with pure terror. This wasn't some story told over and over through the centuries. This was real, and it scared the devil right out of her. It took every ounce of self-control she possessed not to go into full-on panic mode. She didn't want to die up here on the mountain, and she didn't want to lose Shantel.

Daniel took hold of Shantel and moved her toward the steps leading down the mountainside. "It's time." He turned and stared at Johnnie. She could swear his eyes glowed yellow. "If you want to live, you'll be a good girl and stay right where you are. You feel me?"

Johnnie simply nodded. The air around them grew thick, and while he was no god, he was something, and it affected everything. The reality of the creature that haunted her nightmares for most of her life far surpassed the worst of her imagination.

He lowered the gun he'd been pointing at her face and smiled. "Good girl." He turned and dragged Shantel toward the mountain. The air grew even thicker.

"Oh shit, oh shit, oh shit," she whispered as she relaxed her hands and began to work her way out of the zip tie. It might look easy on crappy television shows, but it wasn't, and the longer it took, the more her anxiety ratcheted up. Her wrists grew raw, and blood trickled down her fingers. The clock ticking in the back of her mind began to toll. Time was up.

None of this felt right. Shantel believed when she walked out onto the patio and faced Daniel that she'd be able to stand up to him. That

Johnnie had her back made her all the more assured of the path she'd decided to take. Tonight, she would end it once and for all.

All that confidence flew out the window the moment she stared into his eyes. It wasn't Daniel, and she had no idea who this creature was. One certainty resonated with her: whatever Daniel had become, it was evil.

Even his face changed. Handsome by any measure, he always drew women to him. That wasn't the face she confronted right now. This one had grown hard and mean, and it scared her more than his words.

"Come, come, Shantel. The moon is rising. This is our time."

Frightened as she might be, she refused to cower. If she were to die out here tonight, she'd go out defiant. He would not win. "It's your time, not mine."

He yanked on her hand, bringing her around to meet his gaze. The trees were swaying in the wind that had picked up, and it brought with it a distinct chill. At least she thought it was the wind that chilled her to the bone. Her heart felt as though it were in her throat, obstructing her breathing. Tears would not fall; she would not allow that to happen. She raised her chin.

"Oh, my beautiful, beautiful Shantel, you are so innocent. Your bravado is wasted tonight because it simply doesn't matter."

"Fuck you."

He frowned. "We will have to come to an understanding on your language. I won't tolerate gutter speak."

"I talk any way I please."

"We shall see." His laugh chilled her blood.

He put the gun into his pocket and took her face in his hands. The intense way he ogled her, she thought he would lean in for a kiss, and goose bumps rose on her arms. Not a kiss. Not even close. He tipped back his head and howled. The sound turned the forest silent as the creatures that called it home scurried away, probably in terror. She understood. Terror washed over her like a heavy rainstorm. The sound wasn't human.

When he looked back at her, the wolf began to show his face. The sound of cloth tearing made her shake all over. She wanted to scream and run away. Her voice disappeared. Her feet refused to move. Before she could summon the strength to flee, he smiled with a mouth full of fangs. One hand, morphing as it reached toward her, brought her close, and then she did scream as those fangs plunged into her shoulder.

❖

At long last, she would be his. The moment he sank his teeth into her flesh, satisfaction rushed over him. He'd finally done what he'd resisted for so long. She would be at his side for eternity. The pure perfection of it was orgasmic.

The tang of her blood sent him reeling in delight. Sweet, hot, perfect. Between the pull of the moon and the taste of her sweetness, he could hold back no longer. He morphed from the man to the wolf, and as he did, he watched her crumple to the ground. Not dead, only buzzing with the gift he'd imparted through the joining of his teeth and her blood. His bite had powers that most humans could never comprehend. She wouldn't be able to either. At least not until the magic touched every cell of her being. Only then would she be on board. Only then would their bond be complete.

His paws hit the ground hard enough that his legs vibrated. With his head tipped toward the buttery light of the moon, he roared. The grass caressed his pads, and the hoot of an owl sent his blood rushing. All he needed now was the hunt, and he had no doubt that it would soon start.

The man in him had gambled on the very good odds that Shantel would never come here alone. The wolf salivated, thinking about the prize that would soon be his. No more waiting, no more wanting. Shantel would be his forever mate, and her friend…she would be just plain fun.

He heard her, smelled her, as she moved toward the edge of the patio, just as he'd expected. The zip ties he'd handed to Shantel had never been intended to restrain her indefinitely. Shantel would make sure there was an avenue of escape. His princess never could stand violence. Her whole life had been dedicated to righting wrongs, and thus she would not put another in harm's way. Particularly if she cared for that someone.

He'd gambled on that weakness and had not been wrong to do so. Her smell wafted on the air, and saliva dripped from his jaw. If he could still speak, he'd coax her to step from the patio to the mountain top. He'd encourage her to run into the shadows, through the trees, and into the night, all of it giving her a false sense of security.

His beloved groaned for just a moment, and the sound turned his attention away from the rabbit struggling to free herself and back to his most precious prize where she lay on the ground. With his nuzzle, he sniffed her face. She would be all right. A mere reaction to the gift he'd imparted with his bite. Good. She groaned again, louder. Even better.

"Shantel!" Her friend's cry burst into the night.

He readied himself for the chase, his powerful legs spread, his muscles tight. This promised to be a night to remember.

"You son of a bitch," she screamed, and as she said one more thing, he sprang at her. "Cougar, now!"

The excitement and adrenaline that roared through him propelled him forward. Before he could reach her, a searing pain raced up his rear leg and brought him to the ground. Heat, red and hot, made him shake when he tried to put his right rear leg down to once again push off. He fell sideways. What just happened?

His head whipped around, and his growl embodied the rage that consumed him. Only then did he become aware of the big dog with his teeth sunk into his hind leg, rendering it immobile. His attention focused on the mere Canis lupus that mistakenly believed it could stop him, and as he did so, he failed to see the human come his way. It was a fatal error.

Chapter Thirty-two

As much as Johnnie wanted to go to Shantel, she had to neutralize the wolf first, or neither of them would be safe. Not a wolf, she corrected herself. A werewolf. The scene unfolded before her like déjà vu. Once more she was a young camper staring at something that couldn't be, a vision from one of the horror movies her parents prohibited her from watching, yet she snuck in every chance she got.

The quest she'd been on since that long-ago night had just come full circle. No crazy or imaginative youth here. She stood tall tonight as a mature woman with a clear head. Her eyes had been good back then, and they were still damn good tonight. Shantel's husband—correction, ex-husband—had just turned into a werewolf right before said eyes. Rick and the cavalry might show up any minute, but without witnessing what happened, they'd never believe her, and they'd get here too late to help.

That left her only one course of action. She had to stop him. She was also smart enough to know she couldn't stop a preternatural creature by herself. Not a problem. Her secret weapon had been waiting patiently out of sight for her command. The second she'd freed herself from the restraints, she'd given him that command. Cougar, smarter than any dog she'd ever shared her life with, knew exactly what she needed him to do.

Cougar's instinct to disable the wolf worked perfectly. A well-placed grab to the rear leg brought it down hard. The sound of tearing flesh was loud on the night air, as was the howl of the massive beast. He tried three times to get back up, and each time, Cougar yanked harder on the injured leg.

Immobilized at first, Johnnie stared. Cougar, the driven yet gentle dog, attacked. He employed the same focus he used on search and in trainings to save two women from a creature that shouldn't be. That brought her back into action. The multi-tool still in her hand after freeing herself from the zip-ties, she pulled out the blade. It might be small, but it was all she had, and she couldn't let Cougar do this alone.

Her best intentions went sideways at the sound of Shantel's scream. She raced to her side and jumped back. The multi-tool dropped from her hand, and her first instinct was to run. Instead, she acted on her second instinct, picked the tool back up, and fought the fear enough to get close to Shantel.

The blood on her shirt filled her with terror. That bastard had bitten her, and blood stained the white fabric crimson. Pain twisted Shantel's face, and while Johnnie wanted to embrace naïveté, she couldn't. She must be strong and face the unknown head-on. He'd not only hurt Shantel. He'd done something to her, and she had a hunch, she knew what would happen next.

Not gonna happen if she had anything to do with it. Her mind raced, recalling all the stories she'd read since that long-ago encounter that had her believing in the world of the paranormal. Daniel, the wolf, continued to fight the disabling injury Cougar inflicted, and Cougar, precious Cougar, wasn't letting go. She needed to act before something happened to her hero dog. Daniel wouldn't give up that easy.

One thought kept recurring in her mind: kill the maker. She'd read so many stories, so many folktales from around the world, she couldn't sort through them all fast enough to definitively land on what belonged to what. Did "kill the maker" work with a werewolf? Or did it only work with vampires?

Good Lord, now she was contemplating the existence of vampires. One creature at a time. She looked down at the small knife in her hand, then back down to where Shantel still writhed on the ground. No more time to think anything through. Time to act.

She ran over to where Cougar gripped Daniel's hind leg. Only one thing caught in her mind—hit the carotid artery. She needed to make it quick, and that was the quickest thing she could think of. As she summoned up strength and courage, she also sent up a silent thanks for all her canine first-aid classes. She knew exactly where to plunge the blade of the small knife. She hoped it would be enough.

Staying out of the reach of the powerful wolf's muzzle, she brought the knife down hard, just behind its jaw. The roar that followed sent the message she waited for. Pay dirt. Blood sprayed, and she couldn't jump back fast enough to escape it. Her knife remained buried in its neck. Cougar continued to hold on for what seemed like forever and probably was no more than a minute. When he finally let go, the wolf—Daniel—no longer moved.

Neither did Shantel.

❖

Her body burned from the inside, and Shantel couldn't keep from screaming. Sounds pounded in her ears, and the smell of blood washed over her like a tsunami. Instead of being able to run away, she could only roll on the ground, rocks digging into her back, pine needles poking into her scalp.

And then the sensations faded. She relaxed, and sweet darkness descended. In the back of her mind lingered the notion that it would be a bad idea to give in to the oblivion, yet she couldn't help herself. She let go and allowed herself to sink into the cold earth. Her eyes closed, and the stars disappeared. The scents and sounds of the night were gone. The rocks didn't hurt. The pine needles gone. The nothingness pulled her away. Bliss.

"Come back here, damn it. Come back."

The peace of the last few moments shattered. She shook, and the pain rolled back through her. Heat roared through her veins. Blood filled her mouth.

"No," she moaned. "No."

"Damn you, Shantel. Don't you dare."

The beautiful but fear-filled voice cut through the apathy that made her want to cling to the peace of what she now recognized as death. Johnnie.

With a sharp intake of breath, she opened her eyes. Johnnie leaned over her, tears falling onto her face, shaking her shoulders without a hint of gentleness. Pure terror. "I'm here," she managed to say. "Stop shaking me."

"Thank you, God." Johnnie pulled her close. The shaking she felt now came from Johnnie.

"What happened?" She closed her eyes again as she rested against Johnnie's warm chest. Her arms around her pushed away any lingering desire to descend into darkness, and soon enough, Johnnie stopped trembling.

"He bit you." Her voice was rough.

"That part I remember." The still-throbbing shoulder wouldn't let her forget it anytime soon.

She opened her eyes and pushed back. In the time since she and Daniel had stepped down onto the mountain, full, deep darkness had descended, the only light that of the moon. "You do that?" She pointed to where Daniel, back in human form, lay unmoving on the ground. Cougar sat a few feet away, staring at him as if to make sure he didn't move.

She nodded. "Me and my main man."

Cougar. "He's a special dog."

"That he is."

"Is he dead? Daniel, I mean."

"That would be affirmative. I don't think even a werewolf can come back from a severed carotid."

The way her shoulders relaxed and her soul soared should instill a fair amount of guilt. Taking a life went against everything she believed in. Still...she gazed at her hands and tilted her head.

"Tell me I'm wrong, but is that fur on my hands?"

Johnnie winced. "Yeah. That's all that's left."

She snapped her head up. "What do you mean that's all that's left?"

"You should have seen yourself five minutes ago."

Fear raged again. "Did he make me..."

"He did." She held her hand up before Shantel could cry out. "I'm pretty sure you're okay now. The minute he died, all that shit stopped happening to you. I think if the one who turns you dies, you stay human."

Both she and Johnnie turned at the sound of running feet. Rick, along with two additional officers, raced to them. Rick did a full circle, taking in everything before asking, "What in the world happened here? He pointed to Daniel. "And why is he naked?"

CHAPTER THIRTY-THREE

Johnnie took a great deal of satisfaction in wrapping up the now-infamous serial-killer case. The entire region reverberated with shock after the news revealed his identity as that of the well-known descendant of one of the city's founding fathers. No one saw the handsome and successful Daniel Rodger for what he'd become. Only a very few knew the entire truth, and none of them were talking.

Shantel and the rest of those responsible for investigating crimes pieced together all they needed to tie him to a total of fifteen murders. The recording she'd made with her phone on the mountain that night helped explain the majority of his crimes. Most of the details made it into the reports that closed the cases and brought a measure of closure to the families of the missing. He'd made no attempt to cover up his involvement in the murder of one of his clients, and they were able to figure out that he'd somehow manipulated the degenerate into perpetrating a murder in an attempt to turn their investigation down a false path. He'd then disposed of the client the same way he did with the rest. He'd killed him.

What didn't make the reports stayed with a chosen few. Even Rick didn't get the whole story, though Johnnie was pretty sure he still didn't quite believe how Daniel ended up naked and dead on the top of Mt. Spokane with a severed Achilles tendon and carotid artery. They gave him the most plausible explanation they could and stuck with it. Rick, with a serial killer dead and no longer a threat to the citizens he'd sworn to protect, let it go. Someday he might push it more, but she'd deal with that if, and when, that day ever arrived. They even found a way to explain away the teeth marks on the bones. It took a bit of doing, but they'd come up with an explanation that everyone accepted. No one would believe the truth anyway.

Today, with all the I's dotted and the T's crossed, she and Shantel were beginning the rest of their lives. They'd grown even closer over the weeks since that night on the top of the mountain, and Johnnie had never been happier. Who would have thought a killer, correction, a werewolf, could bring her such happiness? Life worked in some funny, funny ways.

Shantel walked into the kitchen, beautiful in blue jeans and an EWU sweatshirt. Her long black hair hung loose, her makeup-free face smooth and gorgeous. She didn't think she'd ever grow tired of her expressive dark eyes.

"You ready for this?"

Johnnie wasn't sure. While her werewolf theory proved to be a hundred percent true, learning there was a lot more to the story came as a bit of shock. It shouldn't really, considering how aware she'd become through her chosen profession that there was always way more to the story than ever got written. That truly defined their plans for the day.

"I'm ready."

Shantel smiled. "He just pulled up in the driveway."

"All righty. Let's roll."

Ten minutes later she sat in the living room with a cup of steaming tea in her hand, facing a handsome, tall, white-haired octogenarian. Dr. Soule smiled as he sipped his own cup of tea. He tipped the mug in her direction. "Bravo, young lady. This is marvelous."

"I order only the best."

He gave her a nod and looked over at Shantel. "Shall we get this party started?"

Shantel smiled and nodded back. "Let's do it."

"Ladies," he said as he set down his mug. "This is a formal invitation to you both to become members of the Oborot Society."

"And that is?" Johnnie asked.

"I'm so glad you asked." Again, the smile that made him appear fifty-six rather than eighty-six. "We have a society of enlightened scholars with some very specialized knowledge and skills. For centuries, the Oborot Society has tracked and destroyed dangerous werewolves."

Johnnie stopped him. "Dangerous werewolves? Is there any other kind?"

"Actually, there is. Not all who transform evolve into what Shantel's husband became. Those who become a preternatural and yet maintain the traces of humanity that make them good and kind, we leave in peace. The others? You've handled that kind of creature first-hand."

"You destroy them."

"In a word, yes."

"Dr. Soule…" Shantel was turning her mug in her hands.

His smile reappeared. "Ed, or if you insist on formality, Edward, please. After all, we're family now."

Johnnie finished her thought. "We haven't agreed to this."

"Have you not? I would submit that the moment you saved Shantel and destroyed the beast, you joined our special family."

The handsome scholar made a good point. From that moment forward, her life had, in fact, changed. At the time, her sole focus had been to save Shantel. She'd known, though not acknowledged, that love had been developing fast. Too fast for rational people like her and Shantel. That didn't change the facts one tiny bit. Love had its own ideas about how fast or slow it happened.

Later, as she'd thought back through all that happened, she wondered if that werewolf she'd seen all those years ago and that filled her heart with a fear that stayed with her for decades hadn't been a woman after all and had in fact been Daniel. Not that it really mattered as it all turned out. Her quest for validation involved more than confirming her childhood experience. It had been about stopping the very werewolf that haunted her dreams.

That she'd saved the woman who turned out to be the love of a lifetime? That came as a truly special bonus. She turned to Shantel. In her eyes she glimpsed the same love that filled her own. She also saw the truth. Both of them were different now, and the time had arrived to accept that fact.

"You are with us, yes?" Edward held his mug up in a salute.

She winked at Shantel and leaned forward holding her own. They clinked all three together. "We are."

About the Author

Sheri Lewis Wohl lives in NE Washington State where she's surrounded by mountains, rivers, and forests. It's a perfect backdrop for her stories of danger, romance, and all things paranormal. When not writing, Sheri enjoys cycling, and training and working with her search dogs, Zoey and Deuce.

Books Available from Bold Strokes Books

A Different Man by Andrew L. Huerta. This diverse collection of stories chronicling the challenges of gay life at various ages shines a light on the progress made and the progress still to come. (978-1-63555-977-4)

All That Remains by Sheri Lewis Wohl. Johnnie and Shantel might have to risk their lives—and their love—to stop a werewolf intent on killing. (978-1-63555-949-1)

Beginner's Bet by Fiona Riley. Phenom luxury Realtor Ellison Gamble has everything, except a family to share it with, so when a mix-up brings youthful Katie Crawford into her life, she bets the house on love. (978-1-63555-733-6)

Dangerous Without You by Lexus Grey. Throughout their senior year in high school, Aspen, Remington, Denna, and Raleigh face challenges in life and romance that they never expect. (978-1-63555-947-7)

Desiring More by Raven Sky. In this collection of steamy stories, a rich variety of lovers find themselves desiring more, more from a lover, more from themselves, and more from life. (978-1-63679-037-4)

Jordan's Kiss by Nanisi Barrett D'Arnuck. After losing everything in a fire, Jordan Phelps joins a small lounge band and meets pianist Morgan Sparks, who lights another blaze, this time in Jordan's heart. (978-1-63555-980-4)

Late City Summer by Jeanette Bears. Forced together for her wedding, Emily Stanton and Kate Alessi navigate their lingering passion for one another against the backdrop of New York City and World War II, and a summer romance they left behind. (978-1-63555-968-2)

Love and Lotus Blossoms by Anne Shade. On her path to self-acceptance and true passion, Janesse will risk everything—and possibly everyone—she loves. (978-1-63555-985-9)

Love in the Limelight by Ashley Moore. Marion Hargreaves, the finest actress of her generation, and Jessica Carmichael, the world's biggest pop star, rediscover each other twenty years after an ill-fated affair. (978-1-63679-051-0)

Suspecting Her by Mary P. Burns. Complications ensue when Erin O'Connor falls for top real estate saleswoman Catherine Williams while investigating racism in the real estate industry; the fallout could end their chance at happiness. (978-1-63555-960-6)

Two Winters by Lauren Emily Whalen. A modern YA retelling of Shakespeare's *The Winter's Tale* about birth, death, Catholic school, improv comedy, and the healing nature of time. (978-1-63679-019-0)

Busy Ain't the Half of It by Frederick Smith and Chaz Lamar Cruz. Elijah and Justin seek happily-ever-afters in LA, but are they too busy to notice happiness when it's there? (978-1-63555-944-6)

Calumet by Ali Vali. Jaxon Lavigne and Iris Long had a forbidden small-town romance that didn't last, and the consequences of that love will be uncovered fifteen years later at their high school reunion. (978-1-63555-900-2)

Her Countess to Cherish by Jane Walsh. London Society's material girl realizes there is more to life than diamonds when she falls in love with a non-binary bluestocking. (978-1-63555-902-6)

Hot Days, Heated Nights by Renee Roman. When Cole and Lee meet, instant attraction quickly flares into uncontrollable passion, but their connection might be short lived as Lee's identity is tied to her life in the city. (978-1-63555-888-3)

Never Be the Same by MA Binfield. Casey meets Olivia and sparks fly in this opposites attract romance that proves love can be found in the unlikeliest places. (978-1-63555-938-5)

Quiet Village by Eden Darry. Something not quite human is stalking Collie and her niece, and she'll be forced to work with undercover reporter Emily Lassiter if they want to get out of Hyam alive. (978-1-63555-898-2)

Shaken or Stirred by Georgia Beers. Bar owner Julia Martini and home health aide Savannah McNally attempt to weather the storms brought on by a mysterious blogger trashing the bar, family feuds they knew nothing about, and way too much advice from way too many relatives. (978-1-63555-928-6)

The Fiend in the Fog by Jess Faraday. Can four people on different trajectories work together to save the vulnerable residents of East London from the terrifying fiend in the fog before it's too late? (978-1-63555-514-1)

The Marriage Masquerade by Toni Logan. A no strings attached marriage scheme to inherit a Maui B&B uncovers unexpected attractions and a dark family secret. (978-1-63555-914-9)

Flight SQA016 by Amanda Radley. Fastidious airline passenger Olivia Lewis is used to things being a certain way. When her routine is changed by a new, attractive member of the staff, sparks fly. (978-1-63679-045-9)

Home Is Where the Heart Is by Jenny Frame. Can Archie make the countryside her home and give Ash the fairytale romance she desires? Or will the countryside and small village life all be too much for her? (978-1-63555-922-4)

Moving Forward by PJ Trebelhorn. The last person Shelby Ryan expects to be attracted to is Iris Calhoun, the sister of the man who killed her wife four years and three thousand miles ago. (978-1-63555-953-8)

Poison Pen by Jean Copeland. Debut author Kendra Blake is finally living her best life until a nasty book review and exposed secrets threaten her promising new romance with aspiring journalist Alison Chatterley. (978-1-63555-849-4)

Seasons for Change by KC Richardson. Love, laughter, and trust develop for Shawn and Morgan throughout the changing seasons of Lake Tahoe. (978-1-63555-882-1)

Summer Lovin' by Julie Cannon. Three different women, three exotic locations, one unforgettable summer. What do you think will happen? (978-1-63555-920-0)

Unbridled by D. Jackson Leigh. A visit to a local stable turns into more than riding lessons between a novel writer and an equestrian with a taste for power play. (978-1-63555-847-0)

VIP by Jackie D. In a town where relationships are forged and shattered by perception, sometimes even love can't change who you really are. (978-1-63555-908-8)

Yearning by Gun Brooke. The sleepy town of Dennamore has an irresistible pull on those who've moved away. The mystery Darian Benson and Samantha Pike uncover will change them forever, but the love they find along the way just might be the key to saving themselves. (978-1-63555-757-2)

A Turn of Fate by Ronica Black. Will Nev and Kinsley finally face their painful past and relent to their powerful, forbidden attraction? Or will facing their past be too much to fight through? (978-1-63555-930-9)

Desires After Dark by MJ Williamz. When her human lover falls deathly ill, Alex, a vampire, must decide which is worse, letting her go or condemning her to everlasting life. (978-1-63555-940-8)

Her Consigliere by Carsen Taite. FBI agent Royal Scott swore an oath to uphold the law, and criminal defense attorney Siobhan Collins pledged her loyalty to the only family she's ever known, but will their love be stronger than the bonds they've vowed to others, or will their competing allegiances tear them apart? (978-1-63555-924-8)

In Our Words: Queer Stories from Black, Indigenous, and People of Color Writers. Stories selected by Anne Shade and edited by Victoria Villaseñor. Comprising both the renowned and emerging voices of Black, Indigenous, and People of Color authors, this thoughtfully curated collection of short stories explores the intersection of racial and queer identity. (978-1-63555-936-1)

Measure of Devotion by CF Frizzell. Disguised as her late twin brother, Catherine Samson enters the Civil War to defend the Constitution as a Union soldier, never expecting her life to be altered by a Gettysburg farmer's daughter. (978-1-63555-951-4)

Not Guilty by Brit Ryder. Claire Weaver and Emery Pearson's day jobs clash, even as their desire for each other burns, and a discreet sex-only arrangement is the only option. (978-1-63555-896-8)

Opposites Attract: Butch/Femme Romances by Meghan O'Brien, Aurora Rey, Angie Williams. Sometimes opposites really do attract. Fall in love with these butch/femme romance novellas. (978-1-63555-784-8)

Swift Vengeance by Jean Copeland, Jackie D, Erin Zak. A journalist becomes the subject of her own investigation when sudden strange, violent visions summon her to a summer retreat and into the arms of a killer's possible next victim. (978-1-63555-880-7)

Under Her Influence by Amanda Radley. On their path to #truelove, will Beth and Jemma discover that reality is even better than illusion? (978-1-63555-963-7)

Wasteland by Kristin Keppler & Allisa Bahney. Danielle Clark is fighting against the National Armed Forces and finds peace as a scavenger, until the NAF general's daughter, Katelyn Turner, shows up on her doorstep and brings the fight right back to her. (978-1-63555-935-4)

When in Doubt by VK Powell. Police officer Jeri Wylder thinks she committed a crime in the line of duty but can't remember, until details emerge pointing to a cover-up by those close to her. (978-1-63555-955-2)

A Woman to Treasure by Ali Vali. An ancient scroll isn't the only treasure Levi Montbard finds as she starts her hunt for the truth—all she has to do is prove to Yasmine Hassani that there's more to her than an adventurous soul. (978-1-63555-890-6)

Before. After. Always. by Morgan Lee Miller. Still reeling from her tragic past, Eliza Walsh has sworn off taking risks, until Blake Navarro turns her world right-side up, making her question if falling in love again is worth it. (978-1-63555-845-6)

Bet the Farm by Fiona Riley. Lauren Calloway's luxury real estate sale of the century comes to a screeching halt when dairy farm heiress, and one-night stand, Thea Boudreaux calls her bluff. (978-1-63555-731-2)

Cowgirl by Nance Sparks. The last thing Aren expects is to fall for Carol. Sharing her home is one thing, but sharing her heart means sharing the demons in her past and risking everything to keep Carol safe. (978-1-63555-877-7)

Give In to Me by Elle Spencer. Gabriela Talbot never expected to sleep with her favorite author—certainly not after the scathing review she'd given Whitney Ainsworth's latest book. (978-1-63555-910-1)

Hidden Dreams by Shelley Thrasher. A lethal virus and its resulting vision send Texan Barbara Allan and her lovely guide, Dara, on a journey up Cambodia's Mekong River in search of Barbara's mother's mystifying past. (978-1-63555-856-2)

In the Spotlight by Lesley Davis. For actresses Cole Calder and Eris Whyte, their chance at love runs out fast when a fan's adoration turns to obsession. (978-1-63555-926-2)

Origins by Jen Jensen. Jamis Bachman is pulled into a dangerous mystery that becomes personal when she learns the truth of her origins as a ghost hunter. (978-1-63555-837-1)

Pursuit: A Victorian Entertainment by Felice Picano. An intelligent, handsome, ruthlessly ambitious young man who rose from the slums to become the right-hand man of the Lord Exchequer of England will stop at nothing as he pursues his Lord's vanished wife across Continental Europe. (978-1-63555-870-8)

Unrivaled by Radclyffe. Zoey Cohen will never accept second place in matters of the heart, even when her rival is a career, and Declan Black has nothing left to give of herself or her heart. (978-1-63679-013-8)